BEAUTIFUL

ERIC ADOLPH

That night an angel of the Lord went out and put to death
one hundred and eighty-five thousand in the Assyrian camp.
When the people got up the next morning — there were all
the dead bodies!
  — 2 Kings 19:35
  — Isaiah 37:36

IN THE ALLEY

Cara staggered down the dark street, her footsteps echoing off the dingy, gray tenement walls. Her only thought was to get as far as possible from her apartment. She glanced over her shoulder, afraid she'd been seen and followed. Nobody yet. She leaned against the side of a building, chest heaving, breathing ragged. The washcloth she held against her cheek was drenched with her blood. Her clothes were old and provided little protection against the chilly fall night. She shivered, catching her breath and hugging her battered doll, then she continued to run.

She ran for a long time, always trying to avoid people, to avoid the light. If anyone saw her, or if she asked for help, she was afraid they would send her back to the apartment. He would kill her for sure.

Cara realized she was lost. She didn't know in which direction to run. She hid behind a bush, clutched her doll in both hands and whispered, "Emma? I don't know what to do. I don't know where to go."

The doll gazed silently back at her.

She darted out, and almost tripped over two men lying by the street.

"Hey," one shouted.

Cara gasped and raced in the opposite direction with her last remaining strength. To her horror, the men got up and followed her. She tried to lose them by turning quickly into an alley. A dumpster. She cowered between the dumpster and the dirty brick wall, hardly daring to breathe.

"Girlie. Don't run from us. We just wanna be your friend. Where are you, girlie?"

Fear, blood loss, and pain weakened her. She couldn't run farther. She curled up on the ground, still hugging her doll, and prayed silently. *Please, God, help me. Give me strength so they can't hurt me. Help me, please.*

SCARFACE

Seven Years Later

A quick bump, a well-placed elbow, and Cara's books tumbled to the ground.

"Watch where you're going, Scarface," Belinda May said, laughing, lip curled in disgust. She and her friends giggled to each other as they meandered down the hallway.

Cara crouched to gather her books and notes. *New school, same old stuff.*

"L-let me help you," said a boy who was kneeling in front of his locker. She recognized him from her classes. Adam somebody.

"Don't bother," Cara replied as she walked away.

In English class, she watched as Adam stowed his backpack and prepared to take notes. He carefully aligned his copy of *Beloved* by Toni Morrison on the left of his desktop, midway between front and back of the desk. He placed his notebook, equally centered and to the right of the book, and finally a mechanical pencil, vertical, on the right. *His hair is wild, but he keeps his life precise. And they tell me I'm the weird one.* She smiled to herself.

Adam turned and glanced at her. Cara dropped her eyes.

"OKAY," said Ms. Taggart, the AP English lit and composition teacher. "I believe we ended last class with a discussion of the concept of destruction of identity. You were to think of that in terms of some themes present in the novel and be prepared to discuss.

"Jacob, what did you come up with?"

Jacob Andrews looked up from his notes, where he'd been scribbling furiously. "Uh, yes. I was thinking about how slavery changed both the slaves and their owners."

"Explain."

"They treated slaves as subhuman, as commodities that could be bought and sold. How could someone, forced to submit to the indignities of that life, hold themselves in any esteem? How could a slave feel that he or she had value that we see as intrinsic to every human? And slaveowners … how did they rationalize what they heard on Sunday mornings in church with the way they treated black people? 'Us vs. Them' mentality ultimately degrades a person's natural compassion. This is true for so-called 'good' slaveowners, like Mr. and Mrs. Garner, as much as for stereotypically evil owners such as 'schoolteacher.'"

"Adam?"

"I would b-build on what Jacob said. The feeling of low self-worth continued even after former slaves won their freedom. I don't think any former slave in the novel ever truly felt free. Take Paul D, for instance. Through all his wanderings after he escaped, Paul D was never sure he was worthy enough as a man. Let's see … okay, here in Part One, Paul D was thinking about how he couldn't stay in one p-place for very long: '… walking off when he got ready was the only way he could convince himself that he would no longer have to sleep, pee, eat or swing a sledge hammer in chains.'"

Destruction of identity. Cara's thoughts raced back to that horrible day. *I am just a young girl running away from home. From him. Hiding in the alley, curled behind the dumpster, praying to God for help. Praying for strength. Bargaining for …*

"Cara?" Ms. Taggart said. "You seem to be deep in thought. Is it something you can share with the class?"

Cara took a deep breath and gripped the sides of her desk. "What robs a person of their identity and sense of self-worth is when someone in a position of power uses and desecrates a weaker person's body. You never overcome the feeling of helplessness." She paused. "Even years later, the helplessness is always in the back of your mind. Any little thing can set it off and bring back those horrible memories."

Adam turned to look at her. Cara was staring straight ahead, her eyes stony.

"Would you give an example from the story?" Ms. Taggart asked gently.

"In Part Three, Denver is listening to Sethe attempt to explain to Beloved why Sethe felt she had no choice but to slit her child's throat to save her from what Sethe believed was a much worse evil. She says that men 'could take your whole self for anything that came to mind. Not just work, kill, or maim you, but dirty you. Dirty you so bad you couldn't like yourself anymore. Dirty you so bad you forgot who you were and couldn't think it up.'"

Cara was reciting the text from memory.

The teacher looked up. "The quote, I believe, referred to 'anybody white,' not men in particular."

Cara shrugged. "Whatever. In the novel, it was men, 'schoolteacher' and his nephews. Seems it's always men. They're stronger. They take you and then it's never the same for you afterward."

Cara's eyes were moist, but her expression was fierce.

When the bell rang, Cara quickly packed her things and stood up to leave. Adam waved at her. "C-Cara, wait up."

She shook her head and hurried away.

MAD MATH SKILLS

*A*dam caught up with some friends in the hallway between classes.

"What was that?" asked Marianne Bender, one of his classmates in AP English. "Was it me, or did the awkwardness level go way up at the end of class?"

"I don't think it was you," Jessie Farnham said. "I noticed it too."

"W-what do you know about Cara?" Adam asked.

Marianne shook her head, blonde ponytail waving. "She's new this year. Doesn't talk much. Just keeps to herself. My guess is she's not in the running for prom queen, if you get my drift."

"I'm a guy. I don't get drifts and I don't understand girls, at least not well enough to date one. Though perhaps this will be m-my lucky year. Do you know anyone who wants to date a geek?"

"I'll keep an eye out for you," Marianne said, smiling. "But Cara, she doesn't seem to care what people think. Unusual for people our age. We're supposed to be all about fitting in with our peers, not thinking for ourselves."

He laughed. "Are you an average teenager?"

"Yup, according to my parents. And when they point that out, I tell them I'm just doing what I'm expected to be doing."

"You poor abused child."

"I know, right?"

SCHOOLWORK CAME EASILY TO ADAM. Speaking, not so much. He'd stuttered since he was as young as he could remember.

He ambled into his calculus class and waved at his teacher.

"Hey, M-Mr. Harris."

"Morning, Adam. Ready for more math?"

Adam smiled. "Bring it on."

For the first time, he noticed how easily, how naturally the advanced mathematics came to Cara.

"Cara, can you work this problem for us?" Mr. Harris asked her, rapidly sketching a complex differential equation on the whiteboard in the front of the classroom.

Cara walked up to the whiteboard, stared at the equation for a few moments, then wrote something and circled it.

"Without the tedium of the intermediate steps, this is the answer."

"Are you sure?" asked Mr. Harris.

"What else could it be? Yes, I'm sure."

"You're correct, though if this were a test question, you'd have to write out the intermediate steps for full credit." He smiled. "Okay, then how about this one?" Mr. Harris erased the board and scribbled an even scarier-looking differential equation on the whiteboard. Again, Cara thought for a short time, then wrote the answer.

"You did that in your head?"

"Yes, sir." Then, perhaps feeling that she sounded cocky, she explained. "Let me show you the intermediate steps you requested. The second problem appears more complicated, but if we just follow the rules we've been taught, we get this … which then simplifies to this." She was writing on the board as she spoke. "Now we …"

The way Cara danced through the math, she made it look easy. Obvious, even. Adam was impressed.

YOU DON'T KNOW ME

On a warm, bright late August afternoon, after school, Adam headed to the fieldhouse to watch his younger sister Linnea's soccer game.

"I'm so glad you'll be watching me today, big bro," Linnea had said that morning before school as she gave him a hug.

"I wouldn't want to miss my favorite sister scoring the winning goal."

"Your only sister. And I just play for fun."

As he approached the fieldhouse, he saw a group of kids clustered around someone. There was laughter, jeering. He walked over to investigate. His dad often said crowds do stupid things.

There were about eight in the pack, fairly evenly distributed between girls and boys. He recognized the group: smoking, drugs, petty crimes. *Didn't Jelton get expelled? What's he doing here on school grounds?* They'd formed a rough circle surrounding a familiar auburn-haired girl, pushing her, taunting her. She was holding her large cloth bag she always carried against her chest, protectively, but not saying a word to her tormentors.

"Damn you're ugly, girl. Did your mom cut your face when you were born?"

"What's in the bag? Are you a bag lady?"

Adam's first thought was to walk away. He disliked conflict. He especially hated physical conflict. But for some reason that he didn't fully understand, he could not make himself leave Cara to her fate. He took a deep breath, girded himself, and strode up to the group, trying to look bolder than he felt.

"Wh-what's up, Junior, Tommy?" he said. "Look at you all. Eight of you against a girl. Impressive."

"Fuck off, dickhead," Tommy Jelton said. Tommy had the largest gauges in his earlobes that Adam had seen outside of *National Geographic*. Portions of homemade tattoos were visible on his neck and forearms.

Adam shook his head. "You all, leave her be."

Tommy let loose a torrent of profanity.

"B-brilliant command of the language, as always," Adam said in a mocking tone. He stood his ground. There's an advantage to being tall, though he wasn't incredibly muscular.

"Fun's over. You all get lost." Adam glared at the group. Heat flushed through his body. His hands clenched into fists. If it came to making a stand, he decided he would do it. "Jelton, I'll string you up by those ridiculous earlobes!"

The group had largely forgotten about Cara. They looked at each other as though deciding whether to rush him.

"Cara, g-get out of here," he said. She didn't move. *Damn!*

Junior Smith started toward him with his arms extended as though he planned some sort of wrestling move. Junior was at least Adam's height and outweighed him by some fifty pounds. Adam thought it would not go well if Junior grabbed him. With all his strength, he kicked the bully in the crotch. As Junior doubled over in pain, Adam kneed him in the face. Blood poured from his nose. He collapsed on the grass.

"Who's next?" he demanded. "You want some, Jelton?" They murmured uneasily, wondering whether to attack him or leave. "I said the fun is over. Now g-get out of here unless you want to end up like Junior! Go!"

Tommy Jelton turned to his group. "Come on, let's go. You're gonna regret this, Adam."

Adam stared him down. "It'd be a shame if something happened to your bike. I'm pretty good with tools. It'd suck if your brakes failed."

Tommy looked down at his feet. His body seemed to deflate as he slouched. He left without another word, closely followed by the rest of his posse that could still walk.

Adam turned to Cara. "Are you alright?"

She nodded. "I'm okay." Then she added, "You didn't need to do that. You could have gotten hurt."

"I've had m-my own issues with bullies. I've learned over the years that if you confront bullies immediately, they usually back down. B-but if you let them get away with it, they'll make your life a living hell. I couldn't stand by and allow you to be attacked. Some things are just wrong."

"They were right to attack me," Cara said. "I am a monster."

"No, you don't deserve to be mistreated by those animals."

"You don't know me."

Adam nodded. "I do not. Why d-didn't you fight them? You didn't even say anything to them."

"I couldn't allow myself to fight them, and I had nothing to say to them."

"You couldn't allow yourself ...?"

"As I said, you don't know me."

Junior, on the ground, moaned and slowly sat up. Coagulated blood from his nose had soiled his face and jacket.

Adam crouched beside him, his hand on his shoulder, until he could see that his mind was clearing.

"Junior, look at me," Adam spoke slowly to make sure he understood. "You and your gang will stay far away from Cara. I expect all of you to leave her alone. Do you understand?"

Junior nodded.

"I didn't hear you."

"Yes, sir."

"Very good." Adam patted his shoulder. "Now get the hell out of here."

When Junior left, Adam looked at Cara. "I may have missed most of my sister's soccer game, but I'm going to check out what I can, anyway. Take care of yourself."

THAT EVENING AT DINNER, Adam sat with his parents and his sister Linnea, sharing stories of their day. His father, Stephen, winced and rubbed his forehead with his palm, as though trying to push away a headache. "I went into medicine because I hated politics and bureaucrats. Ha! It seems like all I do anymore is deal with stupid people who don't know medicine but who tell me how to care for my patients."

Adam nodded. "You and Mom have said that before."

"And still we labor, hoping to make a difference." Stephen sighed. "How was your day, Adam?"

"S-school was fun today. And became even more interesting afterward."

His mother, Katie, chuckled. "Any idea how many of my friends' kids would not characterize school as 'fun'?"

"I like school," Linnea piped up.

"And your father and I are happy you do," Katie said. "Adam, it sounds like you have a story to share."

"I do," he replied with a smile, "and like all good stories it begins with the three infamous words 'There's this g-girl ...'"

Their eyes were on him now. Too late for him to back out. "So there's this new girl in school this year. Cara. I don't know what to say. She's incredibly intelligent. There's something about her ... hard to describe, but she's different."

"Different?" asked Stephen.

Adam nodded. "Different. Marches to the beat of a different drummer. Kind, but distant. Gentle, but prickly if you get too close. And smart. Beyond smart. In all the AP classes. Gets on the board and does calculus problems as though they're self-evident. Uses language like a rapier. Never seen anyone like her."

"Is my big brother in love?" Linnea asked with a wicked grin.

"Hardly. She doesn't seem interested in making friends. Just does her own thing."

"But this afternoon ...?" Katie prompted.

"Yeah, this afternoon I was headed over to the fieldhouse to watch my favorite sister p-play soccer, and—"

"Your only sister," Linnea said.

"My charming and intelligent sister who listens politely while I tell a story."

Linnea smiled. "Oops, sorry. Go on."

"Do you know Tommy Jelton or Junior Smith? That group?" Head shakes all around.

"Losers. What's your phrase, Dad? Tail g-gunner on a vacuum truck. That caliber of stupid. Anyway, this afternoon there was a pack of them near the fieldhouse. They'd surrounded someone. I walked closer to see what was happening. They were bullying Cara. Pushing her, taunting her. Saying awful things to her. It was strange. She didn't look scared, but she also wasn't doing anything to defend herself."

"So what happened?"

"I c-convinced them to leave."

Linnea raised an eyebrow. "Convinced?"

"It's a detail, sis. You don't wanna know. Anyway, Cara told me afterward that I didn't need to get involved. She said she deserved to be attacked. I didn't expect her to say that. Once again, I don't understand what just happened with a girl."

"Sounds like you were a gentleman," Stephen said.

"I might have strayed a bit from the strict definition of a gentleman while I was convincing the bullies to leave."

Stephen chuckled. "No doubt. But I'm proud of you for sticking up for a friend."

"I'm not sure what pushed me to act. You know I don't like c-confrontation."

"That's true, Adam. You're not a fighter."

"You make it sound like I'm a wuss. I p-prefer to say that I keep focused on what's important. I just couldn't let this go."

"Well, you did the right thing today," Stephen said.

"Linnea, how was your day?" Katie asked.

"It was pretty easy. You know my science teacher, Ms. Hilstrom?"

"Yes, we met on Parents' Night. She seemed nice."

"She is nice. But she needed to explain some things to kids who had trouble understanding. I got bored, so I was reading. I'm about halfway through *Little Women*."

"Really? What do you think of it so far?"

"It's hard to imagine living under the gender constraints that women had to endure in the mid-nineteenth century."

Katie smiled. "It's true, my daughter out of time."

"But Ms. Hilstrom likes me. We talk about things. She's taught me a lot. Do you know she was twelve years old during the March on Washington and thirteen years old when they passed the Civil Rights Act in 1964? We started talking about *Little Women* and gender equality. Then we moved on to civil rights in general. A hundred years after the Civil War, we still hadn't ended racial segregation and discrimination. And even when Ms. Hilstrom was entering the job market, her choices as a proper young lady were basically teacher or nurse."

Linnea's eyes were wide, fingertips against her open mouth. Adam had to smile. Other young girls got excited about the latest boy band; his little sister was indignant about the nation's slow progress in civil rights.

FINDING MEANING IN A
HORRIBLE PLACE

"Good morning, class," the English teacher began.

"Good morning, Ms. Taggart," most of the teens replied.

"I hope," she declared, "that people will never accuse me of teaching to a test. However, the Advanced Placement Literature and Composition exam evaluates certain writing skills.

"Today I will give you a quote from another modern author. You will have forty minutes to write about how that quote relates to our current novel, *Beloved*. There are fifteen of you in this class, so it is possible that your thinking will take you in at least fifteen different directions. After forty minutes we will stop writing, and we will discuss some of your thoughts. There are no intrinsically right or wrong answers for this exercise; the grading of the actual AP exam will be on how well you explain and defend your thinking.

"Questions?"

Nobody spoke.

"Is anyone in this room unfamiliar with the psychiatrist

and writer Viktor Frankl?" Ms. Taggart looked around. One girl raised her hand.

"Marianne? There are probably others, but you were honest enough to recognize the limits of your knowledge. Thank you. Briefly, Viktor Emil Frankl was an Austrian Jewish physician and Holocaust survivor. His experiences as a concentration camp inmate led him to develop a form of psychotherapy built on the idea that all of life has meaning, even the ugly parts. His best-known work is titled *Man's Search for Meaning*. Your quote for this exercise is from that book. Frankl says:

"If there is a meaning in life at all, then there must be a meaning in suffering. Suffering is an ineradicable part of life, even as fate and death. Without suffering and death, human life cannot be complete."

She turned on the overhead projector so the students could refer to the quote as they worked.

"There is no lack of suffering in *Beloved*. Do you believe Toni Morrison would agree with Viktor Frankl, that there is beauty or meaning in suffering? Why or why not? You may use your copy of the book if you desire." Ms. Taggart scanned the classroom and smiled. Adam was already parsing plot lines and characters in his head.

"Does everyone understand this exercise? You're all nodding. Okay, gentlemen … ladies, start your engines."

The classroom grew quiet as they all got to work.

Forty minutes pass quickly when your mind is full of ideas and you are concentrating on how best to express your thoughts.

Ms. Taggart stood up suddenly. "Okay, class, everybody put down their pens. Please arrange your chairs in a circle so we can see each other. Who would like to start?"

. . .

"THE NAME 'SWEET HOME' evokes feelings of safety and family," Marianne began, "though the plantation was the scene of sadness and frequently of horror."

Jacob raised his hand. "Well, the Garners are the ones who named it, far as I can tell, and for them it was a benign place."

Sarah cleared her throat to get everyone's attention. "The slaves called the plantation Sweet Home as well. That was the only name they had. But that's not the same as quote 'finding beauty or meaning in a horrible place.'"

Ken interjected, "What about Denver's 'emerald closet'? Life at 124 was awkward and uncomfortable at best, between the disapproval or even fear they felt from the Black community and the actions of their resident ghost. But Denver found a place in the trees not too far from 124, her so-called emerald closet, where she felt safe and at peace."

THEY CONTINUED IN THAT MANNER, back-and-forth parry and repartee, deftly arguing ideas. But it was as though by unspoken agreement that they all carefully avoided one image.

It had to happen. Jessie Farnham raised her hand. "Amy Denver, when she first meets Sethe and helps her, she says … wait, here it is. This is the conversation, Amy talking to Sethe:

"Hurt?"

"A touch."

"Good for you. More it hurt more better it is. Can't nothing heal without pain, you know."

"That's finding meaning in a horrible place, huh? And then Amy looks at Sethe's back. She describes the wounds on

Sethe's back as looking like a chokecherry tree, complete with leaves and blossoms. I couldn't imagine living with ugly scars like that."

Sudden silence.

Jacob shook his head. "Jesus, Jess! You didn't just say that."

"I … oh." Jessie's eyes dropped to her desk. "Oh, God. I'm an ass. I'm so sorry, Cara. I didn't mean …" Jessie's eyes filled with tears.

Cara stood then, walked to Jessie's side and gently touched her shoulder. "Jess, I'm sure you didn't mean to be hurtful," Cara said. "But I've learned something about scars. There is nothing … there can be nothing beautiful about a scar, because scars are a record of violence to the body. Sethe's scars are not beautiful; they are not a tree. They're proof of a brutal whipping of a pregnant lady. That's all.

"Marianne, there's a spot on your leg by your knee. Looks like a burn. Do you remember how you got it?"

"Yeah, I sure do," she replied. "I was about six years old. Mom was carrying a pot of spaghetti to the sink. She tripped on the cat. Boiling water hit my leg. I'll never forget how much that hurt."

Cara nodded. "My point exactly."

"Cara?" Marianne asked cautiously. "You don't have to say, but would you tell about your scar? I don't mean to be offensive."

Cara sighed and chuckled to herself. "I knew it would be only a matter of time before someone noticed I have a scar on my face."

There were a few nervous giggles around the circle.

She continued, her eyes distant. Cara's voice was so quiet now that her classmates had to focus on her words. "It was a long time ago … a knife. I don't want to talk about it."

Nobody spoke.

"I try not to look at myself in a mirror because when I see

the scar, I remember how I got it. Violence and brutality. I guess Sethe and I have something in common, huh?"

The passing bell rang, but the students sat still, each of them digesting Cara's words in their own way. Adam thought about how Cara handled the uncomfortable situation with grace. She was calm when she could have been righteously angry. Would he have been so kind?

He tried to think of something to say to her. Nothing came to mind. She walked away, alone.

"Cara?"

Cara turned, a little surprised. She was accustomed to conversation-free walks from one class to another. Marianne smiled at her. "Do you mind some company?"

"No, it's fine. What can I do for you?"

"Nothing. I mean …" Marianne hesitated. "I wanted to say I'm sorry for asking about your scar in front of the class. That should have been a private conversation. I didn't think about it until the words were already out. I'm so sorry."

Cara nodded. "It's okay. Don't worry about it."

"It wasn't okay. I wish it hadn't happened."

"Yeah, I wish a lot of things hadn't happened. I try to do the best I can with what I have."

"You do really well, Cara. Jessie felt awful after she said … what she said in class. I would have replied to her with something angry. But you were bigger than that. Kinder than that."

"Marianne, I'm not as together as you make me sound. Often I'm confused, I'm hurt, angry, sad. Sometimes I just don't care. Sometimes I care desperately."

"So you're like me and every other teen."

"Perhaps you're right," Cara said. "I guess I wouldn't know."

"Well, for what it's worth, I think you're pretty cool. You

don't play the victim the way most people in your … um … situation would."

"I have nothing to be ashamed of. I didn't ask for this stupid scar on my face." Cara stubbornly brushed away a tear.

Marianne put her hand on Cara's shoulder as they walked. "I sure know how to make conversation, huh?"

Cara chuckled through her tears. "You could stand to work on your bedside manner."

"Okay, new subject."

"Praise God!"

"Boys."

"Um, that would be a lateral move."

"How about a specific boy?"

"Marianne, I've heard all the platitudes about how beauty is only skin deep. But nobody is sufficiently open-minded that they could look at this face without wanting to gag. I'm realistic. I can't expect a guy to see past my scar. And despite everything you said earlier, I'm pretty scarred on the inside, too."

"So you haven't noticed any young man showing interest in you?"

"Of course not."

"Nobody a bit over six feet tall, kinda cute for a nerd, smart, nice … nobody like that?"

Cara shook her head. "He sounds great, whoever he is. You should date him."

Marianne chuckled. "Two words: Adam. Samuelson. And I already have a boyfriend.

"Here's my class. See you around, Cara."

Cara stood for a while in the busy hallway, thinking, then she shrugged and continued to her next class.

ANTI-GRAVITY STEW

Three days per week Adam worked in the public library: two weeknights after school until close and all-day Saturday. He was returning a cart of books to their shelves when he came across a familiar head of shoulder-length brown hair bent over an open calculus text. She'd spread notes and papers neatly around. He had to admire her focus.

"Cara?"

She looked up from her work.

"Do you come here often?" he asked, then immediately he closed his eyes and shook his head sadly. "Tell me I d-didn't just say that. Nobody outside of a bar should ever say that. I'm sorry; let me start over."

Cara stared at him, a puzzled look on her face.

"Hey, Cara. It's good to see you here in the library."

She said nothing, so he continued. "What are you doing here? No, that's obvious. You're studying calculus. I mean … Okay, let me try again."

Still no response from the girl, just a puzzled gaze.

"Hi, Cara," he said with a smile.

Nothing.

"This is the p-point where you say something."

"I'm waiting till you find a version you're happy with."

"Fair enough," he said, grinning. "I'm happy with 'Hi, Cara' and a smile."

"Hello."

"How's the studying going?" he asked.

"The math is pretty straightforward."

"Straightforward. Yes, that's how most people describe calculus," Adam said with an eye roll.

"But it is. You look at a math problem, and … it just *has* to be that way. Math makes sense. It follows rules. People are complicated."

"So true," he agreed. "But that's what makes life interesting."

"Interesting. Is that the operative word?"

"Silly humans," he said. "They're a problem we won't solve soon."

Cara nodded solemnly.

"Listen, Cara. I don't work tomorrow. I've been thinking it would be n-nice to have a study partner. You learn things better when you explain them to someone else. Can we try it out tomorrow afternoon, to see if it's a p-productive way to spend some time?"

"If you like," Cara said, with no hint of enthusiasm. She said nothing more.

"Okay, I'll see you here tomorrow." He walked away, replaying the conversation in his mind. He'd never been comfortable talking with girls. It didn't seem as though he made any headway with Cara, yet he wasn't entirely sure what he was hoping to accomplish with her.

· · ·

LUNCHTIME. Adam and his friends piled into the cafeteria, loaded up their trays and took seats at their usual table. Brett took a spoonful of mystery stew and held it upside down, so they could all see.

"Look at this slop. It violated the laws of decency when they made it, and now it's breaking the law of gravity."

They all laughed. Marianne held up a hot dog in a soggy bun. "I think I saw a vein."

"Eww gross," they yelled.

Jacob raised his hand. "I can explain the mystery stew. It's ratatouille made with an actual rat."

More laughter. Jessie shrugged and asked rhetorically, "That sign in the bathroom, 'Flush twice. It's a long way to the cafeteria.' What does it mean?" They laughed and made sounds of retching.

"Your turn, Adam," Brett said. Eyes turned to him. He stood up. "Um, okay." He held out his sandwich of 'meat product' between two slices of Wonder bread. "So this morning there was a p-pet iguana in the biology room. This afternoon ... no iguana." He waved the sandwich and raised his eyebrows like Groucho Marx. "Coincidence? I think not."

That earned him laughter and a brief round of applause.

Suddenly they heard the crash of a tray of food hitting the floor. They turned to look.

"Watch where you're going, Scarface." followed by the familiar tittering laugh of Belinda May. Cara had been on her way to the table where she usually sat alone. Adam wondered whether she'd tripped, which seemed unlikely given her usual grace, or if Belinda had given her a discreet push. The latter explanation seemed much more probable.

Cara quickly cleaned up the mess and headed on to her table. He saw that she'd salvaged the milk carton and an apple, but the mystery stew couldn't be saved.

"Excuse me a minute," he said to his tablemates. There

wasn't much of a line to purchase food anymore, so he filled another bowl with stew, bought it and brought it over to Cara. She looked up as he approached.

"Thank you," she said.

"You may t-take that back once you taste this slop."

"You didn't need to buy me another bowl."

"Everyone's not an ass, Cara. Belinda doesn't speak for all of us," he said, then he headed back to his table.

Marianne looked at him. "You're a good guy, Adam. You watch out, or some girl's gonna notice."

"I know your b-boyfriend," he said, laughing. "Don't wanna piss him off. So it should probably be some other girl."

KNOCKOUT GAME

One cold late-September evening, Adam was walking to clear his head. So much to think about. His hands in his pockets against the cold, he walked faster. Cara, as so often happened lately, was on his mind. They'd studied together for three weeks, and he'd learned nothing about her. Why did she have to be so damn prickly? She'd have friends if she let down that wall. Why did he care?

The prior afternoon, in the library study room, he'd gazed at her face as she worked through math problems. There was so much to look at besides the scar. He loved the slight smile she always had as she arrived at a correct answer. Her eyes captivated him: gray like a winter storm, they seemed old … much, much older than the eyes of a teenager, as though she'd experienced things that nobody should ever see. Despite Cara's scar, he found her beautiful. And yet he sensed she had enormous inner strength, and that given the right circumstances she could be dangerous.

He replayed in his mind a conversation with Brett from earlier that day:

· · ·

"ADAM, I noticed you've been studying with Cara. What do you see in her? How can you look at her and not stare at her scar? I want to yell, 'You have a giant scar on your face! Cover up that huge, ugly scar. Scar. Scar.'"

Adam thought for a moment. "So you noticed her scar, I see?" He snickered. "Observant. Nothing gets past you. Did you see her eyes? She has amazing gray eyes."

"Bro, I couldn't tell you what color her eyes are."

"Did you notice her use of language?"

"Do I look like I've ever talked to her?" Brett said. "Anyway, I'm a guy. Hello? Language is not what I notice about girls."

"Did you notice she's in AP ... like ... everything? She's smart."

"Dude, you're in AP everything," replied Brett. "Who besides you would notice that? Anyway, I just don't see it, you and her."

"There's no 'me and her' anywhere. Lord knows she's given me no sign that she's interested. But she's a smart girl. I just wish ..."

"Yes?"

"Never mind," Adam said and playfully punched Brett's shoulder.

"Anyway, yes, I'm aware she has a scar on her face, but no, it's not what I see when I look at her. We gotta get to class. See you at lunch?"

He turned the other way to head towards his next class. He was thinking of those gray eyes that seemed to see through him, and he bumped into their owner.

"Sorry," he muttered.

"I heard what you said. I don't need you to stand up for me," Cara said. "I can take care of myself."

"I'm sure you can," he replied. "I was just telling the truth."

THE SIDEWALK TOOK him behind an elementary school, the playground equipment empty and neglected. Ahead of him, three young men in hoodies were moving in his direction.

They were play-fighting with each other and talking a little too loudly on the quiet street. He drew closer to them, still lost in his own thoughts.

Suddenly a tremendous blow to Adam's head knocked him to the sidewalk. His vision was blurry. He must have lost consciousness. His next memory was of a dull pain in his jaw, and of nausea. He tasted blood. He was cold, and he realized he was lying on the ground. Slowly he rose to his feet, still unsteady. Gazing around, he saw the three thugs lying unmoving, broken and bloody on the ground, limbs askew. Here a leg was bent above the knee, twisted unnaturally, white bone protruding through a rip in his jeans. There a face was unrecognizable, one side of his skull caved in. He could not imagine the force that would have been required to do this kind of damage.

In death, the three men looked young, not much older than Adam himself. Their faces, at least the two that were relatively intact, were masks of terror: eyes wide, mouths open in a silent scream. Adam's lip quivered. Salty tears filled his eyes. His breath caught. *What did they see before they died? So quick ... that could have been him.* Bile rose in his throat. He fell to his knees and retched, but couldn't produce anything but a little spit. He stayed where he was until the urge to vomit had passed.

Feeling steadier, he rose to his feet. He turned and saw Cara standing against a wall, eyeing him uncertainly. "Wh-what happened?" he said.

"The Knockout Game. One of them cold-cocked you."

Adam stared at her, waiting for an explanation.

"Those men were evil. Monsters. But they ran into a bigger monster."

"Did you see what happened to them?"

Cara nodded, her face solemn. "I *was* what happened to them."

Adam stepped back without thinking. Cara reached out her hand toward him, empty, then let it fall back to her side. "Please don't be afraid of me. I won't hurt you."

He thought about that for a while. "No, I don't believe you would hurt me. But I don't understand ..." he gestured toward the bodies. His voice caught, and he fought back tears. "I mean, they're really *dead*. This doesn't happen."

Cara stood in place, a solemn look on her face.

"How did you c-come to be here?"

"I followed you."

"Why?"

"I ... don't understand you."

"Listen, Cara." He enunciated each word. "I do not want you to follow me."

She shrugged. "It turned out well for you tonight."

"I d-didn't say I don't want you around me. I just don't see why you need to follow me. Why don't you walk with me instead of skulking a distance behind me?"

"You want me to walk with you," she repeated as though not understanding.

"Please," he said. "I would really like that."

"But ..." Her left hand started to her face, then dropped.

"You have a scar," he stated. "It's there, but it's not what I see when I look at you."

"What do you see?"

"I see a cute g-girl with a sharp mind and ... dammit ... I like to look at you. There's something about you. Can I say that?"

Cara looked down at her feet. "You're blind. That blow to your head robbed you of sense."

"Maybe so. What should we do about this?" He gestured to the fallen men. "Are we supposed to call the c-cops?"

Cara looked at him. "What would you tell them? These guys attacked you, and now they're dead. You have a motive, and you had the opportunity. Sounds like a deep hole to dig yourself out of."

"We c-can't leave these people here without telling anyone. It's not right."

"Okay, Adam. I'll take care of it. There's an anonymous crime reporting hotline I've … uh … heard of."

Adam swayed slightly. He shook his head to clear it.

"How are you feeling?" Cara asked.

"How am I feeling? There are three dead p-people here on the sidewalk, and I don't understand how they got that way. My head hurts. I'm scared, I'm angry, I'm nauseated. I've never seen a bone sticking out. I hate blood. Should I go on?"

"Take a breath, Adam. There's a coffee shop near here. You can clean up a bit. I suppose we should probably talk about this. I'll call the police as we walk."

She held out her hand, and Adam took it in his for support as he was still dizzy. Her hand was warm despite the coolness of the evening.

The coffee shop was nearly empty. Adam washed his face in the restroom, happy to see that there was not much blood. They sat facing each other at a small table. Cara gazed at him appraisingly, her gray eyes narrowed. "You're right to be afraid of me," she finally said. Then, in a whisper, "Sometimes I'm afraid of me."

"Why is that?"

"Those men," she said. "Did you see them? Did you see how they died?"

He shook his head. "Cara, I'm not sure what I should think. I can't explain what I saw just now. One of those guys punched me, and I guess, knocked me out for a bit. But they died so horribly. Why did they have to die like that?"

Cara's voice grew more agitated. "I saw them hit you and

you fell. You didn't move. I ran to you and then … I don't remember what happened. I never do. I … have no control over the violence."

She said nothing more. Her eyes filled with tears. Adam gently touched her hand.

"It wasn't you that k-killed them. Couldn't have been you. There's no way a teenage girl can do that kind of damage by herself."

"It wasn't me," she repeated slowly, "that killed them? Then how do you explain what you saw?"

"They c-could have been struck by a car," he ventured.

"So," she persisted, "they could have been struck by a car … that was traveling at high speed … on the sidewalk … and then disappeared. That's your theory?"

"Best I got," he said.

"Why would you have been miraculously uninjured by this hypothetical errant vehicle?" She gazed directly at him.

"Look, Cara, I don't have an answer for you that makes complete sense. All I know is that three people who attacked me are gone, and I'm here having coffee with a cute girl. I hesitate to ask too many questions. Perhaps whatever magic happened that g-got you to sit with me will vanish if I look too hard."

"I sit with you in class."

"Yeah, in class, and we've been studying together in the library a couple times a week, for … what, three weeks now? But when we study, we seem to only talk about c-classwork, not about life outside of school. You're the most private person I've ever met. You've never just sat and talked with me."

"You said you wanted to study together, so we've been studying. What were you really asking me for?"

"Fair enough. Moment of honesty, okay? Girls are …

outside of my comfort zone. I was truly asking you to study. I just …" He stopped talking.

"Yes?"

"Like in math class. You make calculus seem so easy. It's awe-inspiring to watch you work a problem."

"If that's a line, it's one I've never heard before. Points to you for creativity."

Adam smiled. "It's not a line. I guess … for me … smart is attractive. I've been wanting to talk to you about things unrelated to school. But I didn't know how."

"I'm here now, Adam. What would you like to talk about?"

"Tell me about you. I've learned nothing about you. Where do you live? What do your parents do? Do you have any interests or hobbies outside of school?"

"Nowhere. I don't know. No."

"This isn't a conversation," he said. "You sound like you're being interrogated. I don't mean to pry. Friends talk."

"I'm not very interesting. Tell me about you, Adam."

"Okay, I have a thirteen-year-old s-sister named Linnea. She enjoys soccer and is fascinated by science and technology. Her bedroom is like a little engineering lab. They say little sisters are supposed to be a pain, but I like Linnea. She's smarter than most thirteen-year-olds. Uh, I have a mom and a dad. My dad is a physician at the university, and my mom is a nurse. Outside of school, I play piano and chess. Now your turn."

"I …" Cara shifted in her chair. She frowned, then stood up. "Thank you for the coffee, Adam. I have to go."

He stood too. "Cara, please, I'm sorry. I d-didn't mean to push. Please don't go yet."

She picked up her bag and trudged toward the coffee shop door, her head down. He walked silently next to her. "I wish you didn't have that scar."

He saw her tense, her eyes darkening. "B-Because I heard

what you said in class when Marianne asked you about it. I wish I could have been there to protect you."

Cara was silent, but she stopped walking. "Cara, you're the bravest person I know."

"I'm not brave."

"Every day you face the world, alone. People can be cruel. Heaven knows you have reason to be hateful, but you somehow choose to take the higher ground. You're a lady, in the best sense of the word. Now please, let me walk you home."

"I don't have a home."

"Everyone has a home," he said, as if stating something obvious.

"No, actually, they don't. I don't have a home."

"Then which way are you heading?"

"It doesn't matter."

"But where will you spend the night?"

"I always find something. Please, Adam, I'm okay. Just go home."

"I c-can't leave you alone at night to walk by yourself."

"After what just happened, you're worried for my safety?"

Adam shrugged. "I'm sorry. Chivalry is hard to turn off. It's how my parents raised me."

She sighed. "Yea, though I walk through the valley of the shadow of death, I will fear no evil …" She looked directly at him. "… for I am the meanest son-of-a-bitch in the valley."

He chuckled. "And that means exactly what? Besides that I'll never look at Psalm 23 the same way again."

"Means this girl is safe on the streets at night. Trust me."

"Okay, I'll take you at your word. Cara?"

"Yes?"

"We're still on for studying at the library tomorrow after school as usual, right?"

Cara shrugged. "I guess so."

"Would you have d-dinner with me tomorrow night? At my house?"

Cara regarded him intently. "I've not done that before."

"You've never been to someone's house for dinner?"

"Never."

"That's unusual, but it doesn't matter," he said. "I've never invited a girl to meet my family. We're a couple of social butterflies, huh?"

She shrugged.

"It'll be fun." He tried to sound confident.

"Okay, Adam. I need to go. Stay away from guys in hoodies."

"I …" he hesitated. "I guess I'll see you tomorrow in school, then."

Cara nodded, then walked out of the café. She turned a corner and disappeared. Back in the direction they'd come from originally, where the men attacked him, Adam could faintly see the flashing lights of emergency vehicles.

MYSTERY GIRL

*L*ate afternoon, Cara and Adam left the library together, headed to his house. She sat quietly in the passenger seat of his old Toyota, though Cara was always comfortable with silence.

"What are you thinking?" he asked.

"I've never done this before."

"Don't worry. They'll like you. I like you, and I learned what to like in a person from them."

"You must love your parents very much, Adam."

"I do. We d-don't always agree, but we always make a point to talk to each other and listen to each other. I don't think every family works that way."

"You have no idea," she said, her eyes downcast.

Adam lived in a two-story brick house of about average size for his neighborhood. His house was on a side street without much traffic. Kids could ride bikes and roller blade down the tree-lined cul-de-sac. He had a comparatively large backyard which sloped down to a small creek. When he was younger, he did some of his best daydreaming as he wandered along the water's edge.

He parked on the street in front of his house, as always. The garage only fit two cars. His parents got the garage because that was how life worked. The walkway from the street to the front door curved a little past flower beds that, in the coolness of the fall, were without flowers. But the mulch and decorative stones were nice, he thought. Should be, since they represented several weeks of his work and sweat this past summer. The oak door stood solidly against the red-brown brick of his house. He squeezed Cara's hand in reassurance, and he opened the door. Usually, he entered and left through the garage, but he thought that bringing a girl for the first time to meet his parents required an official entrance.

"Mom, Dad, th-this is Cara."

"Hi, Cara. I'm Katie, Adam's mom. This is Adam's dad, Stephen." She gestured to him. "The little one on the couch, acting shy, is Linnea." Linnea smiled and waved. "Come in, won't you? May I get you something to drink?"

Cara paused. "Some water, please."

"I'll get it," Linnea yelled as she ran towards the kitchen. "Anybody else while I'm here?"

"Water for me too, Linnea," Adam said.

"Please, sit down. How was your day?"

Adam fielded that question. "School was fun. We have t-tests at the end of the week in calculus and world history, but Cara and I got a lot done today in the library. We're ready."

"Sounds good. Listen, I need to get back to the kitchen," Katie said. "We're having taco soup. Adam loves it."

"We all love it," Stephen added.

Cara looked at Adam's mom. "I'll come with you." The two of them left together.

Stephen looked at Adam, smiled and nodded in their direction. "Point in her favor, son."

. . .

"You have an amazing kitchen," Cara said. "I like the big island, and I like the way your kitchen is open to the living room. I've worked a little in restaurants, so I can appreciate a nice layout."

"Thanks. I love to cook when I have time, and the family loves to eat. We needed a large kitchen with good appliances."

"It was nice of you to invite me for dinner."

"Our pleasure. Adam says you've become study buddies."

"Yeah, we've been getting together twice a week to review classwork. We both take school seriously."

Neither Cara nor Katie spoke for a moment. To Cara, it seemed like a long time.

"I guess I'm nervous," Cara said. She bit her lip and looked away from Adam's mom.

Katie could tell she was anxious. "Would you tell me about you and Adam?"

Cara thought about it for a time. While she was framing her words, she motioned for Katie to hand her an onion, which she peeled and diced competently. Soon there was another pile of chopped onion in the bowl.

"I guess I feel safe with him. He's kind, for a boy." She smiled briefly as she replayed a recent interaction in her mind.

School. A busy hallway. Adam was talking and joking with his friends. She discovered she enjoyed looking at him. This was a strange new feeling for her. She liked his face: honest, direct. He had a ready smile. She tentatively approached the group.

"Hi, Cara," he said. "Are we still meeting after school to review calculus?"

A tall student, she thought his name was Brett, laughed sarcastically. "Adam finally has a girlfriend?"

"Dude," Adam said with a smile. "What the hell? If you were as smart as Cara, I'd study with you. Try focusing more on the books and less on my rich and exotic social life."

WHEN DINNER WAS READY, they gathered at the table. Everyone sat, Cara beside Linnea per Adam's little sister's request. They held hands and Stephen said a brief grace.

"Everyone dig in. Cara, you go first. Would you like some soup?" asked Katie.

"Yes, please, ma'am."

Katie smiled. "And there's bread. Salad." Conversation halted for a while as they ate.

"LINNEA," Cara said, "I saw your game yesterday."

"You were there?"

Cara nodded. "Yes. Adam said you played. He just didn't tell me how well."

Linnea beamed.

"I watched you steal the ball, take it downfield, pass it, take back control, fake out a defender, and make that goal."

"I didn't think anyone was there to see me," Linnea said. "I'm glad you were at the game, Cara."

Stephen caught Adam's eye, smiled and nodded. Another point.

ADAM HAD a lot to think about that night. He lay in bed, restless and half-asleep.

"Adam, wake up a minute."

A warm hand touched his shoulder. He opened his eyes to

see his little sister sitting on his bed.

"May I talk with you? It's about Cara."

"Sure, sis. What's going on?"

"A few minutes ago, I got up to get a drink, and I overheard Mom and Dad discussing Cara. Dad was concerned that Cara was hiding something, deflecting questions about her home life, and that she seemed to avoid him."

"What did Mom say?"

"You apparently told Mom that Cara was homeless. Mom wanted to offer Cara our extra bedroom, but Dad was hesitant because we know little about her.

"Adam, why do you think she's homeless?"

"Yesterday evening we were in a café. It was getting d-dark, so I said I'd walk her home. She told me not to worry about it. I guess I pushed, and she finally admitted she had nowhere specifically to go. She told me she spends the night wherever.

"Linnea, you know that large b-bag Cara had with her when she came for dinner?"

"Yeah, I wondered about that."

"I looked inside today while we were studying in the library. She'd left to use the restroom. Her bag has a couple changes of clothes and some personal hygiene items. I realized I'd never seen her in clothes other than those." He shook his head. "Sis, everything she owns is in that bag she carries with her."

"My God," Linnea said, "I can't imagine how hard it must be to live like that. She's so nice … and I can tell she's smart. I like her, Adam."

"Me too."

"Adam, wouldn't it be wonderful if Cara could stay with us?"

"Linnea, that'd be awesome. I hadn't thought it was even a possibility." His sister had an amazing mind. He'd become accustomed to asking her opinions because they were usually well-reasoned. "What do you think we could do to help this p-process along?"

"It seems to me that everything hinges on Cara. Would she accept help? Would she be willing to open up?"

"I'm not sure, sis," he said. "Cara's p-pretty private."

"Adam, does Cara have a state ID?"

He looked at her in surprise. "What do you know about state IDs? You're thirteen."

She giggled and tapped her temple with a finger. "There are a lot of things in here thirteen-year-olds aren't supposed to know. And I love surprising my brother."

Adam continued. "Because if Cara has a state ID, then that means she has the documentation to *get* a state ID. That's proof of at least some stability. And if she doesn't have a state ID, I'll bet our folks can help her get one. And the process of obtaining the ID would help Mom and Dad grow more comfortable with her. Linnea, you're my favorite sister."

Giggle. "I'm your only sister. So will you talk to Mom or Dad about this tomorrow?"

"Definitely. And thanks."

"G'night, Adam." She left his room.

THE NEXT EVENING, Adam talked with his father.

"Dad?"

"What's up, son?"

"I'd like to ask you about Cara."

"What can I help with? Relationship advice?"

"No. Um, well, yes. Cara's awfully p-private, and I sense she doesn't want anyone at school to know, but she told me she's homeless. I tried to walk her home from a coffee shop a couple of nights ago. She refused, I didn't understand why, and I guess I sort of forced her to admit she had nowhere to go."

"What are you hoping to accomplish?"

"Today in school, I asked Cara if she had a state ID, like a driver's license or whatever. She said she had no way to get one. I didn't p-promise her anything because I'm not sure what we can do. Anyway, I thought I'd run it by you. See if you have any ideas."

"Let me think about it. I have a lawyer friend who might give us some advice."

Adam raised an eyebrow. "Dad, you've told us often enough how you feel about lawyers, so for you, the phrase 'lawyer friend' is an oxymoron, like jumbo shrimp or Army intelligence."

Stephen laughed. "Yes, they're all minions of the antichrist. Nonetheless, I'll discuss Cara's situation with our lawyer, and we'll see what he says."

Study rooms in the library allowed for private conversations without disturbing the other patrons. As Adam and Cara finished their study session, he posed a question.

"Cara, would you be willing to talk with my parents?"

"About what?"

"I imagine you'll t-tell me you're doing fine and it's none of my business anyway, but I was talking with them about … um, about how you're living and that you have no state ID, which means you can't legally work. I thought they—"

"Why are you worrying about this? I'm doing fine! What I do with my life is none of your …" Cara sighed. "You told me I was gonna say that."

"I pay attention to you. I'm getting to know you."

"And you care."

He nodded. "I do."

"Do you think they can help me?"

"I t-trust my folks completely. They haven't ever lied to Linnea and me, so far as I'm aware. Would you eat with us again tonight? And afterward, the four of us can talk."

Cara nodded. "Okay."

That evening after steaks, grilled asparagus, and garden salad, Cara, Adam and his parents sat in their living room.

Stephen began. "Cara, I was talking in very general terms … no names or anything … with a lawyer I've known for a long time and whose opinion I trust, about your situation."

"My situation?"

"Yes. You're a minor, and to the law, that means you're not qualified to decide what is in your best interest. You've taken care of yourself for years, but to some extent, you've been lucky that a well-meaning bureaucrat at one of your schools hasn't taken a personal interest in you and forced you into the foster care system."

"That would be bad," Cara said in a quiet voice.

"My friend says there are two ways to approach this. One would be for Katie and me to become your legal guardians. For what it's worth, you've made an excellent impression on us. Adam and Linnea are your two biggest fans. But you'll be eighteen in less than a year, and you've been taking care of yourself for a long time. I believe the better approach would be to have you legally declared an emancipated minor. That way, the law allows you to make your own decisions as though you were an adult. You can take those papers with you wherever, and they'll protect you till you turn eighteen and become a legal adult."

"Why are you doing this?"

"Because we're in a position to help. Our intention is not to pry into your business, and certainly not to control you. Call it selfishness if you want. We like the feeling of having done something worthwhile."

"Sorry, I don't mean to sound suspicious or ungrateful. You're good people, and I thank you for opening your house to me. It's just that it's been me against the world for most of my life. In my experience when one hand is open to me, the other hand is preparing to slap me."

"I can't imagine what you've been through, Cara," Katie said.

Cara looked down for a minute, thinking, then glanced back at Stephen. "What are the risks to me, short term, if we start the process of emancipation? Up until now, my strategy has been to remain under the radar, so to speak, so that the law doesn't take an interest in me."

"That's an intelligent question," Stephen replied. "I don't pretend to have everything figured out at this point, but I give you my word I will proceed cautiously, in counsel with my friend who has experience with this area of the law. His name is Sidney Cohen. He's a partner in one of the most prominent law firms in the city. He believes, with what I've told him about our situation, that he can arrange for your emancipation without contacting your biological mother. Of course, he would like to meet you and speak with you. With your permission, I'll set up a meeting with him, you, Katie and me."

"You understand how much my freedom means to me, Dr. Samuelson. But I have no reason not to trust you, and you've been very kind to me. I'll go with you."

SIDNEY COHEN WAS a distinguished-looking older man with a full head of silver hair, perfectly coiffed. He wore a dark suit, red tie over a white dress shirt, and expensive-looking shoes.

Katie and Stephen took a half-day off work so they could take Cara to see him.

"Stephen, my friend, how are you?" the attorney said in his deep, resonant voice as he shook their hands. "And Katie, as lovely as ever."

"Sid, I'd like you to meet Cara Ferris. She's a schoolmate of Adam's."

"Cara, a pleasure to make your acquaintance," he said smiling, looking at Cara.

"Please, follow me to my office. We can talk privately there."

An immense teak desk dominated the space. It looked old and valuable. Behind the desk, a large window showed a view over the downtown area. Two walls were almost entirely bookshelves filled with thick leather volumes. Diplomas and awards covered the remaining wall. Cara noted his J.D. Summa Cum Laude from Harvard Law School. *This guy knows his stuff*, she thought.

"Now, as to you," the attorney began, "Stephen has given me some background, but there are several large holes in my understanding of your life to this point. You're meeting me for the first time, but Stephen and I have been friends for over two decades. We met under the worst of circumstances. My wife took suddenly ill, and within days was on a ventilator. Stephen saved her life. Now he's asked me to help you. Please believe me when I say I will do everything in my power to help you. As you trust Katie and Stephen, you can trust me."

"I understand, sir. I appreciate your help," Cara replied, "but I need to say, before I tell you anything else, that not everything about me is entirely … ah, legal. You may decide to involve the authorities, and for me, that could be catastrophic."

Sidney studied her for a moment. "I've been blessed to have had a very successful career. Over the years, I've represented some good people and some who were not so good. In any event, I very much doubt, Cara, that you will be my most evil client. Regardless, I will represent you to the very best of my ability."

"Very well," Cara responded. "Where should we start?"

"Let me paraphrase Lewis Carroll in *Alice in Wonderland*. Begin at the beginning, and go on till you come to the end. Then stop."

Cara nodded. "I was born in Brooklyn, New York, on August 15, 1999. I never knew my father; Mom didn't talk about him. Mom worked off and on, waitressing in bars, stuff like that. Whatever could earn a little money. She had a series of boyfriends. Never kept one for too long. I don't remember any of them being solid citizens.

"One day, when I was ten years old, Mom was at work, and I was home alone with her then-current boyfriend, Les. He'd been drinking all day. He …" Cara paused, swallowed, then continued her narrative. "He wanted to have sex with me. I refused. He pulled me to him, and I hit him. He got furious. He punched me, and he cut me … cut my face. Then he raped me. He was too strong for me. I couldn't fight him.

"Later, he passed out on the couch. I ran away." Cara stopped to let them digest her words. She looked directly at the attorney. "Mr. Cohen, I've lived on the street since then. I've been on my own for seven years."

There was silence in the attorney's office as the three adults considered her story. Katie wiped her eyes and blew her nose noisily. The attorney stared at his desk and shook his head slowly. "Good God," he said finally. "I thought I knew how ugly the world could get."

"Yes, sir," Cara agreed, "but there are good people, too. This year, I met a boy in school. He was kind to me. He didn't seem to mind my scar. Then he introduced me to his mom and dad." Cara gestured at Katie and Stephen.

"But until just recently, you've been on your own?"

"Yes, sir."

"And you figured out how to attend school. You learned about McKinney-Vento, I suppose?"

Cara nodded. "Yes, sir. I like to read. I like to learn things."

"How is school going for you?"

"I have almost a 4.0 GPA. I hope to go to college."

"Tell me this. You started living on the street in New York, correct?"

"That's right, sir."

"How did you end up here in the Midwest?"

"I didn't specifically intend to come to Indiana. If I grew uncomfortable … if I worried I'd attracted too much attention or if someone at a school looked at my situation too closely, I would move to a new city. I've traveled quite a bit around the eastern half of the country. There are ways for a kid to find rides. Truck stops are often good. I would go wherever the ride took me, so long as it was far away from the previous city."

"Cara!" Katie exclaimed. "Didn't you think that was dangerous?"

"Ma'am," Cara said to her, "as a little girl, I was raped. It's like a part of me died that day. I became numb. I had nobody to turn to, nobody to trust. I made the best choices I could, given my options as I saw them at the time.

"It wasn't like I approached truckers and threw myself on their mercy. I'd learned about stealth and silence. I could usually find a trailer to sneak into, where I could hide until we reached another town."

"Nobody to trust …" Katie repeated, almost to herself.

"In seven years, Adam is the first person I felt I could trust completely. Then by extension, you." Cara gestured to Katie and Stephen. "And now you, Mr. Cohen. Please don't violate my trust."

"Cara, I've never heard a story like yours," the attorney said. "I will not be party to hurting you. On the contrary, I'm pretty sure I can help you. Do you have a state ID? Driver license or the like? Do you by chance know your Social Security number?"

Cara thought for a moment. "No, sir. I never had the proof of residence for a state ID, nor do I know if I have a Social Security number. Is that a problem?"

"It will be more challenging, but we can proceed. What's your mom's full name?"

"Kendra Marie Ferris."

"Okay, and do you remember your last address? I mean, at the time you left home."

"I've tried to put that out of my mind, sir. I'm sorry, I can't think of it."

"That's okay, miss. I can proceed with what we have. I have friends in New York. Stephen, I'll contact you when I have a copy of Cara's birth certificate. I will research the question of Cara's Social Security number. We'll either find it or apply for one. She'll need it when we apply for legal emancipation.

"There will be some documents to sign as we proceed. Stephen, I'll send them by courier to your office."

"Thank you, Sid. I'll look for them."

Cara raised her hand. "Mr. Cohen, you're quite certain that starting this process of legal emancipation will not result in me being sent back to New York? I would die before I returned there."

"Yes, I am certain that you will not be sent back to New York. A judge decides legal emancipation. I know who would hear this case. Given the facts of your story and your more-than-satisfactory situation here, there is no chance she would send you back to your biological mom … if, in fact, one could even find her."

Sidney stood up, walked around his desk and shook hands with everyone.

"Thank you, sir," Cara said. "Thank you all."

PART OF THE FAMILY

"Cara?"

"Yes, ma'am."

"I've talked with Stephen. We want to offer you a place to stay. We have a guest room that's empty, and it's not useful to anyone."

Cara stood up straight. "I can take care of myself. I don't need anyone's help."

Katie continued. "I realize you're not looking for charity. We'll expect you to do your share of the chores, same as Adam and Linnea. You're responsible for your room. You're comfortable in the kitchen, so I was thinking you can help with meals from time to time. Things like that. We can talk about it later."

Cara gave a wan smile. "I can see where Adam learned about persistence."

"Let me show you your room," Katie said.

Cara followed Katie up the stairs to the hallway. They entered the first room on the left. A tan comforter covered the bed, to the right as they entered the room. In the far corner, by the foot of the bed, the closet door was ajar. The back wall had a window and a wooden dresser. Across the room from the bed was a wooden desk and a small bookcase. The floor was hardwood.

"This is yours, Cara, if you'll accept it. Sorry, it's not very fancy."

"I've never worried about being fancy. This is nice."

Cara ran her hand along the bed, then the dresser.

"A proper bed …," she murmured as though to herself.

"The kids share a bathroom in the hallway. I hope that's okay. The rule is if the door is closed, you don't go in. Towels are in the linen closet in the bathroom."

Cara smiled. "Thank you, ma'am. This is truly wonderful. Your family is very kind."

Katie shook her head. "It's stupid for us to have an empty room while you're living on the street."

DINNER THAT NIGHT was roast chicken, garlic mashed potatoes, and a chopped salad.

Stephen stopped eating for a moment, cleared his throat and surveyed the table. "I would like to take this opportunity to formally welcome Cara to our family. Cara, thank you for agreeing to stay with us."

"Thank you," Cara replied.

Stephen nodded. "I have some thoughts I want to share in front of everybody to avoid misunderstandings or hurt feelings. Cara, this is what we do in our house. We talk openly about subjects that some other people may find delicate. I hope you won't feel uncomfortable because that's never my intention.

"First, just to get this out of the way because it's awkward but we need to mention it: I couldn't begin to say I understand what you've been through, but I will do everything I can so you feel safe here in our house. I will try not to be alone with you, at least until you're more comfortable here. So please don't worry that I'm avoiding you or that I don't like you or I'm angry at you."

"I appreciate that."

"In the same vein, though, I would ask that you and Adam not be in each other's bedrooms."

"Of course," Cara and Adam said almost together.

"May I go in your room sometimes, Cara?" Linnea pleaded.

Cara smiled at her. "You're always welcome, Linnea."

AFTER DINNER, Cara and Adam walked together in his backyard, slowly moving towards the creek.

"Cara, there's something I want to say."

She looked up at him.

"Cara, you're a s-smart girl. You're aware I like you."

"You've always been very nice, Adam."

"No, I mean, not like a friend. I mean sure you're my f-friend, but I like you more than just as a friend." Why were the words so hard to say? "And now you'll be living in my house, and I don't want it to be awkward. I cannot imagine what your life has been like. But I suspect, from what I've read, that young p-people living alone are sometimes offered shelter and safety in exchange for things."

She was looking at him hard now. "Cara, my family invited you to live here," he took a deep breath, "and I need you to understand there are no conditions. We want you to stay here, and you don't owe my family or me a thing. I will never pressure you, I will never hurt you, and I completely understand the meaning of the word 'no.'"

Cara stopped walking and stood in front of him, very close. Her hair smelled sweet. She looked up at him. Her eyes were moist. "Thank you, Adam. I don't want you to feel awkward. You're kinder than anyone I've ever known."

"It's p-probably better for me to think of you as a sister."

She nodded. "Yes, that would probably be best." But she didn't back away from him.

"Cara, please …"

"Adam Samuelson, you listen to me. I genuinely appreciate the opportunity to have a warm place to sleep, and food … and friends. But I have lived on my own for seven years. I have figured out how to go to school … by myself. I get mostly A's in my classes, by myself. I will find a way to go to college, and again I can do it by myself. I don't need you, and I don't need your family, kind as you all have been to me. So if I left here today, I would be okay."

She reached up and touched his cheek. Her hand was warm.

"Adam …"

Her lips were slightly parted. She moved even closer. He leaned in and gently touched her lips with his. Her eyes opened wide, and she smiled. "Again, please."

Their second kiss was longer, searching. Her breath warmed his mouth and down into his chest. Their tongues touched tentatively. Neither of them was experienced at this.

She laid her head against his chest, her chestnut hair soft, and they hugged standing by the creek.

As the sun fell below the trees and the air cooled, they strolled, hand in hand, back to the house.

"Cara, I said I should think of you like a sister, but I've changed my mind."

Cara smiled at him.

THE NEXT DAY the sun seemed brighter. Adam hummed as he

dressed. He looked in the mirror one last time, smiled at his reflection, and splashed on a little cologne.

Cara was typically taciturn at breakfast, but he thought he saw her stare at him at one point when she didn't know he could see her. That morning, for the first time, she drove with him to school. In the car, she punched up the Mendelssohn Octet on his iPhone. As the uplifting sounds poured from the car's speakers, she relaxed against the seat and closed her eyes. "I love this," she murmured.

They entered the high school together. Cara turned to head towards her locker. Adam pressed his lips to her hair and inhaled deeply. He could become addicted to the scent of Cara.

She turned to him, a look of surprise on her face. "Adam, someone could see you."

"That's a bad thing?"

"It won't do your social standing any good."

He smiled and played dumb. "My s-social standing, whatever that is, will fall if I like a girl? How does that work?"

Cara sighed and talked to him as though he were a child. "You may not have noticed, but I'm not exactly Miss Popular. Kids are cruel, and I don't want you to be hurt because of your association with me."

Fun time was over. He was becoming irritated … not at Cara, but at life. "Cara, listen to me now," he said. "I have no interest in having a secret g-girlfriend. You're the first girl, and so far the only girl I've ever kissed. That's because you're the first girl I've ever really liked. I wasn't ashamed yesterday evening, and I'm not ashamed now. To hell with haters. To hell with Belinda and her friends. They're not worth the time to think about them.

"And so far as my f-friends are concerned, real friends won't judge me."

"Oookay then," Cara said. "I tried."

"Thanks for your concern," he said with a laugh. They headed down the hallway together.

A*T* LUNCH, for the first time, he waved Cara over to the table where he and his friends usually sat.

"Well, this is different," said Brett Stengler. He didn't add anything, though.

Adam stared at Brett, eyebrow raised, a slight smile on his face.

"So does anybody understand trigonometry?" Brett said, apparently glad to have thought of a different topic of conversation. "I couldn't explain Euler's formula if my life depended on it."

"I can show you how it works," Cara offered. "You should join Adam and me in the library this afternoon after school. We always reserve a study room so we can talk without disturbing people."

"I uh … don't want to intrude on anything," replied Brett, surprised at this turn of conversation.

"We study in the study room," Adam said. "And p-people who go to the library know that the study rooms all have large windows that face the main reading room. Not exactly a good place to make out." Then he added, "But seriously, man, show up. Cara can explain math in a way that makes it seem obvious. She's an excellent teacher."

Cara tried to hide her facial expression by looking down at her tray, but she was clearly smiling.

STORIES FROM THE STREET

*O*ne early October night, not long after Cara moved in with the Samuelsons, they were all hanging out in the living room, sprawled on the couch or one of the comfortable chairs, each engrossed in a book. The calming notes of Bach's cello suites poured from the sound system. Linnea furrowed her brow and looked over at Cara.

"Cara, you don't have a family?" Linnea asked.

Katie looked up sharply. "Linnea!"

"It's okay, really," Cara said. "It's my story, and it's my truth. I lived it. Kids should appreciate how lucky they are to have parents who care."

She turned to Linnea. "No, Linnea, I've lived on my own for seven years. Since I was ten."

Linnea was silent for a short while, thinking. Then, "That's three years younger than me. I don't think I could live alone. I wouldn't know what to do."

"You learn," answered Cara. "Each mistake you make, you learn from it. Each person you trust who tries to hurt you, you learn."

"But I mean, how do you pay for stuff when you're a kid,

and you don't have an allowance, and you're too young to get a job?"

Cara looked at Katie for permission. "Ma'am, I'm willing to talk about this. You have a right to know about me. But I need to tell you all up front, my story is … difficult to listen to. Is it okay for Linnea to hear?"

"Mom!" Linnea said.

Katie nodded. "My daughter is thirteen going on forty. She's an unusual child, in a good way. She can process this, and if she has questions, we can answer them."

Cara began, "Linnea, you understand stealing is bad."

"Of course."

"But sometimes, when you're living on your own, you're so hungry or so cold … you do things that you know are wrong because you want to stay alive. And sometimes kids on the street, girls and boys both, are offered shelter and food in exchange for … things."

Linnea gasped. "You mean like sex things?"

Cara nodded. "A lot of kids end up in that situation. You must understand that when you don't see any way out, you do what you need to do. You know it's wrong, and you hate yourself for your weakness, but you want to live. You do what's necessary to survive. Try not to judge those kids too harshly."

"But …"

"I was lucky in a sad way," Cara said. "My face is ugly, so I suspect not many people wanted to be with me. But I don't want to misrepresent myself. I'm *not* a good girl. I've sometimes chosen life over honor."

There was silence for a few minutes. That was a lot to digest.

"What did you do in the winter?" Linnea asked.

"I have my sweatshirt and a jacket," Cara said, "and I used to have a blanket. Someone stole it while I was at school.

There's no honor among thieves, you see. I couldn't bring a blanket to school because kids would laugh at me … more than they already do. I didn't want my classmates to learn I had no home. I've meant to get another blanket. Sometimes you find one in a dumpster. Sometimes, if you have a little money, you can buy clothes and blankets at Goodwill. When it's freezing, there's usually some church group handing out blankets to street people."

"Where did you do homework?"

"Public library. Plus, it's warm inside. And after I'm done with my homework, I can read books all evening, and while I'm reading, I can imagine I'm in a different place. In a story, I can be pretty, and I can be loved." Cara nodded as she spoke. "A public library is a wonderful place."

Stephen had put down his book and was listening thoughtfully. "Cara, if I may, I have a question."

"Of course, Dr. Samuelson."

"How have you been able to go to school? How can a kid, all by herself with no involvement of a caregiver, arrange for school? How did you provide all the documents, you know, proof of residence, immunization records, things like that?"

Cara gave a wan smile. "Sometimes, even if by accident, the government gets something right. There's a federal law, the McKinney-Vento Act, that provides for schooling for homeless kids. The name the law gives kids like me, who have no caregiver, no adult to help them, is 'unaccompanied youth.' I've been unaccompanied for seven years. When I first ran away, after … you know … I wasn't able to go to school for a while.

"Not that I didn't want to attend school," she said. "I loved school. But I was terrified that the authorities would send me back. I needed to learn how to survive first. I needed to find places to sleep, where to get food, where to find clothes, how to keep clean … all without arousing suspicion with anyone who could make trouble for me."

Cara continued quietly. "Over time, I learned some skills. As I said to Linnea, I'm not proud of everything I had to do." She paused for a moment, then took a deep breath and continued. "But I've found I have better-than-average dexterity and a light touch. I learned how to lift a wallet, take the cash and replace the wallet in the pocket or purse. Or I could remove an item from a shelf. No one ever caught me. If necessary, I'd run and disappear. A few times, I had to change cities because I worried I had attracted undue attention or because someone made me feel unsafe. So that's how, over the years, I migrated from New York City to the Midwest. As I mentioned in the attorney's office, I've lived in several cities scattered around the eastern half of the United States.

"I tell you all that as background to answer your question about schooling. After my, ah, sabbatical, as I call it, I learned about McKinney-Vento. Amazing what you can learn in a library. After a few years on the street, I started back in school. I tell the liaison person in a school that my mother cannot meet with them, which is true, and that I never knew my father, which is also true. I look in their eyes, and I talk as though I believe what I'm saying. Public schools have to accept homeless kids, including unaccompanied youth, even without shot records or transcripts from previous schools. It helps that I do very well academically and that I keep a low profile. I've found it remarkably easy to return to school and do well even after my sabbatical."

"Wow," Stephen said. "I had no idea. You're an amazing person, Cara."

"I just do what I can, sir."

"Well, apparently that's a lot."

.   .   .

Six weeks later, Cara and Katie were working in the kitchen, throwing together a quick dinner.

"Cara?"

"Yes, ma'am?"

"Have you ever been to a doctor?"

"No, never. I have no way to pay for care, but more importantly for me, I would risk being forced into the foster care system or possibly even being sent back to my mom … if she's still alive. I've not seen a dentist either." Then she added, "Though I do brush my teeth."

Katie was silent as she thought about this. "I don't mean to be intrusive, but I would like you to consider getting a physical, if for no other reason than to catch you up on immunizations that you should have had years ago. You should also see a dentist. I've had my teeth cleaned twice a year since as far back as I can remember. It's a part of preventative health care."

"We'll see. You're very kind, but I have no insurance. Now that I have a state ID and a copy of my birth certificate, I can legally work. I just started a job at a bakery at spitting distance from minimum wage. And again, I can't risk a well-meaning person asking too many questions."

"The bakery was your idea. We didn't force you to find a job."

"No, but Adam works in the library, so I should work, too. I need something to do with all the time and energy I used to spend looking for food and shelter. Besides, it's nice to have a little discretionary income."

"Don't worry about cost; we will pay for you. And we can mitigate the risk," Katie said. "There's a clinic, staffed by nurse practitioners, that is designed for people with no insurance and, uh, nonstandard medical history. I'll be happy to go with you and sign documents if needed. They won't ask for legal proof of our relationship. And you can see my dentist. Again, all they'll care about is that there's a legal adult to sign consents and that we both look comfortable and agree with me doing so."

"If you have the time to go with me, we can do that," Cara said.

Katie smiled. "I'll make the time for you. You're worth it."

KILLING THE BLUES

Cara and Adam were hanging out at home on a lazy November weekend day. He sat down at the piano and played some smooth jazz. Cara listened for a few minutes, then walked up and gently touched his shoulder.

"May I get the guitar and join you?" she asked.

"Sure, go for it."

She quickly tuned Stephen's guitar and pulled up a stool by the piano bench. He opened a book of standards. Cara leafed through the first few pieces. "I can play these," she said. "Just don't go too fast."

They settled on a piece and a rhythm, and they made music. Cara had a clear, sweet voice, though it was untrained. The first time through was fun, so they repeated it, sounding a little better. They were far from professional, but good enough to have fun. Every so often he'd look up at her, and she'd smile. There was something intimate about making music with someone you love—intimacy without touching.

He and Cara continued to play. They lost track of time. When they finally took a break, they heard applause behind them. Stephen and Linnea had arrived home and were listening.

Stephen smiled. "You're full of surprises, young lady."

Cara grinned. "Thank you."

"Where did you learn to play guitar?"

"There's a lot of troubled souls on the street, and many of them are artists. I befriended an elderly man for a while. He was battling his own inner demons. Struggled with alcohol and heroin. I guess he was old enough and frail enough that I didn't find him threatening. He taught me some things in exchange for money and food that I stole for him. I understand he was quite the bluesman in his day. Played with some famous people."

"What happened to him?"

"Died." She looked down, her lip trembling.

After a moment, Cara looked up again at Stephen. "I don't think people understand how much turnover there is on the street. Not homeless to having a home; I'm talking about homeless to dead. I'm not even an adult yet, but I've been out there for seven years. That gives me more street experience than many homeless people I meet. I'm like the elder statesman of losers. So many people I knew are dead, whether from exposure, alcohol or drugs, street crimes, suicide …" She shrugged. "Sometimes I'm just numb."

"You're not a loser," Stephen said. "You're a survivor. We're happy you're here. You never have to go back to the streets."

"You all have given me so much. I should try only to look forward. But it's hard …" She grasped Adam's hand. "I won't ever forget where I came from."

Stephen's cellphone rang. He glanced at the number. "It's the hospital. Excuse me," he said as he left the room.

"Cara," Adam asked when they were alone again, "where were you b-before you came to Indiana?"

"Boston, why?"

"I don't know. I guess I want to learn more about you, but I'm not sure where to start. You're nothing like anyone I've ever known. The usual questions that young p-people ask when they're getting to know each other … those questions don't apply to you."

"Is that bad?"

"No, you're fascinating. You've lived a hundred times more than any seventeen-year-old I know. You're a survivor. When the apocalypse happens, I want to be by your side … 'cause you'll figure out how to make it through."

Cara chuckled. "Yeah, after Armageddon, all that will remain are cockroaches and Cara."

They were comfortable together, just sitting. Adam absentmindedly played with her hand.

"Why did you leave Boston? Is that something you can tell me?"

"I'll never lie to you, Adam. It's like I told you all a few nights ago. I felt I'd attracted undue attention. So I left."

"Is there a story?"

Cara was quiet for a minute. He thought she'd decided not to answer. "Adam, do you remember the night we had coffee?"

"Of course."

"Before the coffee. On the street?"

He nodded.

"It was like that. I don't like to think about it."

"I'm s-sorry. Please, if I ever inadvertently cross a boundary, tell me. I would never purposely make you uncomfortable."

"I know, Adam. I trust you."

He put his arm around her and hugged her. Cara laid her head on his shoulder. He kissed her silky, fresh hair.

· · ·

LATER, Adam and his mom were talking in the kitchen. Through the picture window, they could see Cara and Linnea kicking a soccer ball around the backyard. Cara's athleticism surprised him. He'd figured that homeless people didn't have much opportunity to play soccer.

Katie turned to him. "Cara fits in here well."

"Yeah," he agreed. "I was a l-little worried it would be awkward … I mean, since I like her and all."

"Everyone established boundaries at the beginning. That's the key."

"And we've kept those boundaries. I don't go in her room, and she's never entered mine. We would never disrespect you and Dad."

Katie smiled and gently touched his arm. "Your father and I appreciate how you, Cara, and Linnea have adapted to living under the same roof. Have you heard that she and Linnea claim to be sisters?"

"Hmm. I'm not sure I like that."

"Why not?" Katie inquired.

"B-Because Linnea is my sister, so if Cara is Linnea's sister, then by extension, she's my sister as well. I can't very well date my own sister."

Katie let out a musical laugh and gently punched her son's shoulder. "Yeah, they call each other 'sister.' I've noticed they spend quite a bit of time together. That pleases me. It would be difficult to find a better role model for Linnea. Talk about work ethic. I've never seen a young person work as hard as Cara."

DANCE

It was the first of December, and the major topic of conversation at school was the winter dance: Who was going with whom? In the hallway, walking with Cara between classes, Adam gathered up some nerve.

"Cara?" he asked.

She glanced at him. "Yes?"

"The winter dance is in less than two weeks and I, uh …?" He looked at his feet.

Cara smirked. "Boys have it hard, you know. Having to put your ego out there and all that …" She paused. "Should I make it easier for you, or is this something you would like to accomplish all by yourself?"

He had to grin. "Why is it I sound so d-debonair in my mind, but somewhere between there and when the words emanate from my lips … I go from suave to pathetic?"

"You've never been pathetic," Cara said. "You're cute. May I say you're cute?"

"Guys don't want to be cute," he said. "Guys want to be respected."

Cara looked directly at him. "You've always been kind to

me, but you treat others with compassion as well. Even if they're not in a position to help you. You, I can respect."

He took her hand and bowed formally. "Would you accompany me to the Winter Formal, Miss Cara?"

She curtsied. "It would be my honor, sir."

LATER THAT DAY, at home, Katie and Cara were talking.

"Adam tells me he's taking you to the winter dance."

"Yes," Cara replied. "But I may have gotten carried away in the excitement of the moment."

"What do you mean?"

"I don't have … I mean I've never had a …."

"Cara, let's go look for a dress and shoes. Just you and me. I don't work on Saturday."

"Ma'am, I can't … I can't afford a—"

"Oh heavens, child!" Katie interrupted. "My son has never taken a girl to a dance. Can a mom get excited about her son's first dance?"

"But … why me?"

"Why you? Why not you? Should I wish he'd found someone smarter, Miss AP Everything? Someone kinder? More resourceful? More of a lady by any measure that's important?

"Cara, I'm watching my son grow up and start making adult decisions. And I wish I could share with you my joy and my pride as I see in Adam the best of my husband and me. Stephen and I are comfortable with you, and more, we're pleased that you two found each other.

"So please, let's you and me take a few hours this weekend and find you something to wear. Women have bonded through shopping for probably thousands of years. I can imagine our distant ancestors deciding together whether to wear the bearskin or the deerskin to the rain dance."

Cara chuckled. "Okay, then. We have a date."

ON THE NIGHT of the dance, Cara slowly descended the stairs from her room. Adam had been sitting on a couch in the living room, but he stood up when he saw her. She paused partway down the stairs and looked at him uncertainly.

She'd brushed her hair to lustrous perfection. Her eyes were large and bright, with no makeup. She needed none. Katie had done some cosmetic magic with Cara's scar, which helped hide it a little. Her dress was cobalt blue, knee-length and modestly cut, complementing the shape of her body and accenting her long legs and small, firm breasts.

"Wow, Cara. You're stunning!"

Cara smiled and walked down to him. He took her hands in his and looked into her eyes. "I've never seen anyone more beautiful."

"You look handsome, Adam. I've never seen you in a suit and tie."

Adam had reserved a table at Amalfi's, an Italian eatery that his family liked. The restaurant was fancy enough that Cara's and his dressy clothing weren't out of place.

The hostess led them to a table for two off to one side, more private a location than he'd dared hope to expect. When the waiter asked them what they'd like to drink, they both ordered Coke "on the rocks" to make it sound more like an adult beverage. They laughed as they clinked glasses and sipped their sodas. Adam enjoyed listening to her take on their fellow students, "the wildlife," as she called them. Their conversation quickly moved on to other topics, ranging from current events to what they thought might replace the space shuttle. She asked if she could taste his chicken lasagna; he tried her tortellini Alfredo with shrimp. Unlike most girls he knew from lunch at school, Cara did not waste food.

He almost hated to leave for the dance. There was a flash of selfish desire to keep Cara for himself and not share her attention with their classmates. *How unlike me*, he thought.

THE WINTER FORMAL was held at a venue near the high school. The parking lot was pretty full by the time they arrived. They waited in line together for the breathalyzer before they could get in the line to show their tickets. The breathalyzer was apparently a recent addition to the high school social scene; Katie and Stephen said they didn't check for intoxication before school-sponsored dances when they were in high school.

Cara stayed very close to Adam as they mingled with the other students. He held her hand or put his arm around her waist. It felt natural, and she didn't seem to mind. He noticed a few people doing double-takes as they walked by them. This wasn't the version of Cara everybody knew. He was thinking he understood their surprise, as though he'd discovered something rare and beautiful and valuable.

The band, a generic rock band that did covers of current pop songs, was louder than he liked. Cara laughed when he mentioned it was a good thing the organizers of the dance hadn't tasked him with choosing the music, or they would have ended up with a chamber orchestra. Neither of them knew how to dance other than traditional slow-dancing, which they did whenever the songs were appropriate. Other times, they stood around and chatted with friends.

After an hour, Cara left to go to the ladies' room. Adam struck up a conversation with Emilie Devereaux, a cheerleader who ran with the other high school nobility and who, true to the stereotype, was dating the first-string quarterback. She was in an ebullient mood and was in the middle of telling him a funny story when he noticed Cara across the room. Cara had returned from the restroom in time to see Emilie and him laughing, but was too far away to hear what they were laughing about. He watched Cara's face change from happy to shocked to devastated. Her eyes were wide, but he saw her shoulders slump as though in defeat. He had done nothing wrong, but then he hadn't considered Cara's perspective. This was all so new to her, and she had reason to be unsure of herself.

He excused himself from Emilie for a moment, took Cara by the hand and walked with her back to Emilie.

"Emilie, you know my g-girlfriend Cara," he said, his arm around Cara's waist.

Emilie looked Cara up and down dismissively. "She almost got that scar covered up tonight," was all she said.

He turned Cara toward him and looked directly into her eyes. She broke her glance and lowered her gaze to the floor. He gently touched her chin and raised her face to his and kissed her lips. Now she opened her eyes, so he smiled and kissed her again. She melted against him and sighed. He pressed his lips into her hair and inhaled her delicate scent. They quite forgot about the dance for a bit. When he looked around, Emilie had left. Oh well.

"Cara, never d-doubt how I feel about you," he whispered in her ear.

She smiled at him in her gentle way. "Adam," she murmured.

Unsurprisingly, Katie and Stephen were awake, sitting in the living room, when Cara and Adam returned home.

"Well?" Katie said.

"Cara was the most b-beautiful girl at the dance," he replied.

HOME INVASION

One cold Saturday evening in mid-December, Katie and Adam were visiting an elderly neighbor, and Stephen had been called in to the hospital. Cara lounged comfortably on the couch, engrossed in a historical novel. Her mind was in eighteenth century France. Linnea lay sprawled beside her, legs up over the back of the couch at an improbable angle, reading science fiction on her iPad. Cara looked at the younger girl and smiled, shaking her head with amusement at Linnea's position.

"I like books," Linnea said, setting her iPad down. "I don't think they're retro."

"Thirteen-year-old girls don't talk about 'retro.'"

"I'm serious. When I read a book on my iPad, it's not the same as reading an actual book. I like real pages. I feel more of a connection to the author."

"John Green said that great books help you understand," Cara said. "And they help you to feel understood."

"I get what he means. Sometimes I feel that a character could be me, and I understand why they make certain choices and why events occur the way they do, and then I can relate it to my own life. I benefit from the wisdom of a skilled writer."

"You are wise beyond your years, Grasshopper."

The doorbell rang. Linnea jumped up. "I'll get it." She skipped to the front door and opened it. Two police officers loomed large in the doorway. They entered the Samuelson's home without waiting for an invitation.

Cara stood. "May I help you, officers?"

"Shut up!" the larger of the two men snapped at her. "I will talk. You listen and obey. Do you understand?"

"What's going on?" Cara asked, her voice tremulous.

"I said shut up," the man growled. Linnea tried to move away, but he grabbed her arm. Her face twisted in pain.

"You're hurting me!" Linnea said.

"We're about to hurt you more." He stared at Cara, licking his lips. "You. Take off your clothes now, or it will go worse for your little friend."

Cara stared at the men, unbelieving, her eyes wide with alarm. She tried, unsuccessfully, to keep her voice even. "You're not really police, are you? I … I have some money in my wallet. You can take it and go. There's no reason to hurt us."

The other man pulled a gun and aimed it at Cara. "I suggest you do what we say, if you wish to survive the next hour till your mom comes back." He laughed. "She's such a creature of habit. Always at least an hour to visit the old man. So come on, bitch," he said, nodding at Cara. "Get rid of those clothes."

"No!" Cara backed away until she reached the couch. "No, you can't be serious. This isn't happening. Not again."

The larger man who held Linnea pulled a knife and traced the point purposefully over Linnea's chest, then down over her belly, as though deciding where to cut first. "Go ahead, do what we say, or I'll cut this little one." The blade moved lower. Linnea stiffened.

They can't hurt Linnea, thought Cara. *Not my little sister!*

For a moment, she felt as though she were ten years old again …

*M*OMMA'S LATEST BOYFRIEND, *Les, stares at Cara with bloodshot eyes, like a jackal surveying a carcass it's about to devour. His dirty t-shirt rides up over his enormous belly. She does not like him. He smells of sweat and something else she cannot quite place. She hates when Momma is working, and she is alone with him. He is meaner than usual when he drinks.*

"Get me a beer, bitch." His voice is low, quiet, dangerous.

She turns towards the kitchen. "I'll get you a beer. But you shouldn't talk to me like that."

He reaches forward, surprisingly fast, and grabs her wrist, pulling her roughly to him. "You're a pretty little one," he murmurs.

She struggles to free herself, to no avail. The man is too strong. "Let me go!"

"Shut up, bitch! Let me see you …" His rough hands caress her shoulders, then down her body to her waist. "Take off your shirt."

"No!" she cries. "Let me go! Leave me alone!"

The man gropes the front of her chest, squeezing her flesh and making her whimper in pain. Without thinking, she slaps his face with all her power. He gives an enraged yell and punches her hard in the stomach. She doubles over, unable to breathe. He rips her shirt over her head, exposing her ten-year-old chest. She tries to cover herself as best she can while struggling to escape. She flails at him to make him release her, but this just makes him angrier. He grabs her hair and lifts her with one arm as he stands up. She sees him pull a large knife from his pocket.

"You want to play rough, huh?" he jeers. "You fuckin' little cunt!" The blade flashes, and a terrible pain rips through the side of her face. There is blood in her mouth, in her eyes. She vomits. He pulls off her pants and panties. There is nothing she can do. He throws her to the carpet, where she lies still and helpless. He lays himself on her and works his knees between her legs. Pressure, then pain down there. So much pain. She waits for it to be over.

When he finishes, he lies heavily on her for a while, then turns her unresisting body over. She feels a worse pain, a tearing in her bottom. He grunts as he works on her, his fat, sweating body making it hard for her to breathe.

Sometime later Les gets up, pulls up his pants and stumbles to the kitchen for his beer. She remains on the floor where he left her, unmoving, blood and vomit pooling around her head. She feels unattached to her body, as though it belongs to someone else. That's all she remembers.

When she regains consciousness, it is night. Les is passed out on the couch, snoring. She needs to escape. This is her chance.

She runs to the bathroom and quickly wipes herself off then finds a hand towel to hold against her bleeding left cheek. In her bedroom, she dresses in some clean clothes, grabs her doll, Emma, quietly opens the front door, and slips out into the night.

THE FAMILIAR ANGER rose in Cara's chest. She did not try to fight it.

The brutish force in her grew as it took over her body. Pain gripped her limbs as she changed. Her chest tightened, making it difficult to breathe. Powerful muscles appeared and rippled beneath her smooth skin. Her clothes stretched over the unaccustomed musculature, threatening to rip. Her mind cleared, and time seemed to slow down. Now she could see each particle of dust in the room. She could hear the rapid beating of Linnea's heart. She could smell the fear in the child and the fetid breath of the attackers.

The creature inside Cara was enraged; its raw ferocity overwhelmed her. It needed to hurt the men, to punish them. It needed to kill them.

Cara bared her teeth and growled deep in her throat as the creature inside her made her crouch to spring.

COME HOME QUICK!

The house was silent but for a little girl curled up on the living room floor, sobbing. Cara was on her knees, still breathing hard. She looked at her blood-stained hands and shirt. *Not again, God. No!*

She saw Linnea huddled near the open front door. "Linnea," she murmured, hugging the younger girl against her chest, gently rocking.

"Cara, are you back?"

"I'm so sorry, Linnea. I never wanted you to see me like that."

Cara looked around. The larger man was slumped in a pool of blood on the floor. The handle of his knife was protruding from his upper abdomen. His face was swollen and deformed, his nose was flattened and displaced to one side, and his upper lip was split. Several teeth lay on the floor near his head. Both of his arms were obviously broken, white bone exposed, as though he had tried unsuccessfully to protect his head from an overwhelming force. His partner had been thrown across the living room. He lay unmoving, partly against a leg of the couch. A shattered lamp bore mute witness to his short, violent flight. His sightless eyes and his mouth were still wide open, as though amazed. Bruising around his neck and the unnatural angle of his head attested to the mechanism of his death.

Katie's cellphone rang.

"Ma'am, you need to come home right now." Cara's voice was unusually urgent. "Please don't ask any questions. Just come."

"Adam," Katie exclaimed. "Something's wrong at home. Let's go."

"What happened?" Mr. Kowalski asked in his wavering voice.

"Probably nothing, Mr. K.," Katie said. "Don't worry about it. We'll be back to check on you tomorrow. Good night."

THEY SAW the open front door and rushed inside. They entered a scene of carnage.

"My God, what happened?" Adam yelled as he saw the two men, obviously dead.

Katie and Adam rushed to the girls. Linnea was curled in a ball just inside the open door, sobbing quietly. Cara was beside her, stroking her gently, spatters of blood drying on Cara's shirt and hands. The acrid smell of gunpowder hung in the air.

Katie gently pushed Cara aside. "Linnea, honey, are you hurt?" she asked.

"No. Because of Cara, no. Those men broke into our house. The big one grabbed me. He ... touched me ... my chest ... and lower. Told me what he was going to do to me. Cara saved me."

"What did Cara do?"

"She fought them. I didn't really see what happened. But she fought them, and I'm okay."

"You don't look okay," Katie said.

"The man wanted to … to hurt me, and I'm afraid he would have killed me afterward. I guess I'm still scared. Cara, you saved me, you know?"

While Katie attended to Linnea, Adam grabbed Cara and hugged her. She laid her head on his chest and grasped him as though he were giving her life. She was still breathing hard from whatever had happened.

"Are you okay?" he asked her.

Cara wouldn't say anything. She just hugged Adam tighter.

"I'll call 911, then I'll try to reach Dad," Katie said. "Cara, you're not to talk to any investigator unless I'm present. You're still a minor."

Cara bit her lip and nodded.

Katie pulled out her cellphone and quickly punched some numbers with her forefinger.

"Yes, I need to report a home invasion. Two people are dead. We need police and an ambulance. Our address is …"

There was silence as Katie listened to the 911 operator.

"No, there's no current danger. Both men who broke into our home are dead. None of us are injured, as best I can tell. I'm a nurse."

"Yes, they were armed." Pause. "Right now it's just me, my two teenagers and my little girl. We're okay, just shaken up." Pause. "Okay, we'll stay here. Our front door is open."

"They'll be here in about three minutes," Katie said, her eyes tight.

They sat together in the living room, the smell of death in the air, Adam's arm tightly around Cara. She was trembling.

"Cara, talk to me," Katie said. "Tell me what happened."

Cara's voice was low. They had to strain to hear her. "I'm sorry. I'm so sorry, I … I couldn't let them hurt Linnea like what happened to me. I just wanted them to leave us alone."

"What did you do?"

Cara shook her head and sobbed. Katie grabbed Cara's shoulders and shook her. "For God's sake, Cara, tell me! Tell me what you did."

"I killed them."

"I saw the bodies. There's no way you did that. Even a full-grown man isn't strong enough to inflict that kind of damage."

"With my hands. I killed them with my bare hands. And I need to leave before the police get here."

"You've always run away, haven't you?" Adam asked.

Cara nodded.

"P-Please stay. Please don't run anymore. I don't want you to leave."

"We urge you to stay, Cara," Katie said. "We'll face this together as a family."

"I don't have any family."

Katie put her arms around Cara and Adam and motioned Linnea to join them. "Family is more than blood; family is a choice. We're stronger together. Please stay with us."

*I*t seemed much less time than the three minutes the 911 operator promised before they heard sirens growing louder. Through the door, they could see flashing blue and white lights.

A police officer appeared at the door, his right hand on his holster. Another officer was visible behind him. "Officer Johnson and Officer Kendrick, ma'am. Is anyone armed?"

"No sir," Katie said.

Officer Johnson entered and stood just inside the door, surveying the scene of carnage. "What happened?"

"Two armed men broke into the house and threatened harm," Katie said. "The men are dead."

"Who killed them?" His eyes fixed on Cara, noting her bloody, torn clothes.

She shrugged. "I had no choice, officer. They attacked us."

"Damn!" Officer Johnson said at last. "Okay, let me have everybody's name and age and some ID, please." He pulled out a small notepad. They all, except for Linnea, handed him their driver's license or state ID.

"I'm Katie Samuelson. I'm forty-two. This is Adam

Samuelson, seventeen years old, Cara Ferris, seventeen and Linnea Samuelson, thirteen," pointing to each of them in turn. "My husband, Dr. Stephen Samuelson, has been at the hospital all evening. I texted him. He's on his way home now."

"Who was home when the break-in occurred?" Officer Johnson asked.

"Cara and Linnea were home alone."

"Is there anyone else at home now? Anyone upstairs? Are there any weapons that I should know about?"

"Nobody else is here, sir. My husband and I have concealed carry permits, but we both work in healthcare, and hospitals don't allow weapons. So we've gotten out of the habit of carrying. Our handguns are upstairs in a bedroom safe."

Officer Kendrick headed to check the upper floor of their house. He quickly returned, signaling to his colleague that he found nobody upstairs. Then he checked the rest of the ground floor: the kitchen, the dining room, the music room and library, Stephen's office, and garage. "House is clear!" he called to Officer Johnson.

"And these two men, who are dead, are the ones who forcibly entered your house?" continued Officer Johnson.

"Yes, sir."

"So there was nobody here but a teenage girl and a preteen?"

"That's true, sir."

"Look, I'm only a patrolman, and I may be speaking beyond my pay grade, but there's something about this story that doesn't make sense. These men obviously sustained incredibly violent injuries. And you say there were just a couple of girls at home. Where were you and Adam?"

"We were at a neighbor's house. Mr. Kowalski lives two doors down from us. He's eighty-seven years old. His wife died last year, so we stop by his house every so often, to make sure he's okay."

"How did you learn about the break-in?"

"Cara called me. We immediately ran back home, saw what happened, and called 911."

"Okay, here's what we need to do. Detective David Anders is on his way here. He'll want to talk with each of you individually. It's important that you do not discuss the case amongst yourselves before he arrives."

"These young people are minors, officer," Katie said.

"Then you'll need to stay with them for questioning."

While Officer Johnson was talking with the Samuelsons, Officer Kendrick examined the two dead men. "We won't be needing an ambulance," he said to nobody in particular.

Officer Kendrick's radio broke squelch. Adam couldn't make out what was being said. The officer spoke into his radio in a low voice.

Outside, Adam could hear more emergency personnel arriving.

A third officer, armed with a small camera, entered and began taking pictures of the crime scene because that's what Adam's home had become. The flash of the camera seemed at odds with the quiet of the room and the stillness of the two dead men. A man and a woman in civilian clothes and carrying official-looking satchels entered, spoke with Officer Johnson, then got to work collecting evidence. Other members of the homicide investigation team arrived over the next twenty or thirty minutes but did not interact with the family.

Adam heard a slight commotion outside.

"Excuse me, sir. You can't go in there."

"Dammit, that's my house and my family. I sure as hell am going inside."

"I'm sorry, sir. I understand this is your house and I

would certainly be upset if I were you. But this is a crime scene, and you cannot enter. Your family is okay. None of them were injured. The two men who broke into your home are dead. That's all the information we have at this time."

"May I speak with my wife, officer?"

"No, sir. Not until Detective Anders arrives and says it's okay. He'll be here shortly."

"Good evening, Detective Anders," Adam heard the patrolman at the door say. "I'd like you to meet Dr. Samuelson. This is his house. We've asked him to stay outside till you got here, and he's concerned."

"Dr. Samuelson, I'm Detective David Anders. Here's what's going on." Their voices grew too distant for Adam to follow their conversation, as though they'd stepped further away from the door. Neither of them sounded angry, which was good.

A couple of minutes later, a balding man in his forties, wearing a rumpled dark suit and a battered overcoat, stepped through the front door. *He looks like a detective from the movies,* Adam thought to himself. The man's face was lined and tired, but his voice was firm as he approached Adam and introduced himself.

"Detective David Anders," he said as he shook hands with each of the four of them in turn. With every handshake, they introduced themselves.

"Are any of you hurt?" he asked them.

"No, sir," Katie said.

"A lot has happened in the last hour. I imagine you may be feeling scared. You may feel angry, violated. This is normal. Let me tell you what to expect at this point.

"We need you to leave your house for a while so we don't disturb the evidence technicians and the medical examiner when he comes. When they're done, unfortunately, your living room will need to be professionally cleaned. There's a lot of blood. I'll leave a list of biohazard cleanup companies with you. You should probably plan on a hotel tonight.

"Our next step will be for me to drive you all to my office, where I can talk privately with each of you about the events surrounding the break-in. I'll be recording the conversations. Do you have any questions?"

"Do we have to talk about this right now?" Katie asked.

"None of you are under arrest," Detective Anders replied. "Home invasion is a felony. The people at home have the right to defend themselves. At this time, nobody is accusing any of you of illegal activities. But there are two dead people in your house, and we need to understand how they got that way." Katie sighed and nodded agreement.

"I spoke with your husband outside. He'll meet us at the police station so he can drive you all to a hotel when you're done."

POLICE HEADQUARTERS

Cara looked up at the massive concrete and glass rectangle of police headquarters. Her mouth went dry, her chest tightened. She gasped.

Adam, in the passenger seat of his mom's car, glanced back at Cara. She was hugging herself, knees drawn up, shivering.

"Cara? What's wrong?"

"I can't. I can't go in there. I've never—"

"You'll be okay. You did nothing wrong. You protected Linnea and yourself."

"No! You don't understand. I've broken so many laws. I can't go to jail. My … the thing would kill … I just can't."

Katie parked the car and opened the rear door. Cara grasped her hand and climbed out woodenly, silent.

"Cara, look at me," Katie said. "We're just here to give our statement. I will be with you the entire time. Then we will leave here together as a family. You have my word."

Cara nodded.

When they learned that they would have to go to the police station for questioning, Stephen decided to involve his attorney friend, Sidney Cohen. He spoke with Cara and Katie in a room with no recording devices, reserved for attorney-client communication.

"Cara," he said in his deep voice, "I mean no disrespect, but I hadn't thought I would see you again so soon."

"No, sir. This wasn't my plan," Cara said.

"Stephen told me a little about the, er, events of earlier this evening. I need you to tell me, in your own words, exactly what transpired at your home. Remember, I'm on your side."

"If I have anything to add, should I do so?" asked Katie.

Sidney nodded. "That would be fine."

Cara began. "I'll do my best, sir. It was about 8:00 p.m. Linnea and I were on the couch in the living room, reading and talking. The front doorbell rang. We thought nothing of it. Linnea got up and opened the door."

"Did she look through the peephole? Did she ask who it was?" the attorney asked.

"The peephole is too high for her," Cara said. "And no, sir, she didn't ask who was at the door. She just opened it."

"What happened then?"

"Two men dressed as cops were at the door. When the door opened, they came in."

"Did they ask permission to enter?"

"No, they just came inside."

"You say the men were 'dressed as cops.' Why did you suspect they weren't real cops?"

Cara paused. "You know, Mr. Cohen, I got a little suspicious when they told me to shut up, when the larger of the two grabbed Linnea by her arm so hard that she screamed, when they said they'd been watching the house and they knew Ms. Katie would be gone for at least an hour, and especially when they ordered me to take off my clothes. I'm pretty sure actual police officers don't follow that script."

Katie gasped, hands at her mouth, eyes wide. Sidney held out his hands, palms down, placating. "I apologize, Cara. I didn't mean to sound condescending. What happened then?"

"The man holding Linnea had a big knife …" Cara stopped.

"Was it a folding knife, a hunting knife, could you tell?"

Cara shrugged. "I don't know. Whatever the police found sticking out of his stomach."

The attorney tilted his head and raised his eyebrows. He opened his mouth to speak, paused for a moment, then continued. "We have a problem, Cara. On the one hand, it is lawful to defend oneself when one is attacked, even if the attacker dies. On the other hand, we have two large, muscular, armed men, known to be extremely dangerous, who are dead, and a normal-sized teenage girl who admitted to the police that she killed them, single-handedly, in what I understand was a most violent manner. There will be questions."

"We understand, Sid," Katie said. "Though the mechanism of the intruders' deaths hardly seems relevant."

"On the contrary, Katie, the mechanism, as you say, of the attackers' deaths can be very relevant. The law says one may forcefully defend oneself or others from an attacker, but the potential problem we have in our situation is that the violence of the defense far outweighed the violence of the attackers.

"The police will probably find it difficult to believe that this defense was the work of a single teen girl who, by the way, was uninjured.

"Whose blood would they find on your shirt, Cara, and on your hands?" the attorney continued.

"The big man who had Linnea, sir. I couldn't let him hurt her. And I guess they may find my prints as well as his on the handle of the knife."

"Have the police taken your prints or tested your shirt for blood?"

"No, sir. Not yet."

The attorney continued questioning Cara. "Do you have martial arts training?"

"No, sir. Not really. I may have learned a few things over the years. But I just got so … angry … I don't know. I don't remember everything." Cara shook her head.

"So it sounds like you had an adrenaline rush, is that right?"

Cara looked up at him. "I'm not sure what you would call it. I guess adrenaline is as good an explanation as anything else."

Katie leaned forward. "Sid, do you think there will be any legal implications?"

"It's difficult to say at this point, Katie, but I strongly recommend that none of you discuss this case with your friends or colleagues … and especially with the media. Do you both understand?"

"Yes, sir," they answered in unison.

"Detective Anders will speak with you and Linnea individually. Since you're both minors, Mrs. Samuelson will be in the room with you. I'll be there too, of course. You should assume that everything you say will be recorded, audio and probably video as well. I have shared clients with Detective Anders before. He is fair, but remember that it's not his job to prove your innocence."

Just then, they heard a knock on the door. "Come in," said Sidney.

Detective Anders entered. He shook hands with the attorney and then Katie and Cara. His handshake was firm, a man who knew his business.

"Please follow me back to the conference room I reserved for us. We can talk there."

A female police officer sat with Linnea while Cara walked with Katie and the attorney to the small conference room. Furnishings were utilitarian. The chairs were unpadded plastic. Cara figured they would be uncomfortable to sit in for an extended period. In one corner of the room, on the ceiling, she noticed a dark glass globe. Video camera, she thought.

When Sidney, Katie, and Cara had taken their seats at the table, the detective began.

"Before we proceed further, I need to inform you all that our conversation is being recorded. I also want it to be clear that neither you, Cara, nor Linnea are under arrest."

Cara nodded. "I understand."

"Cara, you live with the Samuelsons, is that right?"

"Yes, sir."

"But you're not part of the family."

Katie leaned forward, hands on the table. Her eyes flashed. "She most certainly is part of our family!"

"Yes, ma'am," the detective said. "I meant to say that Cara Ferris is not a Samuelson and that, whether by blood or by adoption, she does not have a legal relationship with the rest of you. Is that correct?"

"Why does Cara's living situation concern the police?" the attorney asked.

"Cara is a minor. She was present at the scene where two men were found dead. Where are her parents?"

"I never knew my father, sir. I am not sure where my mother is now."

The attorney jumped into the fray. "It's immaterial where her mother is. Cara is legally emancipated."

"Ah, interesting." Anders rubbed his chin. "How long have you been emancipated, Cara?"

"We've been working on it since late September, sir. The final paperwork came through over a month ago."

"How long have you been living with the Samuelsons?"

"Since late September."

"Who was home at the time of the break-in?"

"Linnea and I were home alone," Cara said. "We were sitting together on the couch, reading and talking. Ms. Katie and Adam were at a neighbor's house a couple of houses down from ours. The doorbell rang. We weren't expecting anyone, but we assumed Ms. Katie forgot her key or whatever. We didn't think of any danger. Linnea got up and answered the door. Two men dressed as police officers were there. They came inside the house without our permission …" Cara swallowed, and her voice broke. She shook her head and looked down at her lap.

"Take your time, Cara," the detective said gently.

"The larger of the two men grabbed Linnea by her arm so hard she screamed. I asked what they wanted. They told me to shut up. They said we had an hour; they'd been watching the house, and they knew how long Ms. Katie would be gone. The man holding Linnea pulled a knife and threatened to cut her." She stopped.

"There was another man," the detective prompted.

"Yes," said Cara. "He was not quite as large as the first guy, and he had a handgun. A semiautomatic, I think. It was not a revolver.

"He looked at me like I was a piece of meat. Said he was going to enjoy this." She paused again, took a deep breath and continued. "He pointed his gun at me and ordered me to take off my clothes. I couldn't let it happen again, not to me and certainly not to Linnea. I … I guess I got angry and then …"

"Yes?"

"And then the men were dead."

"What did you do when you got angry?"

"I don't remember exactly, but I guess I killed them."

"A teenage girl can't do this kind of damage to two armed men," Detective Anders said.

Cara sighed. "I turned into a monster, and I killed them, sir."

"There are no such things as monsters in real life, miss," Anders said, as though talking to a child.

At this, Cara jumped up, eyes glaring, fists clenched. "Detective, look at me! Dammit, look at me. Do you see my face?" she screamed. "I was ten years old. My mom's boyfriend cut my face because I wouldn't have sex with him. Then he raped me!" Cara was crying now. "I was just a little girl. Don't you dare tell me there are no monsters in real life." She broke down in sobs. Katie hugged her.

After a minute, Cara stood and wiped her eyes. "If we're done, detective, I'll bring Linnea here for her turn."

OFFICIAL INDIVIDUAL QUESTIONING COMPLETED, Detective Anders pulled everyone together in the conference room. Within minutes, somebody knocked on the door. The detective stood up and opened it. Carrying some electronic equipment, a young man in a lab coat entered the room and started setting things up on an unused bit of table.

He smiled at them. "Hello, everybody. My name is Mario. I'm an evidence technician here, and I'll be fingerprinting each of you."

They responded with a chorus of "Hello, Mario."

"Detective Anders, should I get started now?"

"Might as well," the detective sighed. "I'm pretty well done making young ladies cry."

"All right, then. Let me explain to you how fingerprinting works. In the old days … and even now in some smaller towns … police used ink pads and fingerprint cards. Today, everything's electronic. Much less messy."

He showed them a small device that looked something like a credit card terminal, though it had a small glass touchpad on top. A USB cable attached it to his laptop computer.

"What I'll have you do is roll the pad of each of your fingers on this glass part here. We'll do three rolls for each finger. The computer will let us know if it captured good fingerprints. I will clean the fingerprint reader with alcohol wipes between each person, so there'll be no contamination. Do all the adults have a state-issued ID?"

They each took their turn with Mario, logging their fingerprints. Other than giving Mario a few bits of identification-related data, nobody spoke further. Then they got up to leave.

"Thank you for your time," Anders said as they walked out.

"Detective," the attorney nodded at him.

IN THE NEWS

*T*he following morning, the home invasion made the national news:

Teen Girl Kills Two Armed Attackers

AP NEWSWIRE.

A home invasion at the residence of a prominent central Indiana physician turned violent Saturday night, resulting in the death of the two intruders. The teen girl, 17, whose name is being withheld because she is a minor, was home alone with a younger girl, age 13. Police say a struggle between the older teen and the men ensued, leaving the two male intruders dead.

The deceased, Manny Van Zant, 34, and Isaac George Rubens, 28, were wanted for six prior home invasions involving forcible rape and robbery. Police believe the men researched each target to be certain the girls were

home alone. Survivors say the two men wore police uniforms and carried official-looking identification to convince targets to open their door. The home invasions grew progressively more violent.

A source at the police department described the scene as "carnage." The two girls were reportedly uninjured. No charges are being filed at this time. The case is still under investigation.

<<<<<>>>>>

Monday morning at the high school there was no topic of conversation other than the home invasion. Everyone had theories, some of which were truly in the realm of fantasy, but nobody had a convincing explanation. Somehow the entire school knew the incident occurred at Adam's house. In retrospect, he supposed the emergency personnel and the police tape on his usually quiet street would have been a clue. Cara found herself uncomfortable in the limelight. She did not enjoy being the subject of peoples' attention.

Adam could feel the stares and could hear scattered bits of conversations as he and Cara walked to classes. He determined to stay with her in school as much as possible; she didn't need to face this alone.

Adam's friend Brett caught Cara and him first. "Dude, how was your weekend?" He sighed. Brett Stengler was not known for his subtlety.

It's worth a try to feign ignorance. "P-Pretty boring, really. Put in some extra hours at work. Did you do anything interesting?"

"Come on, dude, gimme something. What happened at your house?"

"Oh that," Adam said. "Yeah, some jokers broke into my house, and then they died. Caused lots of p-paperwork."

"Okay, I'll play," Brett said. "How did they die?"

He shrugged. "Dunno. Police said trauma or something. I guess breaking into people's homes is traumatic."

Brett soldiered on. "The news said that Cara and your sister were there alone."

"So?"

"So how did they kill two men?"

"The facts are that two guys broke into my house, then they died. I'm not sure how they got dead. Thank God my two favorite girls were uninjured. That's all I can tell you." Technically, he didn't lie, he told himself; he was not one hundred percent sure of the events immediately following the break-in. And nobody knew for certain what happened to Cara. And that was, in fact, all he was authorized to tell anyone.

"Cara," Brett turned to her, "can you tell me anything?"

"Sorry, no. That's about it," she said with a shrug.

"Dude, we've been friends since, like, fifth grade. You'd think I deserve an inside scoop."

Adam shook his head and smiled. "Sorry to d-disappoint, buddy."

THERE WAS no escape from the notoriety, even during class. Mr. Harris, the retired engineer-turned-teacher who taught AP Calculus, finally had to put his foot down.

"All right, class, enough. I'll give you all exactly ten minutes, until 10:30, to discuss whatever has everyone so excited … then we will focus on math. Agreed?"

The class murmured assent.

"Cara, I don't get it," a boy finally asked.

"Yes?" Cara inquired.

"I've heard you take a lot of grief from a lot of stupid people. You just seem to accept it. But you can fight like you did this past weekend? Why don't you defend yourself in school?"

Cara shrugged. "I've been told not to discuss details about the … unpleasantness this weekend. But two armed men broke into our house and attacked us. That's a whole different situation than school. What should I do, kill someone for teasing me about my scar? Do you think that would be appropriate?"

"No, not when you put it like that. It's not my business, but I can't help but see things. It's just not right."

"You can't help seeing things," Cara repeated, "but you can control what you do about them. John Stuart Mill said the only thing necessary for the triumph of evil is for good men to do nothing."

The boy sulked. "You're saying I'm supposed to get in everyone's business?"

Cara shook her head slowly. "Nobody can or should try to right every little wrong in the world. But some wrongs just shouldn't be allowed to continue. What if, say, you were at a party, and you saw some guys molesting a girl? Would you just shake your head and say to yourself, 'Oh, that's a shame,' or would you get involved? Because even if the guys are much bigger than you, you could still call 911 and then yell at the attackers to stop.

"Or imagine you're at that same party with that same poor girl, and she drinks too much and passes out. Now you have a choice. Do you take advantage of her? Or do you take care of her and see that she gets home safely?

"At what point do you get involved? That's a decision we each need to make for ourselves."

There were nods of agreement.

"Let me be clear," Cara continued in her gentle voice. "I am not saying I expect you to stand up for me. But I'm not the only student here at school who gets teased or bullied. And bullying isn't always the worst thing that can happen to someone." She touched her scar for emphasis. "Life is rough. The odds are high, unfortunately, that you'll see true evil in your lifetime. I pray that you'll recognize it when you see it and that when you do, you'll make the right choice."

Thinking about what Cara had said, everyone was silent.

Mr. Harris stood up and cleared his throat to gain the kids' attention. "As you young people gain more life experience, I believe you'll find that compared to what you've been discussing, calculus is a lot simpler."

WHAT LINNEA SAW

At Stephen's insistence, Adam, Cara, and Linnea started learning how to use and care for weapons. Katie and Stephen met while serving in the Army. He retired as a Major in the Medical Corps, she as a Captain. They hadn't thought to teach the young people until the violence became personal. There is nothing as surreal as watching a thirteen-year-old girl field-strip a pistol, clean it, and reassemble it.

A week after the home invasion, following practice at an indoor range, Adam came to Linnea's bedroom door.

"Linnea, do you have a sec?"

"Sure, for you. Whatcha got?"

"I was hoping I could ask you about that night. C-Can we talk about it?"

"I'd like that, Adam."

"You told the detective you didn't remember much about the attack."

She nodded slowly and let out a sigh. "Yeah, I did."

"But I've known you f-for thirteen years. You miss very little."

"You know, she saved me. They would have hurt me bad, maybe killed me. I owe her."

"She's saved both of us now. I didn't tell Mom and Dad, but the evening before I first brought her here to meet everyone, there was an, uh, an incident."

"What happened?"

"I was walking by the playground behind the elementary school. I thought I was alone. Three g-guys were coming the other way. I wasn't paying too much attention to them. One of them sucker-punched me. Laid me out."

Linnea gasped. "Oh, my God!"

"No, I'm okay. But the three thugs were dead … very dead. Killed with extreme p-prejudice, as they say in the movies. When I came to, Cara was leaning against a wall watching me. Maybe she wasn't sure what I'd do. As I replay in my mind the events of that evening, as we talked in the café, I realize she was trying to tell me to stay away. I just wasn't listening."

"Adam … when she was there for you that time, did you see anything?"

"I d-did not. They knocked me out. The excitement was over by the time I woke up, but I don't think I was out very long at all."

Linnea paused, as though to gather her words. "What I saw that night … what I saw Cara do … I'm pretty sure I wasn't supposed to have witnessed. That's why I told the detective I remembered nothing. Nobody expects much from a little girl. I'm expected to be all swooning over boy bands and fashions and who's going with whom."

"You've never been a standard g-girl, little sis," Adam said.

"Thanks. I've learned everything from my big brother."

Adam laughed. "You're a nut, Linnea. But for real, what did you see?"

"It's hard to explain. You'll think I'm crazy."

"I believe you're my brilliant, whimsical and super special little sister. But not crazy."

"It was like … Adam, do you remember last winter when we went to Chicago? Dad was driving on that road that ran along Lake Michigan. There was a storm and high winds, and those enormous waves roared up off the lake and crashed on the rocks. Remember how we pulled off the road for a few minutes just to experience the power of nature?"

He nodded.

"It was like that. Primal. She was a perfect person … but not a person. I don't know. I don't have the words."

"You're a thirteen-year-old girl who uses words like 'primal.'"

"She looked like one of those statues in a museum, with a fierce and captivating presence, heavily muscled like … like a goddess or a superhero. Except that goddesses and superheroes aren't real. She was a bit larger than Cara because she wore Cara's clothes, but they were too small. Her face was different from Cara's. No scar. I don't remember seeing a halo, or weird lights or wings or weapons. She didn't need weapons; she *was* a weapon."

"D-Did you see her change?"

"I thought at first Cara was having a seizure. She gasped and tightened, making little jerking motions. She arched her back as though she was in great pain. And then …"

"What happened then, Linnea?"

"Adam, within probably a few seconds she grew a couple of inches and added oh … I don't know … twenty-some pounds of muscle. Her scar was gone, as I said. Cara is cute, but this … girl or whatever … was extraordinarily beautiful."

"Did she say anything?"

Linnea thought for a moment, remembering. "At first she made a sound deep in her chest, like a growl. She looked directly at the men and said a few words, but I didn't understand them. It wasn't English. In fact, it wasn't any language I'd ever heard. Then she attacked them."

"D-Did her voice sound like Cara's?"

"You know, it really didn't. But her voice was magnificent, like her. Confident, as though she was used to being in command. I would recognize it anywhere."

"I'm sorry. Go on with your story."

"The man with the gun got off a couple of shots. I would have sworn at least one bullet struck her in the neck, but it didn't seem to do any damage. Well, it did, but then it healed. Just like that. Didn't slow her down any. She moved inhumanly fast. I don't know how somebody could fight her. And she was angry, the way a force of nature is angry. She ignored me, thankfully, but I felt … power, incredible energy. It was too much. I remember I curled up … couldn't breathe … I remember sobbing. Then I remember she was holding me and telling me I was safe … and I looked, and it was our Cara. Quiet and gentle Cara. And her clothes and her hands were all bloody." Linnea threw herself at him, shaking with silent sobs. He stroked her hair and let her cry herself out.

"Adam, I don't understand what I saw. I don't know how to process it. I … I just know she saved my life. And I really like her."

"Me too, sis. I really like her."

AUTOPSY

Detective David Anders followed a young woman dressed in surgical scrubs, blonde hair mostly hidden by a protective surgical cap, into the autopsy suite. He thought for sure she was too young to work here. He wondered if he was getting old.

The autopsy room was cold and sterile. Fluorescent tubes buzzed softly overhead. Large stainless-steel sinks lined one wall. Another wall was mostly cabinets. The floor and remaining walls were off-white tiles, dulled from years of blood and cleaning. The room smelled of meat and formalin.

Two bodies, still dressed as they were when they were alive, lay on metal gurneys a few feet apart. Between the gurneys stood a tall, middle-aged Black man in scrubs and a white lab coat with a name tag that said, 'Dr. Marcus White, Pathologist.' He smiled at his visitor.

"It's good to see you again, David. I see you've met my assistant, Marie." He had a firm handshake.

"Thank you for your time, Marcus. I'm curious to know what you make of these two gentlemen."

"Yes, the crime scene was remarkable, to say the least. I

understand the only weapons found were the knife and handgun belonging to these two men."

"That is correct," Detective Anders agreed. "There were two witnesses to the incident, both minors. They deny seeing any other people at the scene. I mean until their family returned home."

"These witnesses, what did they see?"

"They were still in shock when I spoke to them. The older of the two, a seventeen-year-old girl, says she fought with the men when they attacked her thirteen-year-old companion. She wasn't making sense. Thought she killed the two men with her own hands."

Dr. White chuckled and shook his head. "Eyewitnesses. Gotta love 'em."

He pulled on a pair of surgical gloves and turned to his assistant. "Alright, Marie, let's see what we got." He examined the larger of the two men, speaking out loud into a microphone hanging from the ceiling.

"Victim number one is a 283-pound Caucasian male. Estimated time of death is eight p.m. on November twenty-fifth, approximately thirty minutes before our arrival at the crime scene. External examination is most remarkable for a large knife with a leather-wrapped handle which is perforating his mid-abdominal area, with significant hemorrhage. Also, there is massive trauma to his face and head."

Marie placed a rubber post under the dead man's back, thereby lifting his chest. Then she and Dr. White set about taking samples from clothing and fingernails and swabbing the inside of the dead man's mouth. Completing those tasks, they cut away his clothing.

"Early signs of lividity are visible on the victim's buttocks and back, consistent with the position in which he was found at the crime scene.

"The victim sustained compound fractures of both arms,

including an open fracture of his right ulna. The appearance is consistent with an attempt to protect his head against overwhelming force. There are numerous fractures of his facial bones and mandible, a large laceration of his upper lip, and the traumatic loss of several teeth.

"A mid-abdominal laceration is seen where the knife was noted earlier. The laceration is two and one-quarter inches in length, oriented roughly longitudinally."

The examination of internal organs continued in the same dispassionate manner. Dr. White stopped recording and looked up.

"Jesus, David, it looks as though this man fought a gorilla. The six-inch blade perforated his diaphragm and lacerated his heart. To reach his heart from the point of entry of the knife, one would essentially have to impale him and lift his entire 280-pound weight with the arm that held the knife. That would require an unusually powerful man. Or, as I say, a gorilla. But the poor guy was likely unconscious from head trauma before being stabbed in the heart, since he obviously was alert when he fought to protect his head."

"In your opinion, could a teenage girl have done this?"

"Ha, I would hate to meet the lady who pulled this off. But no, in answer to your question, this damage was most likely done by several powerful men. In my professional opinion, no single human of either gender could cause these injuries. With all the blood at the scene, you probably found shoeprints from the people involved."

The detective shook his head. "Nope, nothing. So far I don't have forensic evidence or witness statements to suggest that there were several strong men who violently repelled the two home invaders. The whole situation is bizarre." He sighed. "All right, let's have a look at the other guy."

The medical examiner and his assistant turned to the second gurney.

"Victim number two is a 195-pound Caucasian male …"

They continued with the second autopsy in their usual professional manner.

"Significant recent bruising is noted on the anterior aspect of his neck. His trachea is crushed, leading to death by asphyxiation. His cervical spine is fractured at C2, and there is bruising on his scalp. This is consistent with being thrown across a room and landing on his head, as suggested by the crime scene photos. Again, it defies credulity to imagine a woman throwing a 200-lb man across a room."

Detective Anders closed his eyes, trying to picture the crime scene in his mind. It just didn't fit. Where were these men who protected the two girls? Who were these men? What training did they have to kill so brutally? Could Dr. Samuelson and his son have killed the intruders in this fashion? They had a motive, but the detective doubted they had the training … or the strength. But then why would the Samuelson family deny that there were other men involved?

Anders looked at the medical examiner. "Marcus, these men … the violence of their deaths … it's incredible. Brings to mind those three young men who were found lying behind Pleasant Ridge Elementary School three months ago."

"That's what I was thinking," responded Dr. White. "I won't soon forget them. Three young healthy men in their early twenties, well … healthy except for massive trauma that looked remarkably similar to these two."

"As I recall, the young men were not model citizens. Gang members since high school, all well-known to local law enforcement."

Dr. White nodded. "Toxicology screen on all three showed positive for amphetamines and marijuana. The estimated time of death was approximately seven p.m., if I remember correctly. The bodies were still warm."

"Yeah, we assumed there'd been a gang fight. Someone

called it in on an anonymous tip line. Those three men were brutally beaten. Over-the-top injuries—open fractures, crushed skulls, that kind of thing—similar to what we're seeing on these two citizens. Only it seems exceedingly unlikely that Dr. Samuelson's living room was the scene of a gang fight.

"Dr. Samuelson's a good man. I worked with him when I was at the university. Damned if I understand what the world's coming to."

"That's the truth," Anders said. He paced back and forth, thinking. "All right, Marcus, I appreciate your expertise and help. Please send your official reports on these two to my office. These deaths make no sense to me. I need to talk with some technicians in the lab."

CRIME LAB

nders walked to the lab to confer with the chief forensic technician.

"Mario, what did we find on the hunting knife in the Samuelson case?"

"There's a clean set of prints on the knife handle that match those of the teen girl, Cara Ferris. Other print remnants, probably older, match Manny Van Zant. No thumbprints on the butt of the knife.

"Makes sense for a street fighter, but unusual for an amateur," Anders mused. "Most people with no knife-fighting skills hold a knife blade-down with their thumb on the butt, like Norman Bates in the shower scene from *Psycho*. Experienced knife fighters use the butt of the knife as a weapon when needed, as well as the blade. So we have a teenage girl who knows how to use a knife. Still don't see how she killed two armed men. She would have had to disarm the big guy in order to get his knife. Then she … or someone … threw the second guy across the room. Coroner says he landed on his head. Broke his neck. Shoeprints?"

"Recent shoeprints match those of the two intruders and

the two girls. No evidence of a ninja or two hiding in the closet waiting for the two guys to show up."

"Cute, Mario. What other fingerprints do we have?"

"No surprise that we found prints from each of the Samuelsons all over the furniture, appliances, doorknobs … but it's the Samuelsons' house."

"Yeah, not very helpful. How about the gun?"

"Standard Glock 31 chambered in .357 SIG. Serial number reported stolen three weeks prior in another home invasion. Rubens' prints on the gun and powder burns on his hands. Two bullets missing. We found one round in the couch. The other was deformed, as one would expect when the round strikes a body … but it was lying on the carpet. No blood or DNA on it."

"Mario, nobody present at the Samuelsons' house had a gunshot wound."

"I know that, detective. I have no explanation."

"So the bullet struck a body, but nobody has a bullet wound?"

Mario nodded. "That's what it looks like."

"What if someone were wearing a bulletproof vest?"

"Detective, nobody present was wearing a bulletproof vest."

"Yeah. I'm fishing. Anyone else's blood at the crime scene?"

"No, sir. Didn't find any blood from either of the girls who were present. They don't seem to have been injured. Every blood stain we tested was consistent with Mr. Van Zant."

"Speaking of Van Zant's blood, what did the toxicology screen show?"

"Unsurprisingly, the tox screens for both gentlemen were positive for alcohol and MDPV … you know, that synthetic stimulant they call 'bath salts' on the street. Just a little pick-me-up, like anyone would do before a home invasion."

"Yeah, right. This is damned curious. There's a lot that doesn't make sense about those two young ladies. The room looked like a war zone, but the little one somehow managed not to see anything. And the older girl ... Mario, I want you to run her fingerprints against any unsolved murders or significant trauma involving children or teens in the last ten years."

"The entire United States? You've got to be joking."

"I'm told I don't have much of a sense of humor. Start with the East Coast and Midwest."

"You realize this will take time. Probably a lot of time."

"I understand. Get it done as fast as possible, and let me know what you find."

"Yes, sir."

"Okay, thanks for your help. We'll see what the video people have for us." Detective Anders turned to leave the lab.

HE WATCHED as the police video technician named Daniel, a young man in his twenties, pulled up a satellite view street map of the area around Pleasant Ridge Elementary School.

"Detective Anders, the three bodies were found here." He pointed with his cursor to an area behind the school. "The school itself does not have surveillance cameras, but there are traffic cameras here at this intersection," he said, indicating a busier street a couple of blocks away. "There's a gas station here, and then there's a strip mall next to it. There are security cameras at the gas station and at several shops in the mall."

"Daniel, can we scroll back to around seven p.m. on the night of September twenty-second?"

"The trouble is that most security camera systems overwrite their data after a certain time. It depends on the size of their storage medium. Even if the data is backed up in the cloud, you can imagine that the sheer volume of mostly useless information would eventually become unwieldy. It's been three months now."

"Damn," the detective said.

"Don't despair so fast," said Daniel. "Luck favors the prepared mind. And today we are lucky. I checked all the available cameras from six p.m. to eight p.m. that night." He quickly tapped some keys. "As you can see from this video, a couple is crossing the street at 7:16 p.m., heading away from the school. We pick them up again at 7:19 p.m., entering the coffee shop."

"Can you back up and get a closer view of their faces?"

"Just a minute." The technician clicked and dragged the cursor on the screen, humming to himself. "Here we go … damn! She'd be easy to pick out of a lineup. That's a serious scar."

The picture on the screen was fuzzy but sharp enough to show the two teenagers Anders had met at the Samuelson's house in the aftermath of the break-in.

"Well hello again, Cara," he whispered.

"You know her, detective?" Daniel asked.

"She and I met. And I'm noticing a disturbing tendency for violence and mayhem to follow in her wake."

"She doesn't look very dangerous. Her guy friend either. He looks kind of geeky."

"Says the geek," Anders teased. "Look at the girl and imagine a Hello Kitty sticker on an Apache helicopter."

"No shit!"

"Zero defecation factor."

"Damn! And you think she was involved with the triple murder by the elementary school?"

"Well, we've established that she was close by at the right time."

"Okay, but …"

"Did you read about the home invasion at Dr. Samuelson's house?"

"Sure. Two armed men with long criminal histories broke into the doctor's house. There was a teen girl and a younger girl there alone. The two men were killed, violently from what I understand."

Anders nodded at the monitor that still showed the teen girl with the facial scar. "Meet the teenager."

"No shit!"

"You're repeating yourself."

"But that girl …?"

"Took out two large armed men who were pumped full of bath salts. Destroyed them, very much like the three men by the school, if we're to believe the medical examiner.

"Her statement at the time of the incident was that she got angry and killed them. Initially, I dismissed the claim out of hand. It seemed preposterous that a teenage girl could kill two armed men with such violence. But I'm wondering."

Daniel closed his eyes briefly and leaned against his desk. "I'm familiar with the International High School for kids who want to take all their classes in French or Spanish, and the Hebrew Academy for kids who want fluency in Hebrew. I've heard of a couple of technical high schools for kids who want training as a welder or mechanic or whatever … and, of course, there's a variety of private schools. But do we have a 'military special ops' high school here in town?"

Anders smiled. "I don't believe we do, no."

"Then where did she get those skills? Where did she come from?"

"That, my friend," replied Anders, "is the million-dollar question. She seems to have shown up here in town in time to start her senior year of high school. No past. No family. When she registered for school this past summer, she told them she was homeless. She apparently moved in with the Samuelsons in September."

"Hmm. I guess it's lucky for the Samuelsons she was home that night, huh?"

"Yeah, lucky. Maybe she's just a normal girl with a knack for being in the wrong place at the wrong time. But that's not the way I'd bet."

LATER THAT DAY, Detective Anders reviewed the arguments in his head as he walked to the prosecutor's office. He knew Bill O'Shea as a tough but media-savvy prosecuting attorney. A good man.

"Afternoon, detective!" The prosecutor smiled. "What do you have for me?"

"You've heard about the Samuelson case?"

"Certainly. Not every day a well-respected physician is the victim of a home invasion."

"Here's what I got," the detective said as he pulled papers out of a folder and laid them on the prosecutor's desk. He described everything he'd learned about Cara and the two attackers.

"In sum, we have two men who illegally entered a house but did not injure anybody. These men were then killed most violently. We have a young lady who admits to being at the scene of the crime and actually admits to killing the men. We found her fingerprints on the murder weapon. I would like to bring this case before a grand jury, with charges of two counts of capital murder."

The prosecutor looked with surprise at his colleague. "No, David, there is no need for a grand jury. We are not bringing murder charges against a teenage girl who defended herself and her young friend in a home invasion."

"But Bill, listen to me …"

"David, no. It is not happening. Can you even imagine the public outcry if we file murder charges against a young woman for defending herself 'too vigorously' against attackers who broke into her home and threatened her life? Men wanted for six prior violent home invasions with the same M.O.? Not to mention the fact that our medical examiner wrote in his report that these injuries could not have been inflicted by any single human, man or woman."

"When you phrase it like that, it sounds ridiculous."

"That is how the press will slant it. You have not been able to find evidence of whoever else may have been involved. Just a girl who fought back as best she could. Turned out to be good enough. Two career criminals, violent offenders both, are dead. A law-abiding family is alive. Let's leave it alone, David."

"Very well, Bill. I won't pursue it further with you. But there's something not right about this, and I don't like unanswered questions."

MRS. HAMERSCHMIDT

Detective Anders walked into the Old World Bakery and closed the door. He had buttoned up his long coat against the chilly December morning. Inside the bakery, it was warm. The scent of fresh baked goods reminded him of his grandma's home many years ago when he was a boy. He gazed around the small, tidy shop. European delicacies including Black Forest cake, stollen chock-full of dried fruits, muffins topped with streusel, assorted Christmas cookies, and fragrant loaves of whole-grain bread filled the display cases.

The window display caught his eye. He walked over to examine it closer. There was a miniature gingerbread house, a foot high, decorated with candies and icing. Beside the house was a small frozen pond where tiny candy children skated.

"May I help you?"

He turned to see a rotund lady wearing an apron dusted with flour. Her face was good-natured; her hair was up in a silver bun.

"Yes, ma'am. Are you the owner of this bakery?"

"I am Loretta Hamerschmidt," the lady said with just a hint of a German accent.

"Detective David Anders, Homicide," he said as he showed her his badge. "May I ask you a few questions about one of your employees?"

"My husband and I have just one employee, a high school girl named Cara Ferris. Is she okay?"

"How long has she worked for you?"

"Ah, let me see. Cara came to us in mid-November. My assistant and friend for many years had a heart attack in October and retired. Manfred and I needed someone to come in early and start dough a couple of days each week so we would not be doing that every single day by ourselves. We are getting too old to keep that up, you know. This young girl came to us. She was so polite, and she was looking for work. Well, I did not think a teenager would be willing to start work that early in the morning, especially with school. But Cara has never missed a day. And smart? I will tell you, she picks up things so quickly. She comes back here some days after school to help behind the counter. Customers love her.

"I am sorry, detective. I just started talking. Did you have a specific question? Is something wrong?"

"Has Cara spoken to you about the events of last weekend at the Samuelsons' home?"

"No, sir. She is very private. Not like most young people now. Most of them open their lives to the world. They see no boundary between private and public. Cara says nothing about her life outside of this bakery. I know she lives with the Samuelsons. I thought that was curious, but then Mrs. Samuelson has been a regular customer for many years, and they are good people. I decided that if the Samuelsons are okay with Cara living there, it was not my business."

"But Cara hasn't mentioned anything about that particular evening?" the detective persisted.

"No, sir. I remember reading about it in the paper, and of course, people were talking at Saint Michael's." The lady shook her head sadly. "Church. Those religious ladies have all the best gossip. But Cara, she came to work as always. Did not act like there was anything wrong. Some people at church said that she killed two men who broke into the Samuelsons' home, but I told them that cannot be true. Cara is the kindest, most gentle girl I have seen. And I have met some fine people in the last sixty-five years."

Mrs. Hamerschmidt was pacing behind the counter as she spoke to the detective. Suddenly she stopped and looked him directly in the eyes.

"Detective Anders, tell me and do not lie. Did my sweet little Cara truly kill two armed men that night at the Samuelsons' house?"

"Ma'am, I wish I had a good answer for you. You've probably read in the news that those two men who broke in were suspects in other home invasions involving rape and robbery. Nobody is mourning their deaths. But it's not clear who killed them, with just a couple of young girls alone in the house.

"So now I'm trying to fill in as many pieces as I can. Anything you tell me may be helpful."

Mrs. Hamerschmidt nodded. "I have a story that may interest you. There was something I saw several weeks ago when Cara did not know I was watching. Make of it what you will."

Anders readied his notepad and his portable voice recorder. You can tell a lot about a person by the choices they make when they have an opportunity and they don't know they're being watched.

"Yes?" She could see that she had the detective's full attention.

"It was in the morning, an unusually cold morning. A dirty little girl, nine or ten years old, came inside this shop. She was staring at the fresh-baked bread and sweets. Her face was thin and pinched, with dry lips. Her clothes were dirty and looked slept-in. She was not wearing a coat heavy enough for the weather. Well, sir, I felt bad for her. I knew she could not pay for nothin', but I thought I would give her a roll.

"But Cara, she saw the little girl, she watched her … and she spoke to the child in a quiet and gentle voice so as not to scare her. The little girl looked prepared to be chased from my store as probably happened to her so many times before. But Cara got a bakery bag and knelt by the little girl. I heard some of what she said. She asked if the girl was hungry, and the little girl said she had not eaten in a day. And it broke my heart. Cara filled the bag with fresh-baked savory buns, then she knelt in front of the girl and presented her with the bag, told her she knew she was hungry enough to eat them all at once, but to make them last. And that dirty little girl, she said, 'Thank you!' and 'God bless you, miss,' and she left my store like she was carrying a bag of diamonds, not buns. Then I saw Cara take money from her pocket and add it to the till to pay for what she gave the little girl.

"Detective, I told Cara I had seen the whole thing, and I asked her why she did it. She said she had been alone on the street, hungry, dirty, and cold, and she knew what it felt like." Mrs. Hamerschmidt stopped her narrative and pulled a tissue from her pocket and wiped her eyes before continuing. "Here I am, going to church and thinking I am such a good person, then I meet a little angel, and I realize I can do so much better. I can afford to give a little food to hungry kids. I throw out food every day, just because it is a day or two old.

Since the morning that Cara fed the little girl, though, I have been donating the day-old baked goods to a local mission rather than tossing them."

"That's quite a story, ma'am," the detective said. "I hope you can afford to continue feeding the hungry masses."

"You do not sound like you're a believer, and that is okay. I cannot explain everything that has happened, but I will tell you, sir, that since Cara started working for us, our paying customers have increased by some twenty percent. And our little bakery has been here for three decades.

"We are busier and more profitable than ever, baking more than ever, and I will tell you what: At my age, I should probably think about retiring, but I am happier than I have felt in years. And nobody leaves my bakery hungry."

Mrs. Hamerschmidt handed the detective a sticky bun on a little paper plate and a napkin.

"Here you go, detective. In the old country, they called these *Buchteln*. Nobody can be unhappy when they eat one of these."

"Thank you, ma'am. Your bakery sure smells nice. Reminds me of when I was a kid. In here, I can almost believe in magic."

"May I tell you anything else about Cara?"

"No, I don't suppose so. I've heard the same thing from Cara's teachers that I've questioned. The girl is intelligent and good and kind. They tell me that in school, she takes some grief because of her scar. Have your customers seemed bothered by it?"

"You know, detective, very few of us look like fashion models. Lord knows I could stand to lose a few pounds, though would you trust a skinny baker?" She laughed. "But there is something about Cara that is attractive despite that scar on her face. Even when she first approached me about a job, I noticed her scar of course, but I was so taken by the girl that I did not think much of it. And I have had no comments from my customers other than how sweet she is."

Anders stood, wiped his mouth with the napkin and placed it and the empty paper plate in the metal garbage bin by the door. "Thank you again, ma'am, for your time and the delicious treat." He patted his belly and smiled. "Your products here might be as addictive as anything sold on the street! Thank you again. Have a nice day."

He walked back out into the frozen mist.

WHEN I CHANGE

One frosty day while school was out for Winter Break, Cara and Adam were walking down near the creek behind the house. He heard her take a breath and open her mouth as though she were about to speak, then she shook her head and closed her mouth again. He stopped walking, placed his hands lightly on her shoulders and gave her what he hoped was a reassuring smile.

"I want you to know," she said, "that I never wanted ..." Her breath caught. "Why can't I be a normal girl with a normal life?"

"Cara," he said, "what does it feel like when you change?"

"It's not fun. The change is incredibly painful. My chest, my arms and legs ... I feel like I've caught fire on the inside of my body. The first time it happened, it terrified me. I didn't understand what was going on. I thought I was dying.

"But the worst part for me is the loss of control. It's as though I become someone or something else, as though it takes over my body. I can't control the violence. I feel over-come with rage, and I want to kill. The only times I've ever *not* killed someone near me were with you last September, and then with Linnea during the home invasion. I was following you that night in late September because I didn't understand you. I didn't understand why you were so … nice to me. Part of me wanted to talk to you, but I was afraid. Then when those men hit you, I thought they'd killed you, and I'd missed my chance. I ran to you and saw they were laughing, and they'd hurt you, and I got angry." She hesitated. "Anyway, I changed, and then they were dead. I don't recall everything that happened. The whole incident probably took less than a minute. Next thing I remember, I was watching you wake up."

"D-Does your mind go blank when you change?"

"That's how it's always been for me. I'd come back in my body, and everyone around me would be dead. Horribly, violently dead. But when the two men broke into your home and attacked Linnea and me … I didn't black out. I was conscious and I remember everything, but I swear it wasn't me. The … thing inside me wanted to kill Linnea too, but I made it stop. I was never aware enough to do that before.

"God, Adam, if I had killed you or Linnea, I most definitely would have killed myself, too." Cara laid her head against his chest, and he wrapped his arms around her body, holding her against him.

"It turned out fine," he murmured into her hair. "I g-got the girl of my dreams."

At this, she pushed back a little so she could look up at him. "I feel guilty."

"Talk to me," he said.

"The worst part of living on the street, for me, was not the discomfort, not the hunger or cold. I've learned to be quite self-reliant. The worst part, for me, was having nobody I could trust. Nobody with whom I could relax, nobody to have my back, nobody who would see past my scar.

"Adam, you couldn't know this, but I've been praying for

you for years. I didn't know exactly what you would look like, but I knew how I would feel when I was with you. But now …"

"But now what, babe? Tell me why you feel guilty."

"It's just a matter of time. Something will happen, and I'll feel I have to protect me or you or your family … and I'll change … and people will die. Adam, what if I changed at school? Kids tease me, and of course I wish they wouldn't, but I don't want to kill them.

"Don't you see? The world would realize that I'm a monster, and they would hate me … and they'd be right. They'd be right to hate me, and they'd be right to kill me. But you … you were friends with the monster. You even loved the monster. The world would turn on you, Adam. It would never forgive you. Your life, and that of your parents and sister, would be ruined.

"I should run away. I should start over somewhere else and let you forget about me, let you love someone else who can give you a normal life. But I'm too selfish. I'm too weak and selfish to leave you. I'm sorry."

He took Cara gently by the arms. "Look at me, Cara. Please listen to me. I wasn't looking for a g-girlfriend, to my mother's dismay. I wasn't seeking to find the girl with whom I'm supposed to build a life while still a high school student. But when I met you, I knew. I knew beyond any doubt that you were it.

"Cara, I'm in this for life, not just so long as life is easy. I d-don't want you to run away. I want you to stay with me. If you stay with me, we can handle anything the world throws at us."

"Adam, I'm not a good person. I'm a killer. I don't deserve you. I don't deserve to be happy."

"Cara, you're a wonderful person. And you deserve the best I can give you. Forever."

She looked at him. Her eyes were intense, burning. "God, Adam, you say things like that, and you make me love you."

Adam drew her to him, and he kissed her, hard. Her hands stroked his arms and his chest. Her breathing quickened. He felt her tongue searching for his. Suddenly she pulled away, panting, her eyes wide.

"Adam, I … please …" she started.

He hugged her and laughed. "Well," he said, "I feel like we're physically c-compatible. At least for me … you make me feel … kissing you pretty much rocks my world."

She smiled up at him shyly. "Me too. I never thought my body would do that. I never dreamed I'd be thinking of a guy that way …"

"What guy?"

"You, silly. The guy I was just kissing."

"I love you, Cara. And I will never stop loving you."

Detective Anders pulled his dark blue unmarked Crown Victoria into the covered parking by his apartment. Head bowed in thought, he trudged slowly through the light snow to his front door. As always, Molly was waiting for him, excited he was home.

"Hello, girl!" He scratched his dog behind her ears, and she madly wagged her short tail in delight. Molly was a muscular, medium-sized dog, a rescue, with short brown hair, a broad forehead and brown, intelligent eyes. At the shelter, they'd said she was a pit bull mix, though he wasn't quite sure what that meant. Since the divorce three years earlier, Molly was his friend and companion, the only female in his life at present.

"What's for dinner, girl?"

Molly knew the word "dinner." She ran to the kitchen with a short, excited bark.

Anders chuckled. "You're excited, girl, aren't you?" He freshened her water and added a scoop of dry food into her beige plastic slow-feeding bowl. The dog attacked her meal with single-minded intensity, licking the bowl clean until it glistened.

"I wish I got that much enjoyment out of my dinner," he said. "Momma was a wonderful cook, wasn't she?"

His ex-wife, Carolyn, had been talented in the kitchen. But there were too many nights of her husband returning home late because he was so focused on a case he lost track of time. She decided she'd had enough. Now that he was single again, he ate pre-cooked microwave meals or dined at a local pub.

The thing he regretted most, he decided, was that Carolyn and he never had kids. They had talked about "once things settle down," but Anders never could figure out how to prioritize his family. The timing never seemed right. His window of opportunity closed, and he had nobody but Molly.

He pulled a TV dinner from the freezer without glancing at the contents. By rote, he opened the packaging, peeled the plastic wrap from the top and placed the tray in the microwave. While his dinner was heating, he grabbed a bottle of Beck's Pale Ale from his refrigerator, popped off the cap with a twist of his hand, and took a long, satisfying drink.

Before sitting down to eat, Anders leaned over and turned on the stereo. Public radio was playing a jazz program that he liked. He stared at his Salisbury steak and mashed potatoes, grimaced, and slowly ate. Molly lay half-alert by his feet. He had never fed her from his dinner, but she remained hopeful.

"Okay, girl, let's take a walk." At this, Molly jumped up, eyes alert, tail wagging.

He attached Molly's leash, checked his pocket to confirm

he had doggy bags, and the two of them headed out into the frigid January night. Their usual walk took them through a small municipal park, one block square, with benches, a few trees, and well-manicured paths.

A young couple was standing facing each other, arms around each other's waist, conversing quietly.

An old man sat on one of the park benches. Anders noted his long, greasy hair, his tattered jacket and pants, and the shopping bag he guarded beside him on the bench. A street person, he decided. It seemed to him there were more and more of them lately. As he passed the old man, the faint sweet smell of alcohol in the air, Molly growled.

"Detective?"

He stopped and looked back at the man. "Have we met?"

"Detective David Anders?" the man persisted in a deep, gravelly voice.

"And you are …?"

"I'm nobody important. I was told to give you this envelope." He held out an unmarked white letter-sized envelope in his gnarled hand. His hand had a fine tremor which made the envelope shake.

"What is it?" Anders asked.

"I don't know. I was told to give it to you."

"Who told you to give me the envelope?"

"I don't know, but he paid me."

"What did he look like, this man who spoke to you?"

"Just a businessman. Nice suit. Didn't give me a name."

"You're not exactly a fountain of information, are you?"

"I don't ask questions. I try to stay out of trouble," the old man replied.

He took the proffered envelope and pocketed it. He decided he would look at it back in his apartment. "All right, you did your job," he told the man.

He and Molly continued their walk, passing through the

small park and along a residential street. Every so often Molly would stop to sniff something, then leave her mark in the snow so other dogs would know she'd been there. Eventually, they circled back toward home. In the park, the young couple was still there, now laughing about something. Anders approached them.

"Excuse me, did you notice a man sitting on that bench?"

"What man is that?"

"The elderly man who was sitting on that bench. The man who talked to me as my dog and I passed through earlier. Did you see which way he went when he left?"

"There's been nobody here but us."

"A man was here," Anders persisted. "An old man. He looked like a street person. There was a large bag on the bench beside him."

"I'm sorry, sir," the young man replied. "My wife and I were talking about how lucky we were to have the park to ourselves tonight. I'm quite sure that there's been nobody else here … I mean, other than when you and your dog came through earlier." He turned to his wife. "Love, did you notice anyone else since we've been here?"

The young lady shook her head. "Nope, nobody."

"Again, I'm sorry," the young man continued. "You must have been mistaken."

"You're probably right," Anders agreed. "It's been a long day. Thank you anyway." He turned and headed back to his apartment, noting as he did so that the snow on the bench was disturbed where the man and his bag had been. Molly trotted beside him. As he walked, he put his hand in his coat pocket. The envelope felt very real.

Back in his apartment, Anders inspected the letter. He noted a regular letter-sized envelope, sealed and unwrinkled, with no writing on the outside. It was a thin envelope. He figured there couldn't be more than a page or two inside.

Taking a deep breath, he opened another beer and savored the cool taste of hops. Then, with a small knife, he carefully slit along the top of the envelope.

Inside, he found a single sheet of paper. On it was written, in a neat and flowing script that he had not seen since he was a young teen:

FATHER saw me die.
The man paid the penalty.
There is balance now.

Boston, June 20, 2016
Issa

Anders stared wide-eyed at the paper. He could hardly breathe. How could anyone know?

"Issa?" he whispered. His eyes filled with tears. Molly whined and moved close beside him. He hadn't spoken the name in many years. His older sister always insisted people use her full name, Isabella, except for David. When he was young he could only say Issa and so, for his use only, she allowed the nickname.

He reread the lines. Haiku. It was a private joke between them, communicating in haiku. Nobody else knew, not even their parents.

He closed his eyes, replaying in his mind the last time he saw her.

. . .

I RIDE my bike home from baseball practice, winding casually through our neighborhood. It is a pleasant spring day. I played well today. Maybe I will start on the freshman team this season. How cool would that be?

I park my bike in the garage and push open the door.

"Issa, I'm home!"

Silence. This is unusual. Isabella loves her pop music. Insists on studying to music.

"Issa?" I say a bit louder.

Still silence.

I push open my sister's bedroom door and stop cold. Isabella lies on her bed, arms outstretched, eyes wide and unblinking, mouth open in a silent scream. Her sweater is stained with blood. I run to her and grab her arm. Her body is still warm, but she doesn't move, doesn't react.

"Issa, no! Please, Issa, wake up! Please don't ... no!"

Then it is a blur. I call 911. Police and paramedics. Parents rush home. Mom screaming, crying. Dad characteristically silent, stoic.

HE RECALLED the questioning that followed his sister's murder. His parents fought with each other and divorced. He chose a college in California, because that was as far as he could get from his parents and the bad memories in Boston.

The police never found Isabella's killer.

WOODENLY, as though on autopilot, Anders phoned his office.

"Yeah, Dooley, Detective Anders here."

"Good evening, detective. What can I do for you?"

"Dial up the Boston PD for me. I need police reports of all murders in Boston, Massachusetts on June 20, 2016, give or take a day. Tell them whatever you need to say, but I need that information immediately. I'm on my way to the office."

"Tonight? Why …"

"I'm on my way," Anders repeated brusquely. "I'll see you in a few minutes."

"I'm on it, sir."

Anders disconnected the call. He donned his leather shoulder rig and his coat, which both hung ready by the front door, and headed to his car.

"I'M NOT sure what you're looking for, detective, but other than the beheading and a few minor assaults and such, there wasn't much excitement in Boston that day."

Detective Anders regarded his younger colleague. Tom Dooley was one of the new breed of officers: young, sharp, prematurely cynical, and possessed of a facility with computers and electronics that still eluded Anders. Dooley raised an eyebrow and waited.

Anders sighed. "Okay, Dooley, I'll bite. Tell me about the beheading."

"A certain Mr. Darren Headly. Unfortunate name. A fifty-seven-year-old white male who was a person of interest in the fatal stabbing of a twenty-year-old female college student a week earlier, and the stabbing of a high school girl six months prior. Anonymous police call at around 11:30 p.m. on June 20, 2016. The only witness was a local drunk, Johnny Horn, who says he was seated against a tree, drinking. A girl was asleep on the bench. Says he saw the deceased approach the girl and pull out a knife. Then he started rambling about 'avenging angels' or whatever. As I said, he admitted that he'd been drinking.

"Officers found Mr. Headly lying on a path near a park bench. His head had been partially wrenched from his torso.

Severe trauma to his head and chest, open fractures, internal injuries. Look at the crime scene photos."

Dooley's fingers danced on the keyboard and a series of picture icons tiled on the screen. Slowly, the two officers cycled through the photos.

Anders shook his head. "Damn."

"Yeah, pretty much. From what I understand, Southwest Corridor Park is not a good place for law-abiding citizens to hang out at night. But in the summer, homeless people often stay there."

"What about the girl on the bench?"

"Mr. Horn didn't see what happened to her. She was gone when police and medics arrived."

"Did this citizen describe the girl?"

"Yeah, apparently he didn't find her very attractive. Brown hair, big ugly scar on her face."

"Indeed …" Anders stroked his chin thoughtfully. "It appears the good Mr. Headly tried to stab the wrong girl this time."

"You know this girl, detective?"

"Our paths have crossed once or twice. I'm seeing a pattern. Rate she's going, there won't be any bad guys left."

"Detective …?"

But he was already on his way out the door.

BEFORE HE HEADED BACK HOME, Anders sat in his car and reviewed what he knew. Point: A sweet, polite teenage girl was associated, at least by proximity, with several violent murders that she could not possibly have committed because no human could be strong enough. Point: All the men who'd been killed were themselves violent criminals. Point: His sister Isabella was killed many years ago, yet she wrote him a letter with information that nobody but her could know, and the letter was handed to him by a man that nobody but him could see. Point: A witness, though admittedly unreliable, swore that he saw what he described as an angel kill a man who had attacked this teenage girl.

I need to learn more about angels, he thought to himself. *I find it hard to believe they're real.*

DEATH IN THE TIME OF
CHOLERA

The Department of Religious Studies at the university was in an imposing limestone edifice that gave the impression of great age. Detective Anders could imagine robed monks inside this building hundreds of years ago, copying manuscripts by candlelight. Then he smiled to himself as he realized that hundreds of years ago, this campus was a forest, and the only humans here were Native Americans. Things are not always as they seem.

Dr. Finn McNair, Longworth Professor of Old and New Testament and Chairman of the Department of Religious Studies, was a burly, red-haired man with alert green eyes and a bushy mustache who Anders could imagine screaming out of the Scottish Highlands, claymore in hand. He looked out of place as an academic, especially in religious studies. But several teaching awards visible in his office stood as proof of his commitment to education.

"Dr. McNair, thank you for agreeing to see me."

The elderly academic smiled. "Call me Finn. I'm happy to help you if I can, detective." His baritone voice had a distinct

New York City accent, which was surprising given his name and his appearance.

"Then call me David. What can you tell me about angels?"

"Angels?"

"Angels, you know, like in the Bible."

"And you're a police detective."

"Involved in the investigation of a series of … ah … unusual deaths."

"Who you believe were killed by angels?"

"Doctor … Finn, I'm trying to make sense of things that do not, on the surface, make sense. I have a witness who claims to have seen someone killed by what appeared to be an angel. In Scripture, angels were associated with some serious violence."

"To what are you referring, in particular?"

"Okay," Anders said, "how about the incident between King Hezekiah of Judah and the Assyrians? Not once but twice in Scripture, it says that an angel of the Lord killed 185,000 Assyrians in a single very productive evening."

"Ah," Dr. McNair smiled as he leaned back in his chair, "a man who knows his Bible."

"Sunday school when I was a kid. I'm afraid I haven't been a very good Catholic since then."

"Nor I, David. When I was a child, I spoke like a child, I thought like a child, I reasoned like a child. When I became a man, I gave up childish ways."

"First Corinthians, right?"

Dr. McNair nodded. "As a young boy, I believed all those stories, literally. But the more I studied archaeology, linguistics, and history of religions, and the more scholarly papers I wrote, the less wondrous and—dare I say—magical those stories seemed."

"What do you mean?"

"Take, for example, the incident you mentioned between

King Hezekiah of Judah and Sennacherib, the king of Assyria. Let's go back a little, before the part about the angel of the Lord. What we have to work with, what we think we know, I like to call 'history-ish.'"

"History-ish?"

"Yes. If we define history as a description of what happened in the past, then history-ish is history in which two opposing sides disagree about what happened, and we don't have independent evidence to confirm one version of history or the other. We believe the events in question occurred about 700 years before Christ. Our biblical sources are Isaiah and Second Kings. Speaking for the Assyrian point of view, we have Sennacherib's Prism, which is a four-sided clay piece discovered in the ruins of Nineveh in the mid-nineteenth century, that describes the events of Sennacherib's campaign against Judah."

"So what happened?"

"That's just it. Who knows for sure? Both sides claimed victory. See, about twenty years earlier, the Assyrians, led by Sennacherib, overran the Israelites in Samaria, capturing the citizens of the northern kingdom. At that time, King Ahaz and his son Hezekiah ruled the southern kingdom, Judah, as co-regents. That was a common practice back then. Judah agreed to pay an annual tribute to Assyria, and in return enjoyed a period of stability and economic power.

"Following the death of Ahaz, Hezekiah made widespread changes, including the destruction of religious idols and refusing to pay tribute to Assyria. Not surprisingly, Sennacherib attacked Judah and laid siege to Jerusalem.

"As I mentioned, the Bible describes the siege of Jerusalem. To prepare for the siege, Hezekiah had his workers block springs outside the city to deprive the Assyrians of water. They dug a 533-meter tunnel to the Spring of Gihon to provide Jerusalem with fresh water. They fortified existing walls and built a new reinforcing wall and towers. Hezekiah believed in Adonai—the word the Hebrews used for God—but he hedged his bets by paying a huge tribute in exchange for Assyrian withdrawal. Despite the tribute, Sennacherib marched on Jerusalem with a large army.

"King Hezekiah was demoralized, but the prophet Isaiah assured him that Jerusalem would be delivered and the Assyrians would fall. The biblical books of Isaiah and Second Kings tell the same story, that overnight an angel of the Lord slaughtered 185,000 Assyrian soldiers, thereby breaking the siege. The Assyrian version of events is roughly similar, except that they describe in more detail the sacking of several Judean cities, they claim the tribute was much larger, and they recast their failure to take Jerusalem as having trapped Hezekiah in Jerusalem 'like a caged bird.'"

Detective Anders nodded. "Ah yes, you're saying that 'spin' is an ancient art."

"Precisely. But the point I'm building up to is that modern scholarship teaches that cholera or some similar disease due to contaminated water and rodent infestation probably decimated the Assyrian soldiers. Not a bad-ass angel of the Lord. So you see? Too much knowledge kills the magic."

"No angel, huh?"

Dr. McNair shook his head. "Sorry, David. To me, it would have been quicker, less painful and more honorable to have fallen due to an angel of the Lord rather than dying of dysentery. In any case, many of their soldiers died, and the Assyrians withdrew. It is sobering to consider that had the Assyrians successfully sacked Jerusalem, the entire line of Abrahamic faiths might not exist today."

"Wow." Anders was silent for a while, digesting that thought. "But what of the many other accounts of angels in the Bible?"

"Is the Bible the literal word of God? Or is it inspired by

God but written by men, using images that made sense to people at that point in time? Is it literal history? Or should we see it as parables that show us how to live?"

"I have friends who would agree with one or another of those positions."

"As do I. We each arrive at our core beliefs in our own way. Sometimes in the Bible, angels are magnificent, described as shining, or with wings and swords, larger than life. At other times, angels look like mortal men. Think, for example, of the story of Lot, when God sends two angels to destroy Sodom and Gomorrah. The angels come to Lot as men.

"There are people who are convinced of the existence of a variety of angels who specialize in different tasks. Other people see angels as a metaphor. For me, in over six decades of life, I have seen things that I cannot explain. I'm okay with angels because I've been Catholic all my life. Angels are a familiar part of our belief system, so I'm comfortable with the idea. But if you ask me to prove the existence of angels, I could not. My argument for the existence of God is similar; with God, the universe makes sense to me. I draw comfort from my belief in God, so I don't ask for further proof."

"So you're saying that the question whether angels exist in the real world is up to each of us individually?"

"Basically, yes. I wouldn't know how to settle the question one way or another using science. Think of a measuring cup. It's a perfectly suitable tool for measuring small volumes, right?"

"Sure."

"Now try using a measuring cup to measure distance. It's not that it's an invalid tool, just that it's not the correct tool for the job. There is a role for religion, and there is a role for science. But science is the wrong tool to prove or disprove the existence of angels … or of God, for that matter."

"Okay, Finn, let me try a different tack. Hypothetically, if I saw an angel, what would it look like?"

"Again, perhaps he would look like a man. Perhaps he would be Caucasian and glowing, possibly with wings, as in the paintings of the old masters. Although while we're on that topic, the masters almost uniformly depicted Jesus as Caucasian and blonde. I doubt anyone living in the Middle East two thousand years ago was pale skinned and blonde. So I have my doubts as to the historical accuracy of those ancient works of art.

"Call me a radical, but perhaps 'he' is sometimes a 'she.' Or perhaps angels are somehow beyond gender. Scripture uses only masculine words to describe angels, but we may be reading more into the biblical use of language than is warranted. And don't even get me started on translation errors.

"Finally, some descriptions of angels in the Bible—not fallen angels, I'm talking about the 'good' ones—are downright scary: multiple wings, covered with eyes, stuff like that. And then, of course, demons are said to be able to take any shape they like to suit their purposes. So if you see something frightening, is it a demon or an angel? My thinking is that if I am seeing an angel in retribution mode, it's likely the last thing I will ever see, so I won't be around to describe the experience for posterity."

Detective Anders leaned back in his chair and smiled. "Thank you, Finn. You just cleared it all up for me."

Dr. McNair chuckled. "The mark of a true academic is the ability to pontificate on a subject without the listener gaining any understanding."

"Have you considered running for Congress?"

"Nope, those are all actually demons." He grinned.

"A few final questions, if I may."

Dr. McNair nodded. "Of course."

"In Scripture, what role do angels play in relation to people?"

"Basically, angels serve as messengers or as agents of retribution."

"Do angels have free will?"

"Angels serve God. Fallen angels, who we call demons, are said to have followed Satan in refusing to serve God. So yes, angels have chosen to serve God, but no, they don't go around doing whatever they like. Demons do as they wish."

"What does Scripture say about who is targeted for retribution?"

"Ah, yes. Proverbs Five. Something to the effect of 'God sees everything you do. Wherever you go, God is watching. The sins of the wicked are a trap; they get caught in the net of their own sin. They die because they have no self-control. Their own stupidity will send them to their graves.' That's a well-known passage. There are many others."

"So God sees everything, and the unrepentant sinner will eventually get caught."

"That's right."

Detective Anders rose from his chair and shook the professor's hand. "Thank you again for your time, Finn. If I come up with further questions, may I call you?"

"Certainly, David. I spend my day pondering questions of good and evil, but this is the first time I've played even a minor role in a real murder investigation."

Anders opened McNair's office door, then stopped. He turned as though struggling with something inside himself. Then he pulled an envelope from his pocket.

"Finn, I may have seen an angel."

Dr. McNair smiled and motioned to the empty chair. "Close the door. Sit down, please. Talk."

The detective handed Dr. McNair the envelope. "Look at this, if you would. There's a story.

"One day, the spring of my freshman year of high school, I returned home from baseball practice and found my older sister Isabella dead in her room. Someone had stabbed her, most likely shortly before I arrived. The police never found her killer.

"Isabella and I were very close. When I was a young boy, I couldn't pronounce her name, so I called her Issa. I was the only person she allowed to use that nickname. A few years before her death, Issa wrote me a birthday card in haiku. I returned the favor. Over time, haiku became our secret communication. Nobody knew, not even our parents. Now, with that background, read this letter."

Dr. McNair carefully examined the envelope and the paper, then read the letter. "Amazing. Tell me, David, how did you come by this letter?"

"There's a small park near my apartment. Two days ago, after dinner, I was walking my dog, Molly. As we walked through the park, an old man who looked like a homeless person, and who smelled of alcohol and sweat, called me by name and handed me this letter. He said a man in a nice suit told him to give me the envelope. The old man wouldn't give me any further information. Oddly, as we returned home from our walk twenty minutes later, the old man was gone, and a couple who was still there at the park denied having seen him.

"I don't understand how the man knew me nor how the other couple failed to notice him. I can't imagine who would know enough about my life to forge that letter, nor do I understand their motivation."

"You're a police detective," Dr. McNair said. "I assume you looked at police reports from Boston on June 20, 2016. What did you find?"

"You're correct. I checked the reports. A fifty-seven-year-old man who was thought responsible for the fatal stabbing of a twenty-year-old female college student a week earlier, and the stabbing of a high school girl six months prior, was found dead. His death was … uh … extremely violent. Severe trauma, including partial decapitation. There was one witness, a known alcoholic, who said he saw the man pull a knife on a teenage girl asleep on a bench. The witness, who admitted he'd been drinking, rambled something about 'avenging angels' that didn't make sense to the police. The girl disappeared."

"So you're saying a man who apparently got off on stabbing girls, and who may have been doing so for a long time, was violently killed. Sounds to me like Proverbs Five as I described to you earlier. Or call it karma, or even just an ironic coincidence. The letter would make sense if he were the one who killed your sister years ago.

"What of the teenage girl?"

"The police in Boston never found her, but I have reason to believe she's here in Indiana. The single witness in the Boston incident, unreliable as he may have been, described a teenage girl with a large scar on her cheek. He was adamant about the scar. I can't imagine there are too many young ladies who look like that. But at least twice in the past several months here in central Indiana, violent men have themselves died violently, and both times a teenage girl with a large scar on her cheek was present at or very near the scene of the crime. I can't help but wonder if it's the same girl, if she travels around killing bad guys, or if she's just terribly unlucky regarding being in the wrong place at the wrong time."

Dr. McNair was silent, thinking. He rose and leafed through a couple of ancient volumes that he pulled from the shelf in his office. He found something, sat down at his desk with the old leathery tome, and read quietly for several minutes. Then he turned back to Detective Anders.

"Possession."

"Yes, I know, nine-tenths of the law and all that," the detective replied in a weary voice.

"No, no, no. That's not where I'm going. Let me preface this by reminding you that I am an academic, and I am not at all in the habit of ascribing a supernatural explanation to everything I do not understand. I believe that most cases of so-called 'possession' are either due to trickery or mental illness. There is a long tradition of hoaxes in the field of demonic or angelic possession."

Anders snorted. "You're serious, Finn?"

The professor nodded.

"I've never been a fan of horror movies, but I've heard of demonic possession. Always in the context of fiction. I'm not familiar with the other one."

"Angelic possession? A similar process, except that angels will never take possession of a human host without the freely granted permission of the host or the will of God. Demons, of course, don't care about permission."

"But of course." Anders rolled his eyes, then grinned. "Sorry, I don't mean to be impolite. It's just …"

Dr. McNair held up a hand in mock protest. "No problem, I understand. I cannot overemphasize that this is *not* my go-to explanation for the unexplainable, and I agree this sounds strange to our modern ears. But many religious scholars, including Saint Thomas Aquinas, take this subject seriously. I've never seen angelic possession, or more accurately I haven't recognized it if I saw it, but I've read about it from several reliable sources. So I'm just throwing this out for your consideration.

"Feel free, of course, to come up with your own theory that better fits the facts as you related them to me."

ON THE BUS

An unseasonably warm morning in early March revealed Indiana at its best. Songbirds and squirrels chattered at each other in the Samuelsons' backyard outside the large kitchen windows, arguing over the bird feeders. The sun beckoned through Linnea's bedroom window.

Over two months had passed since the home invasion. Life was pleasantly normal. Linnea smiled as she dressed. She organized the schoolwork on her desk and packed it into her backpack. She reloaded her gym bag with a clean t-shirt, shorts, and socks, then she barreled down the stairs to the kitchen.

"Good morning Cara … Adam … Mom," hugging each of them in turn. "Where's Dad?"

"Dad had an early case this morning," Katie replied.

"Oh." Linnea hugged Katie again. "When you see him, give him this hug from me."

Katie smiled. "I sure will, honey."

"Mom, don't forget my team has a scrimmage after school. Crissa's mom will take me home afterward, 'kay?"

"Okay. Though depending on when I get off work, I may

be able to catch part of your game and take you home myself. I'll text you to let you know."

"That'd be great."

Linnea prepared her cereal, shredded wheat with blueberries, poured in some milk and sat down to eat.

A FEW MINUTES LATER, Adam and Cara got up from the table. "Time to get to it. You're lucky, sis," Adam said. "You get an extra half hour before your bus comes. Enjoy it while you can. Next year, when you're in high school, you'll leave earlier."

Cara leaned over Linnea and kissed the top of her head. Linnea looked up at her and smiled. "What was that for?"

"I want you to start your day knowing that people love you."

Linnea stood and hugged Cara, waved at Adam and sat back down at the table with Katie.

Once the older teens had left, Katie looked over at her smiling little girl. "You look especially happy this morning."

"I am, Mom. I'm so happy Cara's here. It's like she loves so big, you can almost feel it."

"She's a remarkable young person. She has every excuse to be bitter, to hate the world. But you're right; she's kind and sweet and loving. Dad and I are glad you two are close. She's worthy of emulating."

Mother and daughter sat for a few more minutes, talking. Then Linnea jumped up. "The bus is coming in a few minutes. I have to get ready."

Linnea ran upstairs and brushed her teeth. She dashed into her bedroom, straightened her sheets to remove a wrinkle, and grabbed her backpack and gym bag. Then she bolted down the stairs and headed for the door.

"Don't forget your phone, Linnea," Katie called. "And bring a jacket. It's still cool out."

"I got it. Bye, Mom. Love you. See you tonight," Linnea yelled over her shoulder as she shut the front door. The bus stop was only about a block and a half from her house. Already she could see kids gathering.

The school bus turned a corner several streets down, heading toward her stop. Linnea ran, a bundle of energy careening down the sidewalk. She heard laughter and chanting, "Go, go, go!" but Linnea made it with time to spare. She giggled with her friends, exchanging fist bumps and high fives. "Hey Crissa, Danny, Heather, Nate," she called.

The bus pulled up to their stop. The door opened, revealing the bus driver, Mr. Henry. Linnea liked Mr. Henry. He always had a kind word for the kids. This morning, though, he simply nodded as they piled up the steps into the bus.

"Let's sit in the back," Crissa whispered to Linnea.

"'Kay, let's go."

When everyone found a seat, the bus took off for the next stop on the route to school.

"I hope we're on the same team for the scrimmage today," Crissa said.

"Me too."

"Hey, did you understand the math homework? That stuff confuses me."

"I don't have trouble with the math we're doing now," Linnea said. "I'll go over it with you before class if you want."

The bus made the final stop before heading to the school, allowing the last few students to board.

Mr. Henry nodded at the new arrivals. "Ah, good morning, Johnny. Glad you made it," he said to a little boy who, with his mom, had dashed to the bus stop just in time. The driver waved at the boy's mom, who mouthed "Thank you!" through the closing bus door.

The students were chattering happily, energized by the sunshine and the mild winter day that felt more like spring.

A mile down the road, the bus slowed, then stopped as it prepared to cross a railroad track. Two men were standing on the sidewalk, talking. Mr. Henry opened the school bus door to check for a train. Suddenly the men darted up the steps through the open bus door. The driver tried to close the door but was not fast enough.

"Mikhail sends you his regards," the man growled at Mr. Henry. He fired two shots that echoed loudly through the bus. Kids who were not yet aware of the altercation immediately stopped talking, just in time to see their beloved bus driver thrown against the driver's side window by the force of the bullets, then slump down in his seat. Several children screamed.

"Quiet!" the man yelled. The noise stopped.

In the far back seat of the bus, Linnea was thinking as quickly as she could. *If I call for help, the gunmen will hear me. They'll confiscate my phone and probably hurt me. I don't know how to text the police or the school, and they wouldn't believe me, anyway. My parents for sure would call me back, which would be bad for me. But Adam and Cara will know how to follow my phone. If Cara were here, we'd be okay.*

Linnea pulled out her iPhone, tapped a quick message, then stuffed her phone down in the seat, in the space between the seat and the back cushion.

"Crissa," she whispered, "it's very important that you don't say anything about my phone. Please believe me."

Crissa's eyes were moist with tears. Her lips trembled. But she nodded her understanding.

On the bus, children were talking to each other in hushed voices. One young girl was whimpering.

The gunmen pulled the bus driver from his seat and dumped him unceremoniously in the aisle. One of them took the driver's seat. The bus lurched into motion again.

The other man addressed the kids. "See your driver? This is what happens when you don't obey instructions. Understand?"

They nodded. The man held up a small black duffel bag. "As I walk down the aisle, each of you who has a cellphone will put it in the bag. There will be no exceptions."

He proceeded slowly down the aisle, stepping on the bus driver as he passed over the corpse. Most of the kids had phones. The man waited at each seat for them to pull their phones from their backpacks. He held out the bag and nodded as each phone dropped inside. At the back of the bus, Crissa gave up her phone. Linnea shrugged and said her parents didn't trust her with a phone at her age.

The man stared at her doubtfully for a moment, then at Crissa, who met his gaze, then he turned away. Silently, he carried the duffel bag of cellphones to the front of the bus.

When the man returned to the front of the bus, Crissa whispered to Linnea. "I wonder why he took our phones and put them in that bag."

"I suppose it's a Faraday bag. That's the only thing that would make sense."

"What's a Faraday bag?"

"Copper mesh in the fabric. Blocks the cellphone signals, so we can't call for help, and nobody can track our phones. It's like that mesh in the door of your microwave oven, so the microwaves don't leak out."

"Ah, that's why you …" Crissa subtly nodded to their seat.

"Exactly," Linnea whispered.

"How do you know this stuff?"

"Shhh."

"Why did you kill Mr. Henry? Are you going to kill us?" a boy asked.

"You all will do exactly what we say," replied the man. "Otherwise …" He drew his finger across his throat.

The children were silent. The bus swayed a little as a tire rolled over a pothole.

Crissa leaned over to Linnea and whispered, "We're not heading the right way to the school."

"They're taking us somewhere else," Linnea said. "I figured they would. It wouldn't make sense to kill Mr. Henry but drive us to school, anyway."

"What's gonna happen to us?"

"Don't worry. I got us the best help."

"What do you mean? The police?"

"Do you remember what happened at my house back in December? You know, with the break-in and everything?"

"My parents were talking about it. There were two guys. Guns 'n knives 'n stuff, right?"

"And you remember what happened to the two bad guys?"

"I don't know exactly what happened, but I heard my dad say the bad men died."

"Yep. They were gonna hurt me. One of them had grabbed me. But my sister saved me."

"What did she do?"

Linnea shook her head and held up her hand, palm out, in the universal signal for stop. "I promise it'll work out. Trust me, okay?"

"Okay." Crissa nodded.

The school bus picked up speed as it entered the highway. By now, they all realized that they were not heading to school. Worried whispers passed around the bus from student to student, but nobody wanted to risk the wrath of the two strange men.

Through the bus window, Linnea could see a sign for the

local airport. Soon she noted one runway running roughly parallel to the state highway, separated by a field and a metal fence. The bus slowed a mile or so farther and turned in to the airport entrance.

A tall chain-link fence topped with barbed wire protected the runways. The gunman driving the school bus pulled up to the access gate, opened the window and used a finger to punch a code into the keypad. Nothing happened. He tried again, but the gate remained closed. A gray-haired guard exited the adjacent guard booth and approached the driver.

"Good morning, sir. I'm not aware of a school tour scheduled today."

"Plans have changed," the driver said as he shot the guard. The crack of his pistol reverberated through the bus. The old man fell and lay still. The other man ran to the guard booth and hit the button to open the gate.

TEXT

*A*P World History is a difficult class, but in a different way than, say, Calculus is difficult. The tricky thing with world history is in trying to discuss history through the lens of what people consider to be correct behavior today. People are messy. Often things that were acceptable at a certain point in time, in a certain part of the world, are no longer considered appropriate.

That morning, the class was discussing whether capitalism is a more just economic system than socialism. Ms. Davenport, the teacher, was indignant that the benefits and moral superiority of collectivism versus laissez-faire capitalism were not immediately apparent to her students' young and innocent minds.

Suddenly Cara gasped. Silently, with a look of horror on her face, she handed Adam her cellphone. The message, from Linnea, read:

CARA HELP PLS! 2 men w guns on bus. Shot driver ?dead. DO NOT call or txt me. Follow my phone.

. . .

ADAM STOOD up to attract the teacher's attention. "P-Please forgive me, Ms. Davenport. Family emergency. Come on, Cara."

They quickly packed their book bags and exited the classroom at a fast walk.

"Do we have any other information?"

Cara shook her head solemnly. When they reached the school office, they were glad to see the attendance clerk at her desk. Attendance had never been an issue with Cara and Adam, so they were not on a first-name basis with her. "Ma'am, I'm Adam S-Samuelson, and this is Cara Ferris. We're seniors. We have a family emergency, so we need to leave school. Is there something we need to sign?"

She produced a log book. "Sign here on this line. Bring a note tomorrow or have a parent call to excuse your absence, so it doesn't count against you."

"Thank you so much, ma'am. We'll do that."

Cara and Adam ran to the student parking lot and jumped in his old Toyota Celica. He pulled out his cellphone and looked at it. *God, how I hate making phone calls*, he thought. The knowledge that fear of the telephone was common in stutterers did not make him feel any better. He took a deep breath in an attempt to relax enough to call.

"I got it," Cara said. She dialed the middle school, about a mile down the road from the high school. "Hello, this is Cara Ferris, Linnea Samuelson's older sister. Could you please tell me if Bus 47 has arrived at school yet?" Pause. "Sure, I can wait."

Adam could feel his face flush with embarrassment. *Not again. Not in front of Cara.*

While she was on hold, Cara had opened the Find my Friends app on her phone and was examining the icon for

Linnea's iPhone on the map. She frowned. "The bus isn't where it's supposed to be," she whispered to Adam.

The school secretary came back on line to tell her that the bus had not yet arrived but should do so shortly. "Thank you, ma'am, but would you please transfer me to the Transportation Office?"

"Transportation." A brisk female voice.

"Yes, ma'am. My name is Cara Ferris. My sister Linnea Samuelson rides Bus 47. She's in eighth grade. Anyway, she texted me that there's trouble on her bus. Do you know anything about it?"

"We haven't heard anything from 47. I'm sure everything's okay. Your sister was probably joking. Her bus should be at the school in a few minutes."

"Would you check, please?"

"Fine. Hold on." In the background, Cara and Adam could hear the radio call sent to the entire fleet of school buses. A minute later the call was repeated. The lady came back on the line. "I'm sorry, we're not getting a response from 47. Again, they should be at the school by now."

"Ma'am, my sister wouldn't joke about something like this. Please verify the location of bus 47 now, or let me speak with a supervisor."

"No need to be testy. Here, the GPS shows the bus is … oh, hell … it's not at the school. What are they doing on that road?"

"Ma'am, what's going on? Where's my sister's bus?"

"Hold on, our supervisor is here. He wants to talk to you."

"Bill Kitchens here. Who am I speaking with?"

"Sir, I'm Cara Ferris. I'm a senior at the high school. My sister Linnea Samuelson is on Bus 47. She texted me that two men boarded the bus and shot the driver. It is not like her to joke about this sort of thing. I called her school, but the bus had not yet arrived. I asked them to transfer me to Transportation. Where is her bus now?"

"It appears to be heading towards the airport. I'm notifying the superintendent and the police as we speak. Is this the best number to reach you?"

"Yes, this is my cell," Cara said.

"Okay, keep your phone with you. I'm sure the police will have questions."

"Yes, sir. Thank you."

"Cara, m-my folks need to know what's going on. I'll call Mom before we go." *Awesome, another chance to fail on my phone.*

"I n-need to speak with K-Katie Samuelson, please. This is her son, Adam. Sure, I'll hold."

While he was waiting, he asked Cara what her thoughts were about why anyone would take a busload of kids to the airport.

"That's what doesn't make sense to me," she responded. "A school bus can hold fifty-some kids. How would they transfer all those kids to a plane?"

Katie came on the line, so he motioned this to Cara. He put his cellphone on speaker. "M-Mom, sorry to interrupt you at work."

"What's going on?"

"S-Something's wrong on Linnea's school bus. It never arrived at school. Looks like it's heading to the airport. Linnea texted Cara that gunmen shot the bus driver, and that we should follow her phone but *do not* call or text. I have the impression she hid her phone somewhere after she t-texted us. The school and police are involved. That's all we know at this point."

"Shot the bus driver!" Katie said in a high voice.

"Ma'am," Cara said, "please do not call or text Linnea. We

don't want the men to know about Linnea's phone. The police are involved."

"I won't do anything stupid, Cara. I'll leave here as soon as I find a replacement. Keep me informed, please."

"We will, Mom. Love you."

"You too." Adam ended the call.

"What if they weren't after all the k-kids?" he wondered out loud. "What if they were interested in a specific child?"

"So why would they hijack the school bus? Why not kidnap the specific child they're after?" Cara asked. "Linnea is frequently out, riding her bike around the neighborhood, or she's at soccer practice several days a week. I would think if a kidnapper wanted Linnea or another kid, he could find easier places to take her than on her school bus."

Cara examined her iPhone again. "They're definitely going to the airport. Let's head that way while we talk."

"Sounds good. I'll drive, you navigate."

WHILE THEY DROVE, questions ran through Adam's mind. "Cara," he asked her, "what if they want several specific kids, maybe siblings? It would p-probably be difficult to get two or three or more young children away from their parents simultaneously, other than when they're on the school bus."

Cara considered this. "I would think if the kids' parents are drug lords or whatever, they'd drive their kids to and from school because they'd be worried about security."

"So, what if this hypothetical d-dad or mom is not involved in illegal activity and is not security-conscious, but is a decision-maker for something that involves many millions of dollars, so taking their kids is an attempt to influence their decision a certain way?"

"I suppose that's possible. Linnea has never mentioned particularly rich kids who ride her bus, though I confess her bus rides don't come up much in conversation. Adam, you've lived in our neighborhood much longer than I have. Do you know of anyone who lives near us who is extremely wealthy?"

He shook his head. "No, most families in our neighborhood are a lot like us."

As they drove down the highway toward the airport, several emergency vehicles passed them with full lights and sirens. The reality of their situation quickly sobered them.

"Adam?" Cara murmured, her lips tight. "I couldn't bear it if they hurt Linnea."

THE REGIONAL AIRPORT was ten miles out of town. It was an easy drive on the state highway. Adam had driven past the airport many times, though he'd never before had a reason to stop there. The entrance gate by the security station was open, but emergency vehicles blocked access to the airport.

They continued past the airport and pulled off the road behind the hangars, at a neighboring farm. From that vantage point, the airport looked quiet.

Adam locked his car, and they made their way through the fields quickly and quietly.

Cara whispered, "How will we get over the fence?"

"I'm not sure. If it comes to it, we can put my coat over the b-barbed wire. Still, I'd rather not climb."

When they arrived at the perimeter fence, though, it was apparent that no climbing would be needed. There was a defect in the fence through which a person could easily pass.

"What do you think did this?"

"Probably a tractor accident. They haven't fixed it yet, thank goodness."

Crouching low, they crept to the outside of the closest hangar and peered around. Cara pulled Adam back and gestured to the roof of the squat, utilitarian building nearby. A sign identified the building as "Central Indiana Aviation." Below, in smaller letters, was "FBO."

"I see a guy on the roof. Sniper?"

"He's focused in the other d-direction. We need to get closer. Follow me."

The two teens used what cover they could find until they could crawl under a truck to see what was going on. The school bus had pulled up beside the asphalt ramp. Near the bus, a small business jet was waiting patiently, as though oblivious to the commotion. Heat from the jet engines rippled the air behind them. Several police cars and a SWAT van surrounded the bus at a distance of about one hundred feet. Officers wearing bulletproof vests held guns trained on the bus.

From their vantage point, they were close enough to overhear the negotiations that were being conducted by radio.

"You will listen carefully to our instructions." The speaker had a foreign accent, but Adam couldn't place it exactly. "My colleague will exit and retrieve something from beneath the bus. I have grenade in my hand. I have pulled the pin. If you interfere with us in any way, fifty-two children will die. Do you understand?"

"We understand," the police negotiator responded in a terse voice.

A compact, muscular man with close-cropped hair, wearing a black t-shirt and cargo pants, emerged from the bus. Ignoring the police, he pulled out a small flashlight and knelt by the side of the bus. He peered underneath the yellow metal as he played the beam back and forth. After a short time, he rose, strode to the other side of the bus, squatted down again and wrested a small package from underneath the bus. He briefly examined the package which looked to

Adam like a small rectangular black box. Then, as though oblivious to his audience, he re-entered the bus.

Adam still couldn't see how, surrounded by armed police, the gunmen expected to escape. He wasn't confused for long.

<<<<>>>>

THE KIDS on the bus were quiet. A boy across from Linnea gripped the back of the seat in front of him. His eyes were wide. Linnea heard sobbing from a seat midway down the aisle.

She examined the two gunmen. Both looked very fit, muscular, with identical black t-shirts, cargo pants, dark shoes, and thin dark gloves. They carried handguns in waist holsters. Each man had a messenger bag.

One man was speaking on a small radio to the police negotiator. Linnea could hear both sides of the conversation, including the man's threat to blow up the bus if the police hindered his colleague in any way. He'd pulled from his bag something that looked very much like a grenade, at least what she knew from movies. *He's not lying about killing us all,* she thought.

The man who left the bus returned after a few minutes. "Got it," he said, as he showed his partner a small black box.

"Excellent. Then we need to go. We'll each bring a kid with us like we planned." Still holding the grenade, he looked around the first few seats, then grabbed a young boy by the arm. "We're going for a ride."

"Please no, sir," the boy begged.

"You will not say another word, or I'll shoot your friend. Understand?"

The boy nodded silently. His shoulders slumped in defeat.

THE POLICE NEGOTIATOR'S radio crackled to life again. One gunman spoke. "This is how it will work. We will transfer to the plane now. Each of us will bring a kid as insurance. If you make any move, children will die."

The bus door opened again. Adam could see one man clutching an object in one hand, with his other arm around the neck of a young boy. As he watched, a stain grew on the boy's pants. He had peed.

An officer yelled, "Hold your fire!" at the other police and SWAT units.

Cara whispered, "No." She turned to Adam and kissed him lightly on the cheek. Then, without looking back, she rolled from beneath the truck and strode resolutely away.

"Cara, wait," he pleaded, but she did not respond.

She approached and crossed the police line amid shouts for her to get down and stay back. Cara walked directly towards the bus, her face impassive, her hands held open in front of her chest.

One of the police officers ran to pull her back. Two shots rang out from the direction of the bus. The officer grabbed his chest and fell, turning as he collapsed. His face ... Detective Anders.

LINNEA FIRST REALIZED Cara had arrived when one of her classmates said in a surprised voice, "Someone's coming."

Cara did not pause until she reached the steps leading on to the bus. The gunman holding the young boy aimed his pistol directly at Cara's chest. He said one word: "Stop."

Cara held her hands open in front of her chest. She

looked him in the eye. "My name is Cara. My little sister is on the bus."

"Why did you come here?"

"Let the kids go and take me."

He smirked. "Aren't you a brave little girl."

"It makes sense. I'm just a girl. I can't cause you any trouble. I'll do what you say. Let the kids go, and your job will be easier and cleaner. You'll have a hostage and the kids don't need to die."

The other gunman spoke. "Whatever. Just cuff her. We gotta go."

Cara held out her arms. The man put the cuffs on her wrists. "May I see my sister quickly?" she asked.

The man nodded. "Thirty seconds."

Cara mounted the steps, scanned the interior of the bus, then strode to Linnea.

"Cara, no," Linnea said.

"Linnea, listen to me. When we leave, I need you to guide the kids to the police line. Some of the smaller kids may need help. You take charge. Make sure you account for every kid. Will you do that for me?"

Linnea nodded, tears staining her face.

"I love you, little sister," Cara whispered, then gently kissed Linnea's forehead. She turned and walked back to the front of the bus. "Okay, let's go," she said.

The men roughly released the children they'd been holding. One man grabbed Cara similarly to how he'd been holding the young boy. The two young hostages stumbled back to their seats.

The other man spoke to the kids on the bus. "You will all remain on the bus until the plane takes off. If you do not wait, we kill this girl. Do you understand?"

He fixed the kids in a firm gaze until he saw nods and murmurs of "yes, sir" from everybody.

. . .

From where Adam was hiding, he could see the two gunmen exit the bus. Cara was handcuffed. One man had her in a choke-hold. His other hand clutched what appeared to be a grenade. The other man was holding his pistol to Cara's head. In a tight group, they walked the short distance to the jet. It appeared to Adam that Cara was cooperating with her captors.

The airplane door opened downward, becoming steps. The gunmen and Cara mounted the steps and disappeared inside. With a faint click, the door folded up and closed. The muted whine of the jet engines became a roar as the plane moved.

CRASH AND BURN

The sleek silver Dassault Falcon jet streaked down the runway, her three turbofan engines screaming. Slowly the nose lifted, and the plane rose. Higher, ever higher into the cloudless sky it climbed. Adam felt like he'd lost a piece of his heart. *They took Cara.*

A police officer shouted and pointed. The plane was no longer flying smoothly. It dipped suddenly and slowly turned back towards the airfield, wings wobbling in an ungainly fashion. The plane's nose lifted, and it wavered. Then, as though struck by an invisible hand, the plane shuddered, stalled, and fell.

Adam watched, eyes wide, as the jet hurtled toward the ground. At the last moment, engines groaning, the plane's nose rose slightly. The landing gear tried to absorb the impact. With a screech of rending metal and shredded tires, the landing gear snapped off. The belly of the jet scraped along the ground near the runway with a sound like a wounded bull, plowing a three-hundred-foot trench in the soil. The stricken jet slowed, then settled with a final metallic groan. Flames flickered through the port engine. Silence.

Strident sound of alarms and emergency vehicles filled the air. Firetrucks and ambulances raced to the downed plane. As SWAT forces approached the closed cabin door, firefighters began spraying the burning engine with fire retardant foam. Within seconds, they maneuvered a wheeled platform to the cabin door. An officer lifted the exterior door handle. The door slid out and down. Several officers, flashlights and weapons ready, swarmed inside the downed plane. Their examination was brief. The leader called for a stretcher … just one. The officers exited the plane. One young officer staggered down the steps and slowly fell to his knees. He vomited. Adam was close enough to see that he was fighting not to cry.

Two medics raced up with a stretcher. A minute later they exited bearing a bloody body. The face was not recognizable, but Adam knew it was Cara by her clothes. A feeling of icy dread rushed through him. *God, no! Not my Cara.*

Suddenly the firefighters yelled a warning. Everyone scattered. With a roar, a giant fireball engulfed the stricken jet. Adam could feel the blistering heat from where he stood.

Katie and Stephen guided Linnea and Adam through the next hours. The airport was the center of a whirl of activity. Adam answered questions from the police investigators in monosyllables. Their stupid questions didn't matter. His girlfriend was dying, and he could not help her. At one point, Stephen left. Adam assumed he had to return to the hospital.

Even hugs from Linnea failed to lift his spirits. "Thank you for coming for me, Adam," she murmured, looking up at him. He couldn't think of anything to say, so he quietly stroked her hair.

"You're a smart young lady. You handled yourself very well," Katie told her.

"Where's Cara? Is she okay?"

Katie and Adam fought back tears. Katie replied, "They took her away in an ambulance, to the hospital. She was very badly injured when the plane crashed."

"Mom?" Linnea ventured in a small voice.

"Yes, dear?"

"If Cara dies, it's my fault. I shouldn't have asked her to help me."

"No." Katie hugged her tightly. "You thought quickly and well. The policewoman who spoke with us told me privately that you likely saved the lives of all the kids on the bus. Cara did what she felt she had to do. I couldn't imagine her making any other choice. She's so brave. But whatever happens with Cara, please never blame yourself." Linnea nodded but said nothing. She drew her knees up to her chest and leaned against her mom.

"Adam, Dad is at the hospital coordinating care for her. He called me a few minutes ago, and he'll call back with an update after she has some tests. You know she's at the best trauma center in Indianapolis."

"Yeah, Mom. I just feel so helpless, so empty. I c-couldn't imagine her not being here."

"Let's not mourn her before her time. She's in the Lord's hands."

He nodded.

THE NEXT SEVERAL days were the longest of Adam's life. He heard talk of brain swelling, CT scans, at least a couple of surgeries. By day three, they were allowed to visit Cara in the SICU for short periods of time. Her head and face were heavily bandaged. A translucent plastic breathing tube was in her mouth, connected to a machine that sighed and whirred at regular intervals.

A slight Indian woman in a white coat entered. "Good afternoon," she said in the musical accent of the subcontinent. "My name is Dr. Jain."

Katie and Adam, who were visiting, nodded to her. "Doctor."

"I heard you were here. I wanted to speak with you. Cara is a very lucky girl."

"Lucky? She l-looks most unlucky to me," Adam said.

"Yes, well … when she first arrived, her case was more in the purview of neurosurgery than plastic surgery. She suffered significant cranial trauma … uh, to her skull. Initial CT scan suggested some brain swelling, so we gave her steroids and a medicine to keep her asleep. That is why she is on the breathing machine."

"So what happens now, doctor?"

"Brain swelling has pretty much resolved. This does not always happen. We've been decreasing her medication. She's now initiating most breaths on her own. I expect she'll be off the respirator by tomorrow, possibly even this evening, and out of the ICU."

"That sounds good. I mean no offense, but why is a p-plastic surgeon involved?"

Dr. Jain regarded him intently. "In the crash, there were injuries to her face. Broken facial bones. Lacerations."

"More scars? Cara's always been b-beautiful to me. But most people couldn't see past that big scar on the left side of her face. She doesn't deserve more scars."

"Son, after the events at the airport, a lot of people care about Cara. No effort has been spared in her care here. She will always have some scarring, but I hope that when she heals, she will look almost as beautiful on the outside as I'm told she is on the inside." She hesitated. "Back in my home country, we still struggle greatly with proper treatment of women. I heard some of your girlfriend's story. This is one small thing I could do to help."

She touched his shoulder gently and turned to leave. "Thank you, Dr. Jain," Katie said. "For everything."

THE NEXT DAY, as Dr. Jain promised, the doctors transferred Cara to a step-down unit. Adam sat beside her on the hospital bed, holding her hand and talking to her softly. Her eyelids fluttered, then opened. She regarded him intently.

"Welcome back, Cara," he whispered.

She tried to speak, but no sound came out. She tried again. "A'am."

"I'm here, Cara." He thought she tried to smile, but her facial bandages, though fewer than on prior days, were nonetheless covering too much of her face for a proper smile. Still, she gently squeezed his hand, so he'd know she was back.

"Sis … ter okay?"

"Yes, Linnea's just fine, now that you're getting better. She was c-convinced it was her fault that you got badly injured. We'd never seen her so despondent. Now that you're recovering, her smiles are returning."

Cara nodded imperceptibly and squeezed his hand again.

"The other kids are okay, too. You saved every student on the bus. The press is calling you a hero."

"Not …'ero. Jus' Cara." After a few minutes, her hand relaxed and her eyes closed again. Her chest rose and fell slightly with each breath.

"Sleep well, Cara," he whispered, then he wept.

AFTER SCHOOL, Adam was dozing in the chair beside Cara's hospital bed when there was a knock at the door. A young nurse entered and nodded to him. "It is time for medicine," she said in a businesslike voice. Her accent sounded familiar, but he was tired so he couldn't place it. Still, something about this nurse bothered him. He'd spent a lot of time in the room and knew many of Cara's nurses.

"I d-don't recognize you," he said. "What's your name?"

She pulled out a pre-filled syringe from her scrub pocket. Rather than answer him, she was concentrating fully on inserting the needle of the syringe into Cara's IV line. He was pretty sure that syringes for patient use would not be carried in a pocket, and he noted that the nurse did not bother to clean the IV port with an alcohol swab, so he rose from his chair and put his hand on her arm. "What is this medicine for?"

The nurse knocked his hand away with a quick, violent motion and turned back to the IV line. Now he knew things had gone off-track in a big way. He grabbed her syringe arm with both hands. He intended to pull her outside the room and away from Cara. However, before he could move her, she turned, kicked his right lower leg, and then, as he bent over from pain, smashed her elbow into his face. He was momentarily stunned, giving her time to pull a knife. They circled each other. She was clearly a skilled fighter. Why would she want to hurt Cara?

"You need lesson in staying out of other people's business," she said to him. Her accent ... the gunmen from the school bus. Damn!

He feinted to one side. When she slashed at him, he grabbed his coat from his chair to use as makeshift protection from her blade. He needed reinforcements, but how ... ah yes! Without making it obvious, he worked them closer to the wall. She suddenly lunged at him, but he hooked her knife hand with his coat, then he punched the Code Blue button on the wall. From the corner of his eye, he saw the syringe intended for Cara had fallen to the floor during their struggle. An alarm sounded in the nursing station, a blue light flashed above the bed, and a female voice on the hospital intercom began to repeat, "Code Blue, Step-down Unit. Code Blue, Step-down Unit."

The fake nurse seemed to be filled with sudden strength. With a quick series of brutal moves, she had Adam on the floor, choking him with her legs. He was fighting to keep control of the knife, but he could not breathe. His eyesight was growing fuzzy. With one hand, he flailed around for a weapon. His hand closed on something. The syringe. As people burst through the door into the room, he plunged the needle of the syringe into her thigh and pressed it home. The would-be assassin jerked strongly for a second, then collapsed.

ESCALATION

*A*dam rested on the hospital room floor for a minute to catch his breath. As he lay there, a medical team descended en masse on Cara's room. Doctors and nurses rolled the woman off him and started CPR. From what he could tell, it wasn't going well. That was okay with him. He watched a young doctor insert an airway. It looked like that would hurt if one were awake enough to feel it.

Someone brought a gurney. They loaded her on it and headed off to the emergency room.

Once more, the room he was in became a crime scene. As the medical team left, the police arrived. Soon after, his mom arrived, too. One officer took statements from Adam and the nurses while another snapped multiple pictures inside and outside the room. A couple of hours after his struggle, he heard a familiar voice outside in the hallway, a voice he did not expect ever to hear again.

Detective Anders walked slowly into the room, as though it hurt him to move. Adam stood and offered him his chair. He needed it more than Adam.

"Thank you, son." He turned and sat, wincing as he did so.

"I saw you get shot," Adam said.

"Thank God for body armor, huh? But they used good ammo. Cracked some ribs, despite the Kevlar."

"You should be home resting."

"I tried. Got bored at home. I was doing paperwork at the office when the call came through about this death, and I saw Cara's name in the report. I just had to come."

"So the l-lady died?"

"They pronounced her dead in the emergency room."

"I … I've never k-killed anyone before."

"She would have killed Cara. The syringe contained a solution of concentrated nicotine. They could never restart her heart. Nobody's blaming you, son. You did what you had to do."

"Who was she? Why would she want to hurt Cara?"

"Her name was Olga Kronikova. Russian mob, Chicago."

"Olga," Adam said. "I always thought that was a classic name for an evil female Russian."

"There's often some truth behind stereotypes," Anders agreed. "Though Olga Korbut was a Soviet gymnast who won multiple gold medals in the Olympics back in the seventies. Olga Tañón is a Grammy-winning Puerto Rican musician. Oh, and Olga Kurylenko is a gorgeous model and a very talented actress. She was born in Ukraine, but I believe she lives in France."

Adam smiled. "You made your point."

"So what did Olga Kronikova say to you here in the room?"

"I won't forget it soon. She said I need a lesson in staying out of other p-people's business. Her accent reminded me of the men on the bus."

"Yes, they were professionals. They wore gloves so as not to leave any fingerprints on the bus, but our facial recognition software identified them also as Russian mob."

"Detective, what was this all about? What was the p-point of hijacking a school bus?"

"That part we don't know yet. I was hoping to interview Cara. We need to know what happened on the airplane."

"How she was the only one alive?"

"That, and if anyone spoke to her. Maybe she knows what the object was that the perps took from under the bus. Not much remained after the jet caught fire. The NTSB is still investigating, but they may take months to reach a conclusion."

Katie looked over at Cara, who was sleeping peacefully. The portion of her face that was unbandaged was swollen and bruised. "Detective, I don't think she's in any condition to be interviewed yet."

Anders nodded. "Agreed. Not today anyway. I'll have my office schedule with you and your husband ... and your attorney, if you all would feel more comfortable with him there. You know, Mrs. Samuelson, my thinking has evolved over the past few months. Cara certainly has her secrets, and I still have questions, but we have some dangerous criminals to contend with. My focus is on them, not Cara."

"Understood," she said.

"Meanwhile, I'll post a guard outside her room for the duration of her hospital stay."

"Thank you, sir."

THREE DAYS LATER, Cara was alert, restless, and wanted to leave the hospital. Dr. Jain convinced her to stay another day for safety, and to give time to arrange for post-op care at home. Katie offered to take time off work to help. Detective Anders arranged with the hospital for the use of a small conference room, one of those spaces normally used for giving bad news to large families. Katie and Stephen were present, their attorney Mr. Cohen was there, and interestingly, Linnea insisted on attending. Her argument was sound: Her school bus had been hijacked, she'd been forced to witness the murder of her bus driver, she had single-handedly arranged for Cara's involvement which almost cost Cara her life, though likely saved the lives of her schoolmates. After all this she deserved to know, from the source, what was going on. There was a new player as well, an Asian man of indeterminate age.

Detective Anders gestured to him and said, "I would like you all to meet Special Agent Vincent Tanaka from the FBI, Chicago office. He is collaborating with us on this case."

Adam did not find this at all surprising. So much of that very bad day fell under the purview of the FBI: organized crime, violent crime, crimes against children, and more. It occurred to him more than once over the past few days that one would have to be exceedingly stupid or incredibly desperate to hijack a school bus.

Adam studied Vincent Tanaka. Everything about him was impeccable. His hair was flawlessly groomed. His dark elegant suit fit his thin form perfectly. His shoes were unsmudged, his nails short and clean, and his teeth, even and white. Adam was tempted to dismiss him as a poser, but there was something hard in his eyes. Something about him made Adam feel that he'd be a good man to have on his side in a fight.

Special Agent Tanaka placed an omnidirectional microphone on the table where everyone was sitting. "As we agreed, this conversation is being recorded. The FBI will work in concert with Detective Anders' office as we move forward." He paused and looked around at each of them. "Detective Anders and I have already spoken in depth, but I have some questions. Linnea, let me start with you."

Linnea glanced at her parents, who nodded to her. "Yes, sir. What would you like to know?"

"You were a very brave young lady in the face of horrific violence that should never have been part of your life." Linnea looked at Agent Tanaka, holding his gaze. "But I wonder what you were thinking when the two gunmen came into your school bus and shot your bus driver, Mr. Henry. You did not call the police. You did not text or call your parents. You did not even contact the school. Why did you text Cara?"

Linnea regarded the man with calm intensity. Adam could see how she unnerved many adults with her precocious use of language and her advanced way of thinking for a child. "Agent Tanaka, a school bus is not large. The men would have overheard any conversation. I don't know how to text the police or the school, and even if I had, they would not have believed me. They would have texted or called me back, and the gunmen would have confiscated my phone and possibly killed me. Had I texted my parents, I felt they would have panicked. Again, they would have called my phone. Besides … and I mean no disrespect … my parents are not as technologically savvy as my older siblings and would not know how to follow my phone. So I texted my big sister, whom I love and trust completely. And she and Adam came for me, as I knew they would.

"After my one text to Cara, I hid my phone in the bus seat. I don't know how much you're aware of what happened on the bus, but the first thing the men did was to confiscate everybody's cellphones. They placed them in a black canvas duffel that I assume was a Faraday bag. I told them that my parents didn't trust me with a phone. I hope they will forgive my lie."

"You are correct, Linnea. The cellphones were still in the duffel on the bus, and it was indeed a Faraday bag."

"Faraday bag?" Katie asked.

"Copper mesh in the fabric, Mom. Blocks the cellphone signals. Anyway, I didn't know whether the bus had a GPS. Since the incident, I've learned that they do. However, I also have learned the school was not yet concerned that my bus was late. So had I done otherwise, at a minimum two of my classmates would be dead."

Agent Tanaka studied his hands for a minute as he chose his words. "I cannot fault your logic, young lady. Your intellect is formidable. I hope, when you're old enough to work, you choose to work on our side."

Linnea nodded. "I appreciate that, sir."

He turned to Cara. "You've been through a lot in the past ten days. How are you feeling?"

"My head hurts. No surprise, I guess. My body hurts too. I got pretty banged up in the plane crash."

"What were you thinking, that made you cross a police line and approach the school bus?"

"I saw the hijackers had taken a young boy to use as a human shield as they transferred to the jet. I overheard the negotiations by radio, in which one of them said, 'Each of us will bring a kid as insurance.' I was afraid the children would die. Hopefully, I could convince them to release the kids and take me instead. That way they wouldn't have to kill two innocent children."

"But then what did you expect would happen once they got you in the airplane? You saw people's faces; you would have seen and heard too much. Once the plane took off, you would have been no further use to them. Surely you knew they would kill you?"

"But they didn't kill me, did they? I'm here, and everyone else who was on that plane is dead."

Agent Tanaka held out his thumb and forefinger a quarter-inch apart. "And you came that close to being dead yourself."

Cara shrugged. "Okay, so in retrospect, I wish the pilots hadn't died. I know a lot of things, but as you can see, I do not know how to fly a plane."

Agent Tanaka regarded her curiously. He started to speak, but Sidney Cohen stood up briskly. "Cara, I recommend you stop talking."

Agent Tanaka smacked the tabletop with his fist and stood, facing the attorney. "Mr. Cohen, this is not a game. We need to know what happened on that plane," he snapped. "What did she learn? Why did the plane crash?" He paused for effect. "And why, Mr. Cohen, did someone try to kill her three days ago?"

Cara raised her hand in a calming motion. "Gentlemen, please. The enemy is still out there, and we must work together." She looked around the table. "Agent Tanaka, I will tell you what I remember. But I remind you that I sustained a significant head injury ten days or so ago." She gestured to her bandages. "As I said, I will tell you as best I can what I remember."

Agent Tanaka gave her a curt nod. "Please continue, then." He sat back down.

"The two men dragged me up the stairs into the jet, then threw me into a seat. They had handcuffed me on the bus. Besides the two gunmen and the two pilots, there was another man who seemed to be in charge. He had short gray hair and a goatee. Probably in his sixties. Very fit. Foreign accent."

"Go on."

"He asked if they found the box. One of the hijackers pulled it out of his messenger bag and held it aloft. The man nodded and said something like, 'Michael will be pleased.'"

Linnea held up her hand. "Agent Tanaka, when the

gunmen first boarded the bus, one of them said, 'Michael sends you his regards,' then he shot Mr. Henry."

Agent Tanaka nodded. "They were referring to Mikhail Alexeyevich Sokolov. Based in Chicago. Head of the Russian mob in the Midwest. He's a very dangerous man."

"Would he really be willing to kill children?" Linnea asked.

"At your age, you're not supposed to know what an ugly world this is."

"Sir, at my age I watched my bus driver get shot to death right in front of me as I was on my way to school. At my age, I survived a violent home invasion a few months ago. From what, precisely, do you think you're protecting me?"

"Okay, miss. Mikhail Sokolov is one of the most cold-blooded killers I've ever encountered. Yes, he has killed women and children to teach people lessons, or for reasons of his own. He most likely would have ordered the murder of the kids on your bus who were the original hostages. He would have killed Cara, no question in my mind. Now he's lost whatever was in that box, and Cara is alive. The woman who attempted to kill Cara here in the hospital three days ago was Russian mob. That's not a coincidence. She failed thanks to a heroic effort by this young man. I take no pleasure in saying this, but Sokolov is a vindictive man. He does not like to lose." He turned to Detective Anders. "The Samuelsons should have police protection until this is over."

"I'll take care of it," Anders said.

"Cara, did the man on the plane, the one with the goatee, say anything else? Do you remember if you heard any names?"

"One gunman called him ... Yuri, I think."

"Yuri Kozlov. He is, or should I say was, a very close associate of Sokolov."

"Yuri said this would be a 'game changer.' He used those

words. He said they would soon become very wealthy. That's all the conversation I remember concerning the package from under the bus."

"What else did they discuss?"

"Basically, that they would sell me as a sex slave."

"What happened then?"

"I'm sorry, Agent Tanaka. I became … disgruntled. I'm not at all pleasant to be around when I'm angry." Cara paused. "Then the plane was falling, and I do not know how to fly one. There wasn't much time for me to figure it out."

Anders gave a short laugh. "Not pleasant to be around? Cara, you have a way with a phrase like nobody I've ever known."

Tanaka shook his head. "I'm torn. Part of me wants to ask you more questions, and part of me wants to give you a medal." He sighed. "All right, I know how to reach all of you. Is there anything else? Yes, Linnea?"

"Why the school bus? As I remember, there was something off about Mr. Henry when I got on the bus. He's usually quite jovial. That morning … it's crazy, but it almost looked as though he'd been crying. I wonder if something happened to him before that morning's ride. I'd be interested to know the status of his wife and children, or anyone else who could have been used as leverage against him."

"We certainly will look into that, though of course I cannot promise to share the information with you. I say again, you are a most unusual thirteen-year-old. I mean that in the very best way. With your parents' permission, we'll talk again. Thank you all for your cooperation. Dr. and Mrs. Samuelson, you have a most … interesting family." He nodded to Anders. "Detective." Agent Tanaka shook hands all around, gathered up his microphone and left the room.

IN THE SPOTLIGHT

Adam had hoped that now Cara was healthy enough to return to school, their family could regain some semblance of normalcy. But the squad car parked on the street outside their house was a constant reminder that their lives had changed.

Detective Anders was adamant that none of them should be alone. Katie and Stephen were equally adamant that they had work to do, that there was no specific threat or time limit. Life would continue. The detective and the Samuelsons met in the middle: Cara and Adam would drive Linnea to and from school, and she reluctantly agreed to take a break from her beloved soccer for now. Anders assigned additional police to their schools and to the hospitals where they worked.

The school system arranged for a new driver to cover Linnea's bus route, though few kids were willing to ride Bus 47 anymore. Adam could understand their parents' hesitation.

The big change was that they were now in the public eye. Following the home invasion, Cara suffered through a few days of celebrity status within their high school itself. Then their classmates moved on to something else. Now, however, they were in the national news. The press dubbed Cara "Teen Hero." There were photographs of the school bus and the downed airplane, but also photographs of their house and even Cara's school picture. She was not at all pleased that her prominent scar was plastered all over the news media. The Samuelsons read of interviews with their friends, their neighbors and even with people who they knew only peripherally, and with the usual panoply of "experts." Interestingly, there was no mention of the incident in the hospital.

Reporters left requests for interviews on their home voicemail. When they stopped answering the landline, reporters began calling and texting their cellphones. A couple of the more shameless ones knocked on their front door, ready with a camera and shouting questions the moment they opened the door. Stephen spoke with the police, and this practice ceased.

They assumed, naively, that after a few days the spotlight would move somewhere else. But it seemed that the longer they refused interviews, the crazier the narrative grew. A friend from school pointed Adam to an interview on Good Morning America. Linnea and Adam watched it together.

"Good morning, I'm Roberta Robins. By now, we're all familiar with the story of the teen girl from Indiana who everyone is hailing as a hero for saving the lives of a busload of children after their school bus was hijacked and the driver brutally murdered before their eyes. Today I have here with me a seven-year-old, Sarah Newsome, and her mother, Anita. Sarah was one of the students on the bus, and she saw something very interesting.

"Welcome to the program."

"Thank you, ma'am."

"Mrs. Newsome, let me start with you. This must be

every mother's worst fear, that their little one may have been injured or killed in a place where they're supposed to be safe. How did you first hear that your daughter's bus had been hijacked?"

"I was at home drinking my coffee, getting ready to head out to the office. The school called and said there'd been an accident … that I needed to go to the fire station immediately. Something about my daughter's bus. They wouldn't give me more information than that over the phone."

"This must be difficult for you. What happened at the fire station?"

"The fire station where they told me to go is located a mile or so from our local airport. Ordinarily, I would have driven past the airport to go there, but the state highway was blocked. There were lots of emergency vehicles. They were directing traffic to a side road. As I drove by, I could see that out in the field there was an airplane on fire. I couldn't tell if the school bus was there or not.

"I turned into the fire station along with a lot of other cars. All the kids were there. They were crying. Parents were crying. Sarah came to me, and I just hugged her."

"And then?"

"There was another girl with her, an older girl who Sarah told me helped her off the bus. Her name was Linnea. Everyone was talking so fast. I didn't understand what happened at first. Then they told me that Mr. Henry, the bus driver, had been shot. Two men with guns drove the bus to the airport. They threatened to let go of a hand grenade if the police did anything to stop them. They were going to each bring a child to use as a shield as they transferred to the airplane. Then a teenage girl walked up and offered herself as a hostage. Surprisingly, the gunmen released the children and took the young lady instead. Then they went on the plane. It took off and then … then something happened, and it crashed. That's all I know. The children on the bus were all okay."

Roberta Robins nodded. "Later that day, when you were talking to Sarah … Sarah, can you tell us in your own words? What did you see when you were on the bus?"

"I saw a angel."

"An angel. What did this angel look like?"

"She was tall with long dark hair. She was more beautiful than anyone I'd ever seen, even in movies. The way she walked … like a ballerina, I knew she was special. A policeman tried to stop her, and the bad men shot him. But the angel kept walking to the bus.

"She talked to the men. They handcuffed her and let the kids go. I remember thinking that was silly. Can't they see that handcuffs could never hold a angel?"

"Did other kids see the angel also?"

"I don't know. She didn't have wings or anything like that, but there was something about her that …" She shrugged. "I knew she wasn't just a girl."

"Would you tell us, Sarah, what she was wearing?"

"She weared jeans, a blue shirt, running shoes. Yeah, just normal stuff."

"I would have thought angels wore robes or something," Roberta said with a smile.

"No, just regular clothes."

"Mrs. Newsome, you and I have already talked. Tell me again why you came forward with this story."

"Yes, of course. It was the details. And Sarah was so insistent that this is what she saw. It's not like her to invent tales. And honestly, I guess it made sense, in a way. It's not harder to believe than saying some random normal teenager just happened to show up, crossed a police line during a hostage situation without getting shot, then offered to sacrifice herself in place of a busload of children."

As Adam and Linnea watched this, they looked at each other. "Through the eyes of a child," he murmured. Linnea squeezed his hand.

"Do you think it's possible the girl really saw what I saw?"

"I d-don't know, Linnea. I wonder."

"Cara is going to have a cow," Linnea said.

THAT EVENING AFTER DINNER, while Adam and Linnea cleared the dishes, Cara and Katie stayed at the table, talking.

"Cara?"

"Yes, ma'am?"

"I understand how uncomfortable you are with all the media attention."

"I mean no offense, but I wonder if you do. I have lived my entire life under the radar, invisible, if you will. This crazy media frenzy makes me terribly uncomfortable. And there's a feeling, way back somewhere in my brain, that it will make all of us less safe."

"It's not like you to run and hide," Katie remarked.

"I don't know what to do. How do I fight this? What do I say about crazy people who call me an angel or whatever?"

"You take control of the story. Tell it your way."

"I don't want people to think I was looking to be famous. I'm just a girl who was in a position to make a difference."

"Then tell people what happened. The ones who are open to the truth will believe you. Those who have already made up their minds won't be swayed no matter how much evidence you give them, so don't worry about them."

"What's okay for me to say? I don't want to undermine the FBI investigation."

"That's wise. We should discuss this with Special Agent Tanaka."

<<<<>>>>

Adam sat with his parents in the audience when Ellen DeGeneres interviewed Cara and Linnea.

"Good afternoon. My guests today are two young ladies who the world has been talking about for a couple of weeks now. We all know the story. Two men hijacked a school bus filled with kids en route to an Indiana elementary school. The men shot dead their beloved bus driver, then they drove the bus to a local airport. The gunmen were preparing to transfer to a jet, using two children as human shields, when this brave teenager offered herself as a hostage if the children on the bus would be set free.

"Would you introduce yourselves, please?"

"Yes, ma'am. I'm Cara Ferris and …"

"I'm Linnea Samuelson," Linnea piped up.

"It's a pleasure having you here. I'm aware that you resisted speaking directly to the media for a long time. Why did you change your mind?"

Cara took this question. "Ellen, when you decide to be a public figure, someone like you, for example, you accept that in exchange for money and fame you will live, in essence, in a glass house. You work out some arrangement with the paparazzi and your fans, and you get on with your life and your work. But the key thing is that you chose this life. My family never wanted the spotlight; we never wanted the attention. We just wanted to be left alone to do the best we can in this capricious world.

"We thought, naively, that if we ignored the commotion, it would pass. We assumed that, over time, people would find something else about which to obsess. Instead, the stories have grown ever crazier. So … here we are."

"Cara, we've heard what happened on the bus. But when

you arrived at the airport and saw what was going on, what were your thoughts?"

"Just that I couldn't allow the gunmen to use children as hostages. My thought was that if they saw an option to killing children, an option that would let them still achieve whatever they were trying to accomplish, they would agree. So I walked up to the bus and offered myself as a hostage. That's it."

"A young girl named Sarah, who was on the bus and saw you approach, has recently been in the news describing you as an angel."

Cara smiled. "That's very kind of her. But I expect any parent of teenagers would tell you that teens are no angels. I'm certainly not."

"You offered your life for the kids' safety. That's not … that's kind of exceptional, wouldn't you agree?" Ellen persisted.

"No, I don't think so. To save the lives of over fifty children? Many people would do that. Any parent would take a bullet for their kids."

"But those weren't your kids."

Cara took Linnea's hand. Her voice was firm and her eyes were moist. "I love my sister. I'll protect her with every breath in my body."

Ellen paused for a moment and wiped her eyes. When she spoke, her voice was husky. "You're not supposed to make me cry on my own show." She smiled, then she said, "'Greater love has no one than this: to lay down one's life for one's friends.' I feel I understand what this means a little better now."

Linnea leaned against Cara and laid her head on her shoulder for a moment. Cara kissed Linnea's hair, then turned back to Ellen.

"Okay, so the gunmen took you into the airplane, correct?"

Cara nodded. "Once we left the bus, I knew Linnea would take responsibility for helping all the kids get to safety."

"That's what I heard. You're quite an amazing young lady, Linnea."

"Thank you, ma'am. But at that point, my life was no longer in danger, so I just needed to be responsible, not brave."

"Cara, what happened on the airplane?"

"I'm sorry, I remember little about it. You probably know I suffered head trauma when the plane crashed."

"Yes, you spent a few days in the ICU, from what I understand."

"And you can see that my face is still a little the worse for wear." The camera panned in, revealing the swelling and bruising that was slowly resolving. Steri-strips still held some lacerations closed. "Ellen," Cara said in her gentle voice, "this is not the face of an angel, wouldn't you agree?"

Ellen gave a warm smile and leaned forward in her chair. "I imagine that everyone watching us wishes they had a sister or a friend like you. So yes, Cara, you look to me like an angel.

"This has been an eventful year for you, hasn't it?" Ellen continued.

"To what, in particular, are you referring?"

"You two girls were involved in a home invasion this past December. Is that true?"

"Yes, ma'am."

"What happened?"

"You understand that it's still an active investigation, so we can't discuss the details. But basically a couple of armed men broke into our house. My sister and I were home alone. We did what we could. Luckily, it was enough."

"I understand the two men were killed."

Cara nodded. "Yes, ma'am."

"But active investigation, can't discuss details, yada yada?"

Cara smiled at this. "Yes, ma'am."

"And before that?"

Cara wrinkled her forehead and frowned, waiting.

"You showed up in a small town in Indiana at the beginning of the school year. No past, no home address. At least twice since then, you were in the right place, at the right time, to save lives. One could be forgiven for thinking you're an angel."

"A girl has no secrets on national television, huh?" Cara closed her eyes and took a deep breath. Her cheeks flushed as she shook her head slowly. Linnea took one of Cara's hands in hers.

"It's okay," Linnea said to Cara. "You have nothing to be ashamed about."

Cara leaned forward and looked directly at Ellen. "You asked me earlier why I'd tried to avoid the media. This is why. There's a perfectly mundane explanation for why I 'showed up,' as you put it. I hadn't wanted people to know … I was embarrassed. Ellen, I've been homeless for many years. I've lived alone on the streets, like untold thousands of people in this greatest country on earth. We may be invisible as normal people go through their daily lives, but we're not nameless or faceless.

"Last fall, the Samuelsons offered to let me live in their house, to be part of their family. These are people who live their faith, not just on Sundays but all the time. Linnea and I unofficially adopted each other as sisters, but I couldn't love her more if we'd been together all our lives.

"And so, Ellen, if I've been a blessing to them, it's nothing compared to what they've given me."

DISGRUNTLED

$\mathcal{C}$ara returned to school two weeks after the plane crash, trying to fit back into a world that had irrevocably changed. She had never been very comfortable in her own skin, and now people were saying she performed miracles. Adam's friends tried in their own way to relate. Her first day back, as Cara and Adam were walking to class, Brett Stengler approached them. He looked at Cara, uncomfortable, as though he wanted to speak to her. Adam gave him an encouraging smile, then turned to Cara. "I'll see you in c-class in a few minutes."

"Cara?"

"Hi, Brett."

"Listen, I …" He looked at the floor.

"It's okay, Brett. We move on."

"No. I read that once you say words, they take on a life of their own. You can never take them back. All you can do is apologize. I'm sorry for being an ass.

"Cara, that was my little brother they were going to use as a shield. You saved his life." His voice broke. "I owe you." He gently touched her shoulder and walked away.

. . .

LUNCH WAS awkward that first day Cara was back. Adam's usual table sat together as always, but it was as though nobody knew what to say.

"Why is everybody so t-tense?" Adam asked nobody in particular.

Silence. Finally, Marianne said, "I guess … I've never known anyone who faced down men with guns and who saved a bunch of kids and who survived an airplane crash. A lot of us had younger siblings on that bus, or at least we know people who did. It's like … something from an action movie, except that this really happened. I've met Brett's little brother. I know Jessie's kid sister. That little girl, Sarah, who was on TV, who said you were an angel? She lives on my street.

"I guess I'm just sort of intimidated."

Cara looked around at her friends. "I understand. But I wish I could convince you that I'm just … me. Though now with even more scars on my face." She paused to gather her words. "When I first started at this school, I sat by myself at lunch. Nobody talked to me. I felt like I didn't fit anywhere. Then I met Adam and through him, all of you. I had a place to sit, people to talk to. I don't want to lose that.

"Please don't put me on a pedestal, because when you're on a pedestal, you're all alone."

Marianne stood up, walked over to Cara, and hugged her.

TWO WEEKS PASSED since Cara's release from the hospital. The very bad day was past tense. It was history. No longer was there a police car parked in front of the Samuelsons' house, though they patrolled the neighborhood more frequently than in the past. Katie and Stephen returned to their usual work schedules. Adam still drove Linnea to and from school, but she began pushing for permission to return to soccer.

Adam found it interesting to note the different types of books his family of voracious readers devoured. After the bus incident, Linnea brought home books on homemade weaponry, survival, evasion, and escape. She memorized the books, then left them for the rest of the family to read if they liked. Adam could imagine how helpless she and the other kids must have felt on the bus, so he understood her need to empower herself through knowledge.

They had heard nothing from Detective Anders at the police department or from Special Agent Tanaka of the FBI. Is it true that no news is good news?

No, Stephen says the media would argue that *bad* news is good news ... for the media. Nothing sells newspapers like a tragedy. And yet another calamity graced the front page of their local paper. A couple of young boys were playing in a field outside of town, where they discovered the partly decomposed body of a middle-aged woman. She'd been shot once in the forehead. Her name was Elizabeth Henry, an office manager who by all accounts was well liked by everyone who knew her.

The following day, Detective Anders received a call from Agent Tanaka. "We need to talk. Tonight."

Anders pulled up behind a black Mercedes parked on a side street. Tanaka left the Mercedes and walked around to the passenger side of the dark unmarked Crown Victoria. Anders unlocked the door, and Tanaka climbed inside.

"Nice car. Unobtrusive." Anders chuckled.

"You laugh, but I'm investigating the Russian mob. Compared to what some of those guys drive, this is nothing."

"What's on your mind tonight, Agent Tanaka?"

"That girl, Linnea, her suspicion about the bus driver's family was spot on. Richard Henry's wife, Elizabeth, was found yesterday in a field near town. A couple of kids discovered her body. She'd been shot in the head, gangland style."

Anders nodded. "That was in the report. What have you found that explains why Mr. Henry was a target in the first place?"

"Initially, we were operating under the assumption that Mr. Henry was supplementing his income by working as a drug runner. But we examined his bank records, and there is no evidence of unusual profits or exorbitant purchases. He and his wife were living as one would expect of a school bus driver and an office manager."

"So why …"

"We believe it was to provide access to his brother-in-law, Dr. Malcolm Hosta. Dr. Hosta is a respected expert on the psychopharmacology of addiction. He and his lab journals have been missing since the day of the bus hijacking. His wife died four years ago of breast cancer. Never had kids. Lives alone. So presumably they could find no strong leverage against him directly."

"Dr. Hosta doesn't sound like a dangerous man," Anders said.

"No," Tanaka agreed, "not in the sense you mean. But some of his emails to colleagues suggest that he was working on the most addictive drug ever known, such that after a single exposure one would do anything to get more. His idea was to study it, to find ways to block its effects.

"We believe he succeeded. Mr. Henry visited his brother-in-law the day before he was shot in his bus. We believe the package that Mr. Henry hid under his bus contained the formula for this super-drug, and possibly samples as well. It appears Sokolov was holding Mr. Henry's wife, Elizabeth. Following the plane crash and fire, with the loss of everything inside, Elizabeth had no further value to him."

Anders nodded. "I wonder why the gunmen didn't confront Mr. Henry at his home and take the package before killing him. It seems like it would have been easier."

"That was most likely the original plan. We searched Mr. Henry's home after the airport incident. Someone had ransacked his house. At this point, there's no way to be sure of the order of events or what Mr. Henry was thinking when he hid the package under his bus. Perhaps he didn't believe anyone would attack a school bus."

"But why would the gunmen have thought the package would be under the bus, to begin with? It's a strange place to hide something."

"Another good question to which I don't yet know the answer. Could there have been a tracking device on the package? Might his wife have been pressured to suggest what Mr. Henry would be likely to do?

"It looks to us as though the criminals' plan changed at the last minute, as though they were improvising. But now everybody who was involved in the caper, both the perpetrators and the victims, are dead. So all of this is speculation."

"What do you think Sokolov's next move will be?" Anders asked.

"It's difficult to say for sure. Sokolov has a history of being extremely vindictive. What happened that day in the jet was a blow both to his bank account and to his sense of honor. Kozlov was his close friend since childhood as well as his business associate."

"You're saying we've likely not heard the last of him. Wonderful. I'd like to maintain some security around the Samuelsons, but the parents are not terribly cooperative with this. At least we'll watch the two schools and outside their home."

"Good idea. There's another topic on my mind, detective, that I'd like to discuss with you."

"What's that?"

"I sense there is something important that I don't know about that girl, Cara. That family talks around something. You talk around something. Detective, I need to understand. I believe they're in grave danger, and I want to protect them. But I need to know what I'm dealing with."

Anders' face was stone. He said nothing.

"David, I have been on Sokolov's trail for six years. He is my target. I will bring him down. I give you my word I will hold what you tell me in confidence. Forever." He waited.

"Okay, Agent …"

"Vince, at least here in the car." He smiled.

"Okay, Vince. What do you know about Cara?"

"She lives with the Samuelsons. She has no criminal record. Got her driver's license this past fall. She's clean."

"Yes, she is clean," Anders said. "She's a really sweet young lady. Does very well in school. A good person who has had an incredibly hard life. She was homeless for years, a kid living by herself on the street. It's an amazing story. Anyway, she met the Samuelsons this past fall, and they invited her to live with them. Just in time, as it turns out."

"What do you mean?"

"What do you know of the home invasion this past December at the Samuelsons'?"

"Not much. From what I can see, the Samuelsons are okay."

"Two armed men, violent, on drugs, wanted for rape and murder, broke into the Samuelsons' house. Cara and the thirteen-year-old, Linnea, were home alone."

"And?"

"When the police arrived, they found the two men dead from injuries so extreme, the coroner felt they could not have been committed by a human … at least not a single human. The two girls were fine. I arrived at the crime scene about an hour after the 911 call. Cara initially told me she killed the men with her bare hands. Of course, I said that was impossible. She stated she turned into a monster and killed them. I told her monsters aren't real. We left it at that.

"When I attended the autopsies, the coroner reminded me of similar extreme injuries in three young men about three months earlier. The men were frequent low-level offenders, nothing that would interest the FBI. I reviewed street cameras from the night of their murder, and I found … Cara Ferris was in the immediate vicinity at the correct time.

"Last June, a man was found in a park in Boston, partially decapitated. A witness said the man had been about to stab a young lady who was sleeping on a park bench. Please don't be shocked when I tell you he gave an accurate description of Cara.

"Vince, think about these stories when you consider what likely happened inside the jet after it left the airport with Cara."

"Damn," Tanaka said. "And how did Cara put it? That she became disgruntled? That she's not pleasant to be around when she's angry? Damn.

"Do you know how she does … whatever she does?"

"Sorry, I do not. Other than that one time, when Cara and I first spoke, she has not directly admitted to killing anyone. She only makes veiled references similar to 'not pleasant to be around.' And their family attorney is as close to a stone wall as one can get."

"Do the rest of the Samuelsons know what she can do?"

Anders considered the question. "Linnea was there when the two intruders were killed in their home. She told me she didn't remember what happened. But you spoke with her. You know how incredibly perceptive she is. I suspect she saw how the men died.

"Consider this: When her school bus was hijacked, and she had time for one text, who did she choose? Yep, the most bad-ass help she could think of."

KNOW YOUR ENEMY

Danny Gold's stomach churned. He rubbed the back of his neck and swallowed compulsively. The supple gray leather of his white Cadillac Escalade was cool on his skin and did little to reassure him. By rote, he left his office in Chicago, heading north on I-90 to I-94. The thirty-five-minute drive to Highland Park seemed to take hours. Mikhail did not sound happy; he sounded like somebody was about to lose their skin. *Please God*, he thought, *let it not be me*.

Gold pulled up in front of the wrought-iron gates and waited. He studied the intricate scrollwork of the gates while, he was sure, hidden cameras and facial recognition software studied him. He pondered how there were so many paths to the life of a billionaire; some built business empires that were proud monuments to the power of capitalism, that made the lives of many people better … and then there were the few who made their fortune a much different, much darker way. The gates opened. Gold drove along the gently winding drive. Meticulously groomed trees, still devoid of leaves, and manicured gardens surrounded him as he approached the massive estate. By the infinity pool with its central island, he stopped his car and got out at a gesture from the valet. It occurred to Gold that the gentleman was more muscular, and more heavily armed, than was strictly necessary for a valet.

"Follow me, please," the valet said in a deep inflectionless voice.

MIKHAIL ALEXEYEVICH SOKOLOV leaned his muscular, six-foot frame back on his plush leather couch. His blonde hair was cut short, military style, in contrast with his tailored suit and manicured hands. The one thing people most commonly noticed about Sokolov was his eyes—they were cold and pitiless, shark's eyes.

Sunlight streamed in through multiple large picture windows, highlighting the opulence of the room. Teak and marble, crystal and the latest electronics; all of this was his, for his enjoyment. But his heart was heavy, and his mood was black. His prize had been so close, almost within his grasp, then it had been wrested away. But how? From what? What happened to his jet? How did he lose both the drug formula and the life of his closest friend? *Yuri, what did you see in the seconds before you died?*

Danny Gold followed the guard through the massive front doors, across the ornate entryway, and up the curved marble staircase. Down the hall on the left, the guard dropped off Gold at Sokolov's study.

"Sit." Sokolov's voice was high and soft, incongruous to his large, muscular body.

"Yes, sir." He was sweating, though he hadn't exerted himself. Could Sokolov sense his fear?

"My plane."

"Sir, I have no explanation. The jet underwent routine

maintenance no more than a month ago. Both pilots and the other two men have been with our organization for years. Their backgrounds are clear; I ran them again after the incident."

Sokolov scowled at him. "What of that damn teenager who's been all over the news? Why the hell was there a teenager on my plane? The plan was for my men to take a couple of young kids with them for the transfer to the plane."

"I'm sorry, sir, I can't answer that. Unfortunately, your men aren't in a position to answer that either."

"Do I look like I'm in a mood to joke?"

"No, sir. Not at all. You know that the girl, Cara Ferris, survived the crash, yes?"

"It would be hard not to know. You'd think there was nothing else newsworthy anywhere in the world."

"I sent Olga to take care of her, sir, while she was still in the hospital. But Olga was unsuccessful."

"I'm aware of that. Olga has never before failed to complete an assignment. How did she die?"

"We hacked into the hospital medical records. Apparently, there was a struggle in Cara's hospital room. During the struggle, the syringe of concentrated nicotine that was intended for Cara was plunged into Olga's thigh and hit a major vessel. She went into cardiac arrest. They could not resuscitate her."

"So Olga died by accident? Such a waste of talent."

"Sir."

Sokolov glanced at his accountant. "This Cara Ferris. What did you find out about her?"

"She's just a teenage girl. Lives with a family in Indiana along with one of the little girls on the school bus, Linnea Samuelson. Apparently, Cara was homeless before that."

"She sounds pathetic. Why would she survive a plane crash where I lost so much?"

"I can't answer that, sir."

"I need to know what happened on my jet."

"Sir, do you have any ... uh, friends at the NTSB, the National Transportation Safety Board? That plane was large enough that it should have had a flight data recorder and a cockpit voice recorder. We may find answers there. The information is not supposed to be publicly available, but if you know someone ..."

Sokolov thought for a moment. "Yes, I believe I do. I'll send you his file. You will fly to Washington, DC, and take care of this personally. I must have this information. I will not forgive failure."

"Of course, sir." Gold bowed obsequiously and left the room. He felt dizzy, so he paused in the hallway to catch his breath. *Shit*, he thought, *I'm a goddamn accountant.*

BRIAN PETERSON, Deputy Director of the Office of Aviation Safety at the NTSB, had a problem. Well, two problems, really. This plane that crashed in Indiana had attracted a lot of attention. The media were interested, naturally. But the media were easy for him to deal with. All he had to do was say, "No comment until we complete our investigation." Easy. But the FBI had come to visit, and they're not so easily put off. Still, the law is clear that nobody outside of the NTSB is to have access to the flight data recorder and the cockpit voice recorder until the investigation is complete, and even then, there are restrictions.

Peterson's second problem was that he liked to bet on dogs. But he'd had a run of poor luck and accumulated a strong six-figure debt to the wrong people. He had a very disturbing meeting today with a Danny Gold, who had come all the way from Chicago to visit with him. Gold had shown a video of Peterson's daughter, Karen, who was in college in

North Carolina. The video showed her leaving her dorm, walking to class, eating lunch, studying. Nothing scary, yet it was surprisingly intimate.

"Why are you showing me this?" he'd asked.

"Mr. Peterson … Brian, you're not an ignorant man. So don't say ignorant things. My boss wants his money, or he'll take Karen and sell her for the money. She'll be worth six figures to some of his … clients. One way or another, he'll get what you owe him."

"My God, no! Please don't hurt Karen!"

Gold sat quietly and studied him.

"I don't have the money right now." Peterson's voice broke. He sobbed. "I'll do anything you ask. Just tell me what I can do."

"Now you're talking sensibly. Maybe there is something you can give me …"

SOKOLOV LISTENED AGAIN to the audio of the final few minutes of his jet's flight.

His men were laughing, mocking their unwilling passenger. The men's conversation became sexually explicit. Then …

Snarling as from an enraged animal. "What the hell?" Yuri's voice.

Metal bending, then giving way. Then screams. Someone yelled "God no!"

Several gunshots. More screams and sounds of struggle, another gunshot. A sound like a melon breaking apart from being hurled against a concrete wall.

Then silence.

Then, less than a minute later, buckling sounds from the cockpit and a girl's voice talking to herself. "Landing gear, where the heck is the landing gear? Ah, here, okay. Crap, what do I do with all these lights? How do I steer this damned thing? Aim for the airport. Don't wanna hit houses."

A raucous alarm jarred the cockpit.

"The steering thing is shaking. The light says 'stall.' What should I do for a stall? Gotta get the nose up …no, down. I can't get it to do anything. Oh, God, it's falling too fast."

A short time later a mechanical voice exclaimed, "Terrain. Terrain. Pull up. Pull up."

"Damn, this is gonna crash! Pull up, come on, pull up." The girl grunted with the effort.

Then the sickening sounds of a crash. Rending of metal, the roar of the wind. Silence.

What the hell did this girl do? Who or what is she?

ONLY LATER DID SOKOLOV THINK, "How can I control and use her?"

SPECIAL AGENT VINCENT TANAKA pored carefully over the preliminary dump from the flight data recorder in Sokolov's jet. His source at the NTSB had come through for him once again. According to the staff engineers at the FBI who examined the data, there had been no malfunction of any part of the jet. Not the controls, not the engines. Nothing. The preliminary conclusion from people who were qualified to interpret the data was that the jet had been flown inexpertly at the end, that it had stalled at too low of an altitude to recover. But the pilot in command, as well as his copilot, both had many thousands of hours of flight time in this or similar aircraft. This was a rookie mistake.

Only then did Tanaka listen to the audio from the cockpit voice recorder. Holy crap. Detective Anders had not been bullshitting him. This explained why, after the crash, Cara was found in the ruined cockpit; *she* was the jet's pilot for the final few minutes before the crash, and she had never flown an airplane. Everyone else on the plane must have been dead.

He needed damage control. Neither the government nor the media must learn about Cara; that would not end well. She would be exploited or killed, and the family that took her in would be endangered. Tanaka thought—and not for the first time—that with all the spying and hacking going on between the various U.S. Government agencies, there was no need of Russia or China. He shrugged. Ah, well. Time to make this cockpit voice recorder, and all the copies at the NTSB, disappear.

Just one final listen, for one more person, before he ordered the cockpit voice recorder data destroyed. He owed Detective Anders that much.

THERE ARE NO SUPERHEROES

The Sunday after Cara returned to school, the Samuelsons and Cara went to church. They were not consistent in their attendance at services, but that particular Sunday, they felt the need to re-ground themselves.

Adam thought Cara looked especially nice in a new dress she bought with money from her job, though he was unabashedly biased. His other thought, when they arrived at the church, was that the crowd was unusually large for a service other than Christmas or Easter. People came up to them, wanting to touch Cara, to thank her. She pasted a polite smile on her face, but her stomach fluttered, and she fought the urge to flee. She pressed against Adam as if he could provide her some protection from the throngs. Katie leaned over to Cara and whispered something in her ear. Cara laughed nervously. Adam raised an eyebrow in question.

"Your mom said I was probably less intimidated by two men with guns. She has a good point."

"Yeah, this is hard to fight," he agreed.

A young girl and her mom worked their way towards

them, focused on Cara. The girl walked with a wide, awkward gait as though she was always on the cusp of losing her balance. Adam noticed leg braces under her dress. Then he recognized her from TV—the girl who saw an angel.

"Cara?"

Cara turned to the girl and smiled. She leaned down to the younger girl's height. "What's your name?"

"Sarah. Sarah Newsome. This is my mom," she added as though there were some question.

Her mom held out her hand. "Anita. It is such a pleasure to meet you, Cara. I could never thank you enough."

Cara smiled at her. "I'm glad the kids are okay." She stroked Sarah's hair. "You look so adorable in that dress, Sarah." The girl beamed.

Her mom spoke again in an earnest but quiet voice. "I saw your interview on Ellen. It made me think perhaps I ought not to have spoken about … what Sarah saw. I apologize if I caused you any distress."

"It's okay, ma'am. I'm just not comfortable in the spotlight. I wasn't looking for recognition, and I don't know what to say when people call me an angel. In my mind, angels are beautiful and strong and perfect. I'm scarred and ugly and confused, trying to do the best I can in an often strange and imperfect world.

"But I'm pleased that on that day I could do some good."

Their pastor, Tim Holden, approached the Samuelsons with a warm smile. "Stephen. Katie. It's good to see you all."

"Tim, how are you?" Stephen shook his hand.

"The past few months have been rough for you guys, huh? Is your family doing okay?" the pastor asked.

"Things are getting back to normal. The kids are in school. Katie and I are back at work. By the way, thank you for visiting Cara in the hospital."

"That's what I'm here for. Cara, it's great to see you up and around. You had us all scared for a few days."

"Thank you, sir," Cara responded. "It was certainly more excitement than I'd hoped for. I'm glad it ended well."

"As are we all, Cara." Pastor Holden smiled and pressed her hand. "Let me get this party started."

He nodded to the organist who started playing the intro to a familiar hymn. Everybody found seats and began to sing.

AFTER A FEW HYMNS, Pastor Holden stood up to speak. He gazed around the congregation. "Welcome. Welcome, everyone.

"It warms my heart to see the pews so full. I understand why many of you felt the pull to come to church this morning, to pray in fellowship with your neighbors and friends. Three weeks ago, we were shocked out of our routine. We feel mortal … and a little afraid. Mostly we feel thankful. We want to believe that God works in our life, that His hand guides us and protects us. And yet tragedies happen. Innocent people die. And then, sometimes, lives are saved in a manner that defies simple explanation.

"When I was a kid, I collected comic books. You know, I often preferred the Marvel Universe or the DC Universe to our actual world. Those of you who are old enough will remember January 28, 1986. The eyes of a nation were glued to our TVs, watching the launch of the Space Shuttle Challenger. A minute and thirteen seconds into its flight, the shuttle broke apart, killing all seven crew members. Seven lives lost, including Christa McAuliffe, a high school teacher. At the time, through my tears, I remember thinking that in the Marvel Universe, this disaster would have been the origin story of seven new superheroes. But in our universe, this was not the beginning of a grand new adventure; in our universe, we lost seven brave, innocent souls.

"So we can be forgiven if sometimes we think that the magic, the miracles, are gone. God doesn't speak to us from a burning bush, there are no pillars of fire other than from thermonuclear weapons, and God hardly has a chance to smite anyone because we're so busy smiting each other. And yet, all over the world, babies are born, men and women reach out their hand to people in need." He paused. "Then three and a half weeks ago, a school bus full of our children was saved from death by hand grenade. The moment was captured for us in the news media and witnessed by many people present at the scene. There were no superheroes, no old white man in a cloud throwing thunderbolts. No magic. Just a girl who walked in faith, and we watched God work through her.

"Friends, God cannot steer a parked car. Faith is an action verb. 'Wishing in faith' accomplishes nothing. It's a waste of time. Walking and working in faith allows God to act through you. With His help, we're all superheroes. Think about that the next time you see something, and you say to yourself, 'Boy, I wish that situation would resolve itself.' Situations never resolve themselves. We cannot afford to wait for a Superman or a Wonder Woman to appear and save us. We must act, and when the bad is too much for our human power to handle alone, trust that God will be with us.

"Let us pray."

And the congregation prayed, they sang some more hymns, then people headed home.

"Mom," Linnea said in the car, "don't forget Crissa is coming to our house this afternoon for a sleepover."

"I remember. That'll be a great way to start Spring Break."

THE UNUSUAL ROOM

The Samuelsons had barely arrived home from church when the front doorbell rang.

"Hey, Crissa. Hi Mrs. Robinson. Come in. Mom's in the … I mean, uh … she'll be here in a minute." Linnea turned red.

Crissa's mom laughed. "Got it. Listen, is Cara here by chance? I'd like to thank her personally."

"I'll get her, ma'am. Come on, Crissa." They thundered up, and a minute later, Cara descended the stairs with the two younger girls.

"Cara, this is Mrs. Robinson, Crissa's mom."

"How do you do, ma'am?"

"I wanted to thank you, face to face. I … don't know what I would have done if we'd lost Crissa."

"I'm glad I could make a difference," Cara said. "But I wouldn't have been there if Linnea hadn't thought to text me. She's the hero."

"That's my friend," Crissa said.

. . .

THAT NIGHT, the two girls sat on Linnea's bed, talking. Crissa looked around Linnea's bedroom, her face a mix of curiosity and amusement.

"Every time I'm here, it amazes me. I've not seen another girl's bedroom that looks like this."

"Like what? This is my bed. There's my desk. Dresser. Closet over there. It's just a bedroom."

"Computer with the cover off, tools next to it."

"I'm getting ready to upgrade the motherboard."

"You're a kid. You're in middle school."

"It's not that hard. I can show you. Look …"

Crissa waved dismissively. "No, that's not the point. Look at all this electronic stuff. And glassware. And tubes. And chemicals. And … I don't even know what that huge thing is you built in your basement."

"I like science. Physics. Adam and I built that device downstairs. It uses a strong magnetic field in a vacuum to accelerate—"

Crissa threw her arms in the air. "Stop. You're frying my brain."

"What? It's a hobby. Everyone needs a hobby."

"I like theater, but I don't have Neil Patrick Harris hidden in my bedroom closet."

Linnea laughed. "I could imagine you hiding Lin-Manuel Miranda in there. No, no. Hugh Jackman. I can totally see that."

Crissa giggled and turned red. "Maybe … speaking of which, Linnea, what do you think of Jimmy Dougherty?"

"He's okay."

"I heard he likes you. Well, he said he thinks you're pretty, though he wishes you had bigger … uh …"

"And there you have it, Crissa. That's all you can expect from a boy. All they see is your bust. I'm waiting, and I know what I'm waiting for. Someone who will look north of my chest, who will love me for *me*."

"What will he be like?"

Linnea pondered for a minute. "He'll have Adam's intelligence and morality and demeanor. But Adam's in love with Cara, and my ideal guy will be in love with me. And, of course, he won't be my brother."

"How does that work? I mean, since she lives with you guys and their bedrooms are down the hall from each other. Isn't that awkward?"

"Crissa, that's what I'm talking about. They've never … I mean, it's not my business, but they've both told me privately. They've never been in each other's room. They're waiting for … you know … till they're married, which won't be for a while since they're in high school and can't support themselves. I've seen them kiss, though they try to be discreet. But mostly, I see how they look at each other. That's what I want."

"Imagine if Jimmy were my boyfriend. How long do you suppose he would wait?"

Crissa chuckled. "Two weeks maybe?"

"And another thing. It was my brother and Cara who came and saved us. They didn't let a police blockade and snipers stop them." Then quieter, "You talk about Jimmy, who is so cool because he's an outstanding athlete and might like me even though my breasts aren't big enough for him. Do you think he would have risked his life to save me?"

"Of course not. But Jimmy's our age, so that's not really a fair argument. What's a middle school kid supposed to do?"

"Yeah, that's a good point. Anyway, that's why I'm waiting for a real man. But I'm thirteen years old, and I'm not in any hurry."

"You sure put it in perspective for me."

"That's what friends are for."

"No, it's like … you're different from anyone else."

"Different how?"

"Your music. I don't know anyone else who listens to classical music."

"My entire family loves classical."

"And you all eat together almost every night. And you all sit in your living room and read while you listen to that classical music. And … and the way you talk to your parents."

"What? I'm not disrespectful."

"No, no, I mean you give your opinion like you're an adult. And you guys talk about things—important things—at dinner. I've never really paid attention to what's going on in the world. I'm a kid. I thought it didn't matter to me. But you know all about that stuff, and you talk about it. And … like every girl at school wants a boyfriend. But you, you don't want just a boy. You're holding out for a real man. And … I don't know … you're just not like anyone else."

"Crissa, why do I have to be like everyone else? Why can't I just be me? And why can't I wait till I find someone who likes me the way I am, small bust and all?" She smiled. "Why can't I like the music that touches my soul? There's nothing wrong with following the latest boy band or whatever, but it's not me."

"No, I can see that wouldn't be you. I'm glad you're my friend, Linnea. You make my world seem … I don't know … bigger, brighter somehow."

"Thanks. Friends make each other better."

Crissa pursed her lips and wrinkled her forehead. "What do I do for you? I'm just a theater nerd. And, I guess, soccer. I don't have any special skills."

"No? Think back to what happened on the bus. Remember when I texted Cara then I hid my phone?"

"Yeah. I'll never forget that day."

"Your acting skills saved all of our lives."

"I didn't do anything special."

"When the man came around to collect our phones, and he paused at our seat, you acted as though you believed I really had no cellphone. Anybody else, they wouldn't have been able to stop themselves from glancing at the seat pocket. But the man never suspected."

"Huh. I never thought about it that way."

Linnea put her hand on her friend's arm. "Crissa, I know you were terrified. We were all terrified. Things could have gone horribly wrong for all the kids on the bus."

Crissa's eyes grew moist, her voice husky. "Does it come back to you at night?"

"What do you mean?"

"At night … I'm on the bus and I hear the gunshots … and Mr. Henry is dead and … I wake up screaming. Do you know I …" Her voice broke. Her lips quivered as she fought not to cry. "I haven't ridden the bus since then. I just can't."

Linnea hugged her. "As scared as you were, you acted your role perfectly. If you hadn't been strong in that one moment when I needed you, we probably wouldn't be alive to be having this conversation. You're stronger than you think."

"Thank you."

For the first time since that horrible day, Crissa Robinson slept through the night with no bad dreams.

INVASION OF PRIVACY

One night, two weeks after her sleepover with Crissa, Linnea lay awake. Something felt wrong, though she couldn't pinpoint what it was. She listened but heard nothing unusual. She glanced at her phone. 2:17 a.m. Maybe if she read for a while, she'd be able to sleep. She turned on a small reading light and opened her current novel.

A generic off-white van pulled up to the curb of a side street a couple of blocks from the Samuelsons' house. The large man with the high voice turned to his compatriots. "Weapons check. We carry only air guns with darts. We cannot risk accidentally killing either of the girls."

"Check," each man replied.

"Smoke grenades."

"Check."

"Gregori, you have the glass-cutting tools, correct?"

"Yeah, boss. Got 'em."

"Police?"

"Drive by on schedule. Each hour. Due any minute now."

"Alarm system?"

"Doors, windows, glass break. No motion. I was there

yesterday as a technician from their alarm company, to 'check their system.'" He smiled and made air quotes as he said this. "I caused it to report a malfunction. They called for someone to repair it. They took me through the house so I could check all the windows."

"Excellent. Bedrooms?"

"Top of the stairs, teen girl first on the left, younger girl second room on the left."

"Correct. Remember, we take only the little girl. And the most important thing?"

Sigh. "Anesthetize the teenage girl while she's still asleep."

"Yes, why?"

"Because you've said, more than once, that if she wakes up, we're all dead."

"You don't sound like you believe me. How long have we worked together?"

"A long time, Mikhail. Years."

"And would you describe me as a nervous type?"

Quick head shake and a chuckle. "No, not nervous. Don't worry; she won't wake up." A thought occurred to him. "Any special instructions for the parents and the boy?"

"Just pop the two girls and leave with the young one. We don't need complications."

"Got it."

"Okay, the police just drove by. Let's move."

Without making a sound, four men in dark clothes glided into the shadows behind a stand of bushes and low trees. Staying in the cover of vegetation, they made their way to the back of the Samuelsons' house. One man affixed two large suction cups to the sliding glass door by the rear patio. While a colleague held the suction cup handles, the man ran a tool around the perimeter of the window. Together, they lifted out the window and placed it gently on the patio. Silent as shadows, the men entered the house, verified that the ground floor was unoccupied, and crept up the staircase to the second floor.

ADAM AWOKE SUDDENLY, roused by a quiet creak of wood. Was it one of the steps or in the hallway? He opened his eyes in the darkness of his room, sat up in bed and listened. Probably Cara or Linnea going to the bathroom. Recent events had made everyone in the house jumpy.

ENGROSSED IN HER NOVEL, Linnea sensed rather than heard the door open without a sound. She looked up in surprise when she felt a sharp pinprick on her chest. A man, dressed completely in black and holding a gun, stood at her door. Linnea tried to sit up, realized she had no control over her muscles, and collapsed back on her bed, unconscious. Her book tumbled to the floor. The man picked her up as though she weighed nothing, slung her over his shoulder and left the room.

ADAM THOUGHT he heard a sound like something falling, but then it was quiet. *Damn my nerves,* he thought. *Now I'm imagining things. Still, I'd better check it out.* He walked to his door and opened it. The hallway was dark and quiet. Bedroom doors were all closed. The bathroom door was open, the light off.

With care, so he wouldn't scare his sister, he opened Linnea's door. A reading lamp over her bed was on, so he could see her bed was empty. The window was closed and locked. A book was lying on the floor. *Is that what I heard?*

Worried now, he rushed to Cara's room. He paused a moment by the door because he had never gone inside her room since she had come to live with them. *Probably Linnea fell asleep with Cara. They spend a lot of time together. I should go back to bed*, he thought. Then he shook his head and quietly opened the door. In the faint glow of a nightlight, he saw Cara asleep … but no sign of Linnea.

"Cara," he whispered. No response. "Cara?" he said a little louder. Nothing. Adam entered her room and stood beside her bed. She lay on her back. Her face was calm, peaceful. Her chest rose and fell with slow regularity. He reached, intending to gently shake her awake, when he noticed the three small darts protruding from Cara's upper chest and left shoulder. "Cara!" He shook her, with no response. She was unconscious. *Shit.*

Then, from downstairs, Adam heard a faint sound of someone stumbling, followed by a whispered expletive. He rushed out of Cara's room and down the staircase. The living room was empty. He headed toward the kitchen just in time to see several figures exiting his house through the rear patio door.

"Hey!" he shouted. One turned and fired at him. The silenced round whizzed past his ear. Adam ran for the alarm panel and tapped the three-digit emergency code. He felt a sharp pinprick, then another. His world went black, and he collapsed.

Several police cars and two ambulances appeared within minutes of Adam's silent alarm. Again, the entire Samuelson house was a crime scene. Bright lights illuminated their yard, front and back, barricade tape marking the perimeter. Police scoured the surrounding area for several blocks in all directions, but the intruders, and Linnea, were gone.

I'VE GOT NO STRINGS

*A*dam woke up, and he panicked. He was in a small space. He couldn't move his head.

"Shhh," a lady said as she sat next to him. "You're in an ambulance. We put a brace on your neck because you may have fallen. Standard protocol. My name's Marci. EMT. My partner, Ken, is driving. We're only five minutes out from the hospital. Your mom's meeting us there."

"Oh." He tried to relax, with little success. "H-How did I get here?"

"We found you collapsed on the floor in your living room. Someone shot you with darts. Not sure what was on them, but I put you on oxygen and started an IV. Your vital signs have been fine. I spoke with the emergency room doctor. In the ER, the doctors and police will question the heck out of you, so you may want to save your conversation for them."

"K," he tried to nod. It was too hard to think just yet, so he let his mind drift for a while. "Wait, wh-what happened to Cara and Linnea?" He was agitated again.

"Who are they?"

"Cara. Teen g-girl about my age. Linnea, my little sister."

"Ah yes, the teen girl is in the other ambulance. Someone shot her with darts, too. I didn't see a younger girl."

"I need to know Linnea is okay. She's only thirteen years old. C-Can you call someone, please?"

"We're pulling into the ER now. I'm sure the police will be here. They should be able to answer all your questions."

A STOCKY, brown-skinned man in blue scrubs stood by Adam's cot. The small room was surrounded by drapes that had been pulled closed. The man smiled. "Good morning, I'm Dr. Soria. You're Adam Samuelson?"

He nodded. "Yes, sir."

"Would you prefer Adam or Mr. Samuelson?"

"Adam is good."

"How are you feeling now?"

"I feel okay," he said. "Nothing hurts, other than a bit of a headache."

A police officer poked his head through the drapes. "May I join the party?"

Dr. Soria waved him in. "You don't mind if I do a quick exam while you talk, do you? I expect that our conversation would cover the same material, so we can both work together. Are you okay with that, Adam?"

"Sure, that's fine."

"Hello, son. I'm Officer Gladden." They shook hands. Officer Gladden looked to be around Stephen Samuelson's age. He had a round, friendly face, short blond hair cut military style, and pale skin.

"Do you take any medications?" Dr. Soria asked Adam.

"No, sir."

"Any allergies?"

"No."

"Chronic illnesses? Major surgeries?"

"Nothing."

Dr. Soria ran through a quick physical exam and neurological exam. "Everything looks good."

"What do you remember about this past evening?" Officer Gladden asked.

Adam paused, thinking. "I woke up. Thought I heard a noise. Something falling. I d-decided to check it out. The hallway was quiet, and all the bedroom doors were closed. Something … a feeling, I don't know … led me to check on Linnea. She wasn't in her room. I thought maybe she was sleeping in Cara's room because, you know, girls do that sometimes. B-But she wasn't in Cara's room either, and I couldn't wake Cara up. Then I saw Cara had been shot with darts.

"I heard a sound in the kitchen, so I ran downstairs to see what it was. Some people, I assume men, all in black, were leaving through the p-patio door. One of them shot at me. It sounded like an airsoft gun. You know, not loud like a normal gun."

"And then what?" the officer pressed.

"As fast as I could, I hit the silent alarm on our security panel. Then they got me with those darts. That's all I remember."

"Why didn't you wake your dad? Do you know he was still asleep when the police arrived?"

"Gosh, not a g-good way to wake up. I'll have to apologize when I see him."

"I think he's more worried than angry at you, but I got the impression that he feels kind of silly that he slept through all the excitement."

"I'm sorry. I didn't have much time to consider my options. Officer, was anyone hurt besides Cara and me? Where was Linnea?"

"Then you don't know."

"I d-don't know what, officer? What happened to my family?"

"Cara's in a room nearby, and she's awake. A female officer is talking with her. Your mom is here, filling out paperwork."

"And Linnea?"

"Son, they took your sister. I'm sorry." Officer Gladden laid his hand on Adam's shoulder to comfort him, but he jerked away and sat up on his cot.

"They k-kidnapped Linnea?"

Officer Gladden nodded, his expression somber. "The police and the FBI are working on her case now. We'll find her."

"She's only thirteen years old!" he shouted at nobody in particular. His voice was hoarse.

"Yes, son, I'm aware of that. My daughter's in her class." He paused. "This is personal. We will find her."

"Doctor, I need to leave."

"Adam, we don't know yet what was in the darts. For all we know, you'll collapse again in a while. If you're driving, you could kill yourself or someone else."

"Did you give me any medication to counteract the d-drug that knocked me out?"

"No."

"So we're not worried that a medication you gave me to reverse whatever was in the darts will wear off, leaving me unconscious again, b-because you didn't give me any medication. Why would you think I'd collapse again, doctor?"

"I don't know what they put on the darts. The tox screen is pending. I'm trying to be conservative. I'd like to watch you and Cara for a few hours. Make sure you're okay. Your parents have enough to worry about right now, from what I understand."

"I'll wait with Cara. Where is she?"

"I'll take you to her. She's been asking about you as well. Give me a moment to get you a wheelchair."

"I can walk."

"You were brought in by ambulance. Humor me, please."

THE DOCTOR CHECKED that Cara was dressed, then opened the drapes and let Adam in. He left the drapes open. Then he turned and was called to see another patient.

Just then Katie joined them. "Damn paperwork. How are you two feeling?" She hugged them both. "I'm glad I'm allowed to come in your room, now that the doctor and police are done with you. As a nurse, I understand the rules, but as a mom, I hate them."

"We're g-good. Is there any word on Linnea?"

"Nobody's contacted us yet with demands. I'm sure the FBI has hooks to our home phone and our various cellphones."

Katie's gaze was clear and direct. She did not appear to have wasted time crying; she looked ready to do whatever was necessary to protect her children.

"D-Did she leave anything in her room? Any clues? Does she have her phone?"

"Apparently she was in bed reading a book. The reading light was still on, and the book was lying on the floor as though it had fallen. Her cellphone was still plugged into the charger by her bed. Other than the fallen book, there were no signs of a struggle. They probably used those damn darts on her."

"Crap!"

"There's something I'm wondering about," Cara said. Katie and Adam looked at her. "I guess I understand why they shot you, Adam. You interrupted them as they were leaving with Linnea. But notice they got me while I was asleep but did not try to neutralize your parents. It makes me think that their intention when they broke into the house … whoever they are … was to kidnap Linnea and to ensure that I was not awake to stop them. They had no intention, going in, to shoot you or your folks. I believe that they specifically wanted me incapacitated while they took Linnea. It's as if they knew me, knew what I could do. This smells of that Sokolov guy who I inadvertently pissed off with that whole school bus and airplane thing."

"This d-doesn't make sense. If they wanted to stop you, they could have shot you in your sleep with something that would kill you."

"So they apparently want me alive. They may know what I can do. And they probably heard me say on national television that I would do anything to protect my little sister. I wonder if they intend to control me, to use me, through Linnea."

"I c-can't envision anyone controlling you," Adam said.

"They miscalculated. I am nobody's puppet."

RED CHIEF

*L*innea awoke. She lay still and inventoried. It felt and sounded like she was in a vehicle, probably in the back of a van. She cautiously moved her arms and legs. Good, she was not tied. She patted herself down to see what was available to work with. Not good, still wearing her pajamas, barefoot, and no cellphone.

What did she remember? She thought about it for a while. She remembered not being able to sleep, remembered reading her novel … then a man was standing in her doorway. He shot her with something sharp, like a dart. Then she couldn't move. She remembered falling, then … nothing until now.

How long had it been? Where would the man be taking her? What would happen to her?

Linnea started to panic but then recalled reading about situations like this. She needed to stay calm and think. An opportunity would appear; they always do, she'd read. What was in her favor? First, they didn't know her. They would see a thirteen-year-old girl and assume she was helpless. But she was not weak and stupid, more like strong, and smart.

Second, she'd been reading a lot about survival, escape, homemade weapons, that sort of thing. They wouldn't know that she remembered everything she read. Third? Well, they wouldn't know that she knew how to use guns. If she got her hands on one, things could get interesting.

Was the dart still in her chest? She checked but couldn't feel anything. Too bad, it might have been useful.

The enclosure she was in was pitch black. No windows. She carefully felt her way around. There was a mat covering most of the floor area; the edges were metal. The walls were metal and smooth. There was what felt like a door in the back, but it appeared to be locked from the outside.

Now, what happened at home? Was anyone else hurt? If Cara was still alive, somebody would pay for this, for sure.

Who would have a reason, and resources, to break into her house and kidnap her? That was a short list: Mikhail Sokolov. Cara had killed his lieutenant, destroyed the super-drug Sokolov had stolen, and crashed his plane. But what would he gain by kidnapping Linnea? She pondered that question for a time, as the van continued on the highway. Her folks didn't have enough money to interest a billionaire. Perhaps Sokolov planned to use her to try to control Cara. Yes, that could be it. Somehow, he must have learned what Cara can do, and he'd decided he'd rather own her than kill her.

With this reasoning, where would the van be headed? Sokolov would only feel comfortable if Linnea were physically in his control. Agent Tanaka had said that Sokolov lived in or near Chicago. So it would not be a long ride. Once she arrived at his lair, she'd need to figure out how to direct Cara there. She clenched her lips in a grim smile. He thought he'd control Cara, huh?

<<<<>>>>

KATIE SIGNED THE REQUISITE PAPERS, the three thanked the caregivers and headed home. In the car, Cara and Adam got up to speed on the investigation.

"So the FBI is still there?"

"Yes, there have been agents in and around the house for several hours. They've photographed and fingerprinted everything. Took samples of her DNA from her hairbrush. We gave them copies of her medical and dental records, such as we have at home, school pictures and some more recent photos from my phone. They already have her fingerprints, of course, since the home invasion. Linnea's cellphone was charging by her bed, but it's locked, so it's not much help to us."

"Any leads yet?" Cara asked.

"They brought in dogs. Let them smell some of Linnea's dirty clothes. The trail led out the sliding glass door at the back porch, across the lawn, through bushes to a street a block and a half away. Apparently, the dogs lost her scent there. The men must have had a vehicle waiting."

WHEN THEY ARRIVED BACK at the house, they found Stephen seated in the living room smoking a pipe. Adam knew he only smoked his pipe when he was under great stress.

"Dad, I apologize for not waking you up. It's just that Cara had been shot with those d-darts, and she wouldn't wake up. Then I heard a noise in the kitchen, so I ran downstairs. The men were on their way out the back. I yelled, then I hit the alarm. Then they shot me with those damn darts, and I don't remember anything else till the ambulance."

Stephen spoke to his pipe. "I was asleep in bed when the police came. I had no idea … felt stupid."

"I can imagine. I'm s-sorry."

Stephen nodded curtly but didn't speak further. Adam waited a minute, then touched his dad's shoulder and left.

Cara and Adam walked outside around the neighborhood, where they could talk freely, while a repair person worked on their sliding glass door.

"Adam, you know that Linnea and I are very close," Cara began.

"You're a wonderful role model for her."

"Where I'm going with this is that I feel I have some insight into how Linnea thinks and what she might do. We all know Linnea is unusually intelligent."

"Yes."

"She has a photographic memory. Since the bus incident, Linnea has read a stack of books about survival, hostage situations, evasion, escape, homemade tools, and weaponry. Adam, I believe she has full use of that knowledge, as though she had the books right with her at all times."

"I can see that."

"She's very comfortable with computers, including networking and controls. And your folks taught her about firearms."

"This is all true."

"I'm just saying that Linnea thinks way outside of the box, and she has tools at her disposal that nobody would expect of a thirteen-year-old. She is a brilliant and determined girl. She would be a very dangerous hostage."

"Do you think we should call Sokolov to warn him?"

"It's not funny."

"Yeah, I'm nervous so I s-said something stupid."

Cara stopped walking and put her arms around him.

"You're far from stupid. Most of the computer stuff she learned from you.

"I'm not even completely sure Sokolov is behind her abduction."

"Occam's razor," Adam said.

"Yes, I know, the simplest explanation is most likely the truth. If Sokolov didn't do this, then we would have to postulate yet another, unrelated, bad person who wished to harm our family. But whoever took her, they may be in for a surprise."

"What do you mean?"

"Have you ever read stories by O. Henry?"

"Sure. They're sort of quirky, often with surprise p-plot twists."

"Are you familiar with 'The Ransom of Red Chief'?"

"Yeah, I remember that one. A couple of men kidnap for ransom a wealthy man's little boy. But he's such a rotten kid, he drives the men crazy. They end up having to p-pay the dad to take him back."

"Exactly. That was a comic story, while obviously there is nothing at all humorous about our current situation. Consider this, though: They think they've kidnapped a typical cute little girl. I don't mean to imply that she's not in grave danger, but I believe they'll soon wish they'd never met this particular girl."

"You think so?"

Cara nodded.

"Damn." Adam found himself at a bit of a loss for words. "How do you think we should help her?"

"I don't know. For now, all we can do is wait until we get more information.

"Adam, there's something specific we need to discuss. If we assume Sokolov is behind this, it may be that he's learned what I can do. He may plan to use Linnea to try to control me. You know, Cara needs to do X, or something bad happens to Linnea. Knowing Sokolov, the demand will be grossly illegal, possibly involving murder. I do not know how your parents, or law enforcement, will react. If Sokolov can divide us, if he can make us mistrust each other, then he has a tremendous advantage. I'll be most effective if I can stay free to act, but law enforcement may try to restrain me."

"What will you do, Cara?"

Cara looked directly into his eyes. He felt as though she could see his soul. He knew he would believe whatever she said. "I will disappear. Go underground. I've done it before. I swear to you I will kill Sokolov—quickly if Linnea is okay, slowly and painfully if she's hurt. I will destroy his organization. To do that, I will send to hell as many of his thugs as necessary. Sokolov is a dead man. He just doesn't know it yet."

"I'll g-go with you," Adam blurted, without thinking.

She smiled a grim, quiet smile as she gazed at his face. "Adam, I'm going to a place where you can't follow. I will always love you. I will never forget the kindness of your parents. I'd never had a sister until I met Linnea, and there's a place in my heart that will always be hers.

"I told you months ago that I wouldn't have been able to bear it if I had killed you, Adam. I can't put you in harm's way, either from me or from those bastards who took our little sister."

"I'm a big boy now, Cara. I can choose my own path."

"I don't think you understand what's inside me. I'm only now beginning to see. There is something merciless in me. It kills, and it enjoys killing. Even now, the thought of harvesting so many souls is pleasing in a very strange way. Adam, I'm told the thing in me looks beautiful, like an angel, but it doesn't use weapons. It speaks some strange, inhuman tongue, it growls and snarls like a beast. I don't want to say the word, but I don't think I'm an angel. I don't want you to see how ugly I truly am."

"What about our talk of b-building a life together? Getting married after college? Having a family someday? You have scars, Cara, but they never bothered me … I mean, apart from hating how you got them. From the beginning, I've been attracted to what's inside you. You're b-beautiful to me, intelligent, strong and kind. You're my missing half, Cara. My friend, my partner, and someday, God willing, my lover.

"But Cara, you are not invincible. You n-need someone to have your back. I'm not saying this lightly: I will stay with you, whether through hell or through an eternity of nothing. I'm hoping, though, we can still look forward to a long and satisfying life together. Besides," Adam smiled and kissed her forehead, "better the devil you know …"

She kissed him, hard.

Just then his iPhone buzzed. Adam glanced at the screen. "Mom wants us. Maybe there's new information. Cara, if things go badly at home and you need to leave, we need an FBI-resistant way to c-communicate. This is what I have in mind." They discussed the details as they walked through their neighborhood back to the house.

Inside, they immediately noticed that the atmosphere had changed, had become thick with tension. Adam's mom was unusually quiet and serious.

"Ms. Katie?" Cara said to her. "What happened?"

Katie turned to Cara, regarding her silently, her face grim. "Did you get a message recently, Cara?"

"An email? I haven't checked since we got home from the hospital. Why?"

"Sit. Both of you. I've called Special Agent Tanaka. He'll be here shortly."

That turned out to be an understatement. Several dark

sedans pulled up in front of their house. Numerous agents spilled out, spreading from the vehicles. Adam turned to look behind his house and saw that armed agents also surrounded it in the back. Someone knocked on their front door. Without a word, Stephen opened it. Tanaka stepped across the threshold.

"Dr. and Mrs. Samuelson," he nodded in quick greeting, his tone grave.

"Please come in," Stephen told him. "Let's sit and talk."

Katie, Stephen, and Agent Tanaka joined Cara and Adam in the living room. Everyone sat. The silence was awkward.

Cara started. "Agent Tanaka, what is going on? Adam and I came home from taking a walk, and it's like everything changed. Please tell us what's happening."

Tanaka gazed at her, his face imperturbable. "You don't know?"

Cara shook her head. "No, sir."

"Did you receive an email in the past hour?" Tanaka asked.

"Ms. Katie asked me the same thing. I check email a few times a day, but I don't allow email notifications because my phone would buzz all day with spam."

"Interesting. Take a look now."

Cara held her cellphone so that Adam could see as well. There was a new message from a sender named papa.bear@gmail.com with a subject line that said simply "Linnea." There was no body to the email, just an attachment with the title "help me." Cara tapped on the attachment, opening a little viewer.

Linnea sat on a plain wooden chair. Her hands appeared to be fastened behind the back of the chair. The room was dark except for a light shining on the girl. Her hair was messed. Her left cheek was red, as though someone had slapped her. She was still wearing her pajamas from when she was abducted. She looked directly at the videographer and spoke as though she were reading. Linnea was serious yet calm. Her eyes were clear with no evidence of crying. Her mother's daughter, Adam thought.

"Cara, you must kill FBI Special Agent Vincent Tanaka. You have twenty-four hours, or they will kill me. It is Tanaka or me. You choose." The video went dark.

CARA REPLAYED THE VIDEO, then put away her phone. She stared at her lap for a minute to get control. Adam could see emotions playing across her face, only because he knew that face so well. When she looked back up at them, her gray eyes had turned hard like stone. Her voice was firm.

"Very well. I have chosen."

CHOICE

Cara stared directly at Agent Tanaka, as though there were nobody else in the room.

"Sir, I will start with the bottom line, so you know where I'm headed. Then I will explain my reasoning. At that point, you only need to decide whether you will help me or whether I'm on my own.

"Bottom line, I do not have only two choices. I am going to kill Mikhail Sokolov and save Linnea. If Sokolov hurts Linnea, he will die slowly and painfully; nonetheless, he will be dead before tomorrow.

"Sokolov is clever. He knows that if he can divide us, if he can sow mistrust, he'll have a powerful advantage. I can't imagine why he thought I'd attack a federal agent simply because he told me to do so. On the contrary, I need you to help me pinpoint Sokolov's lair."

Tanaka answered with a faint smile. "First, Cara, you're not in a bargaining position. Twenty armed agents are surrounding the house. Second, what do you expect me to do about your assertion that you're going to kill someone, considering that I'm a law enforcement officer?"

"Agent Tanaka, if you and I were actually at odds which, as I've said, we are not … the teams of armed agents would not be a challenge. The, uh, thing inside of me is too fast, too strong and is not bothered by bullets. Regarding my mindset, you saw that I protected Linnea during the home invasion. You saw that I saved a busload of children when given the opportunity. Finally, you know that I changed back when I was in the jet, even though I believed I would probably die, so I could try to land the plane without killing innocent people. I could easily have stayed as that creature, let the plane crash where it may, and walked away unscathed. If you haven't yet figured out that I'm one of the good guys, I don't know what further I could do to convince you.

"You and your teams of armed agents that you're so proud of are welcome to go kill Sokolov yourselves, if you think you can accomplish that without Linnea paying a terrible price. Agent, you have an idea of what I can do. Together, we can save a little girl and stop a madman. We don't have to work together officially, on paper. You're welcome to take all the credit when it's over. I just want my sister back."

Katie jumped to her feet. "Damn all of you! While you two are dancing around, there's a terrified little girl who thinks she's going to die."

At this, Cara rose from beside Adam and walked over to his parents. She stood in front of Katie and took one of her hands in her own. "Ms. Katie, Linnea was talking to us in that video. She was telling us, by her affect, that she is in full control of her amazing brain, and that she expects to live. I understand the reality of the danger she's in, and I swear to you I will bring her back. Sokolov will rue the day he took her."

Cara turned again to Agent Tanaka. "You must know where Sokolov lives. My best guess is that Linnea is there.

You go ahead and do whatever FBI special agents do, but think about what we discussed. This is much more likely to end well for Linnea if we share information and do not, whether inadvertently or on purpose, hinder each other. I'm going to disappear now. If you decide to help me, leave useful information here with my family."

Cara walked out of the room toward the kitchen, not looking back. They heard her footsteps … and then they didn't. Adam crossed the room to his parents and took Cara's place by Katie. "She's gone," he said. "I c-can't imagine why you guys thought Cara was dangerous. She loves you. Even now, she called you family."

Katie's eyes were wet with tears. "I'm sorry. I'm not thinking well. When I saw the video, I … I guess I thought only of the two choices, and I panicked. I should never have mistrusted Cara. She's never given us a reason. Adam, please tell her I'm sorry."

"I will, Mom." He squeezed her hand, then stood up and kissed her cheek.

Agent Tanaka rose and walked in the direction Cara had gone. After a minute, they heard several agents enter the house from the rear. They did a quick search. Tanaka returned to the Samuelsons. "She's gone. How the hell …?"

Adam looked at him. "She's on our side," he said. "Time is running out for my little sister. You need to work with Cara. If she were going to kill you, you would already be dead. The person who should worry is Sokolov."

"Dr. and Mrs. Samuelson, I've said it before, but it bears repeating. You have a very unusual family. Stay by your phones, please." With that, Tanaka and his associates left the house and drove off.

"Adam, what will she do now?" Stephen asked.

"Cara's had years of experience staying under the radar. She can live anywhere. She doesn't need infrastructure as we do. I p-presume she'll head to Chicago. She'll get information from the street, searching for Sokolov. Someone like him cannot be invisible."

"I didn't realize she could … uh … change at will."

"She hates it. She hates her angel or whatever it is, but she seems to be getting better at controlling it. For the longest time, she would only change to save her life. Her mind would go blank, and when she came back to her body, everyone around her would be dead. But during the home invasion, her mind did not go blank, and she could prevent her angel from killing Linnea. She told me that in the jet, for the first time, she realized she could stay in that form for a while. I'm not sure exactly how long. B-But a few minutes ago, you heard her explain to us why she changed back anyway, even knowing that it would probably cost her her life.

"This is what I worry about, Dad. When she's a girl, she can be injured or k-killed. Someone needs to have her back. It obviously won't be the FBI. She needs me."

"Son, I see where you're going with this. You're not a fighter. Please, Mom and I can't lose you and Linnea both."

"Dad, I intend for all of us to come back home. Deep down you understand how it is with Cara and me because you know how it is with Mom and you. When I met Cara, I wasn't looking for a g-girlfriend or a soul mate. Over time, as I came to know her, I realized that she fit with me in a way that nobody else ever could, that she is The One. I trust Cara implicitly, I love her with all my heart and, come what may, I will always have her back. I believe that together, Cara and I can overcome anything.

"You s-say I'm not a fighter. Maybe I never before had anyone worth fighting for."

"I understand how you feel, son, but I can't let you do this. These aren't schoolyard bullies pushing Cara around. These are criminals, killers, with real guns. This is what the FBI is for. Just let them do their job."

"They've impressed the hell out of us so far, haven't they, Dad?"

"That's not fair. They …"

Adam was too angry to watch his words. "Fair? Those b-bastards kidnapped a thirteen-year-old girl and you talk about fair? Fair is where you buy candy apples. This is real life. In real life, a teenage girl is ridiculed because of a scar on her face. Hell, in real life a little girl is raped and cut. In real life, my little sister is taken.

"Dad, Mom, there is a twenty-four-hour timer that is c-counting down. Linnea needs us. And frankly, you didn't raise me to sit here at home and hope for the best."

Without another word, Adam turned away and climbed the stairs to his room. He packed a small day bag and brought it down.

"I'm sorry. I wish I didn't have to leave on an unpleasant note. I love you both."

He gave his mom and dad a quick embrace and left the house. Katie was stone-faced as he walked to his car.

SMOKE SIGNALS

After Sokolov forced Linnea to make the video, he laughed at her. "You know, little girl, it doesn't really matter what your monster friend does. I will send you back in pieces. You won't leave this room alive."

He turned and exited. She heard the door lock. She was alone.

Linnea looked around her, to the extent that she could with her hands tied behind the back of the chair. The room had no windows and not much furniture. There was an awful smell, like stale urine. She noticed a small table with some supplies on and under it, and another chair besides the one she was currently using. Light was a single low-wattage bare bulb, though now that her eyes were accustomed to the low light, she could see fairly well. Other than the light bulb, the only other feature of the ceiling was a large air vent.

The first thing to do is to free my hands.

She stood up and was relieved to find that her hands rose with her; her hands were not bound to the chair. When her wrists cleared the back of the chair, she could move to the floor.

What did the book say to do? Reposition hands?

Linnea pulled her wrists apart as hard as she could and then, bending at the waist, she lowered her hands past her butt. She then pulled her knees against her chest, dropped her hands behind her knees, then stepped through her wrists one leg at a time. Now she could examine her restraints more closely. They'd used a heavy-duty black zip tie.

Zip ties can be defeated with a bobby pin. But I don't see one lying around here. What else? Zip ties can be broken by quickly and violently pulling my elbows back to the sides of my chest.

She attempted the maneuver with no success. The second try hurt so badly she felt like crying. She explored the room with her hands still together. *It's good they didn't bind my feet, too.*

She tried the door which was locked as she suspected. The source of the disgusting odor became apparent. A bucket in the far back corner of the room was partly full of stale pee. So she was not the first "guest" to stay here. How long had that urine been sitting there?

Linnea walked over to the table and examined the contents. There was an assortment of medical supplies, including scalpels, clamps, gauze pads, bottles of iodine crystals, hydrogen peroxide, alcohol, and chloroform. *Scalpel. Excellent.* Holding a scalpel with her hands, she directed the blade against the zip tie on her wrists and cut the plastic without injuring herself. She saw that there was also a jug of ammonia, as would be used for cleaning, a pile of rags, a flashlight, and a row of glass bottles on a small storage shelf near the table filled with a clear liquid. She stooped to read a label. *Sulfuric acid.* A large utility sink with a porcelain interior occupied one corner of the room. She was pretty sure these medical supplies were not being used for medical purposes, but something far more nefarious. *Sokolov told me I wouldn't leave this room alive, and I have no reason to doubt him.*

Agent Tanaka said that Sokolov had killed women and children. I need to find a way out of here. I need to call for help. And I need to hurt whoever tries to stop me.

Linnea pulled the table beneath the ceiling air vent, placed the chair on the table, then carefully climbed onto the chair. The vent had a catch which, when unfastened, allowed the grate to swing down on a hinge. She pulled herself up and looked around. *Yes, this vent is large enough for me to crawl through it. Probably couldn't fit an adult, though.*

Back to the door, she now noticed that the door handle itself was like that of any typical bedroom or bathroom door. She pressed the little catch on the stem of the doorknob inward, pulled, and verified that she could expose the mechanism of the knob. Above the doorknob, she saw the flat backplate of a lock that was accessible only from the outside. *A deadbolt?* She could turn the knob, but the door remained firmly closed.

What can I use to booby-trap the door? Ah, iodine crystals, ammonia. I can work with that. I've read that nitrogen tri-iodide has no practical applications because it's too unstable. They say it's not reasonable to make enough for a bomb because most likely it would explode before it was meant to. But I don't have a lot of options.

Linnea pulled on a pair of rubber gloves, huge on her small hands. She poured the iodine crystals on the table, then used the bottle to crush them to powder. She then transferred the powder to a large glass jar and added the ammonium hydroxide most of the way up the jar and gently stirred the orange-purple mixture. She filtered it through a rag, washed it with alcohol, and then, while the purple paste was still wet, she put as much as she could into the doorknob, then gently closed it back up. *God, please don't let it explode while I'm near it.* She soaked the rag in the bucket of urine, so the fabric would stay wet and not accidentally explode.

While she was at it, she figured she might as well do something with the light bulb. She turned off the light. Working by flashlight, she unscrewed the single light bulb and let it cool. When it was no longer at all warm, she made a little hole near the base of the bulb using a scalpel, poured in some chloroform, then sealed the hole with a tiny piece of duct tape. Finally, she screwed the bulb back into the socket.

I'm pushing my luck. It's time to leave this room.

She grabbed the flashlight, a new scalpel with a blade guard, a medical clamp, and a bottle of sulfuric acid, then pulled herself up into the vent. She pulled the grate closed and manipulated the catch with the medical clamp from inside the vent. Carefully, she placed the bottle of sulfuric acid on the inside of the closed grate, so it would fall if the grate were unlatched. Even with the flashlight, the vent was dark and claustrophobic. Slowly and carefully, she crawled along inside the vent, the flashlight in one hand, aware that any sounds she made might be audible in a room.

Suddenly a support gave way from the unaccustomed weight inside the vent. The section Linnea was in lurched downward so that her head was a little lower than her feet. Surprised, she spread her hands to stabilize herself. As she did so, she dropped the flashlight. It rolled forward … and disappeared. She heard it tumble a long way down and to one side. The vent was now pitch black. She could not see her hand in front of her face. The walls of the vent seemed to close in on her. Terror rose in her heart. She reached her hands forward. Ahead of her, the vent went straight down.

If I back up, I'll die. If I fall headfirst down the vent, I'll die.

Panic overcame her. Her heart was racing. It was hard to breathe. No, this could not be the end. She forced herself to slow her breathing. Her life depended on her being able to think clearly. Okay, now, how wide was the downward vent? She reached as far as she could. Nothing. She scooted further forward, wedging her legs in the vent behind her. Still just empty space. There was not enough room to turn around, to reach with her legs. She scooted herself yet further into the opening, operating only by touch, her thigh muscles trembling with the effort.

There. With her fingertips, she could feel a ledge. She continued slowly forward, now bridging the downward vent with her forearms and shins. So far as she could tell, the vent continued forward as well as downward. Her best hope, she judged, was to keep moving. She wriggled forward until much of her torso was on the far side, holding herself in place now with her arms and toes. She turned on her back and wriggled further. When she was all the way across, she rested until her breathing evened out. Then she continued, in the dark, for another ten minutes by her estimation.

In the distance, she could see a faint light reflected into the vent from inside a room. She carefully approached until she could see through the grate. Below her, Sokolov sat at his desk, working on his computer. Seeing him so close almost froze her with fear. She closed her eyes and focused on her breathing until she was calm again.

Please, get up and leave your office.

A loud bang sounded behind her. She could feel the shock wave in the vent. "My goddamn hand!" a man yelled. "Son of a bitch!" Then she heard the door of the room she'd been in open. Someone must have switched on the light because there was another explosion followed by loud screams of pain.

Sokolov stood up from his desk and strode from his office. Quickly but quietly, Linnea opened the ventilation grate and dropped to the floor. Her first move was to lock the door and look around. The office was enormous and filled with plants. Large windows revealed a garden outside, but even inside the office, there were exotic flowers and small trees. *A sadistic criminal who loves flowers? Go figure.* There was an attached full bathroom with shower. A small closet held a couple of suits, still in their dry cleaning bags. Beneath the bathroom sink, she saw assorted janitorial supplies, though she very much doubted that Sokolov himself used them. There was a glass door on the other side of the bathroom. She could see that it opened into an indoor pool.

She returned to the desk. *Oh my gosh, his computer is still on and open.*

Linnea sat, opened a browser and typed rapidly. *I don't have time to look at everything right now. What can I find that looks important, that I can dump to the FBI? And give Cara a heads-up.*

Sending a sizeable amount of information over the internet would take time. She needed to secure her position, both in the real world and on the network. Fingers now flying over the keyboard, she isolated Sokolov's computer from the network so that nobody else in this building could interrupt her.

Next, she turned her attention to the room itself. She grabbed a roll of duct tape and taped all around the perimeter of the locked door, except for the opening between the door and the floor. She removed the clear plastic dry cleaning bag from one suit and used the duct tape to seal the bottom of the bag to the opening beneath the door. She checked carefully to ensure that the seal was as airtight as possible.

From under the sink, she brought a bucket, a gallon of chlorine bleach and a jug of drain cleaner. She placed the three items inside the dry cleaning bag, then sealed the top.

There, now we'll see what happens when they try breaking down the door. What else can I use?

Linnea rifled through the remaining bottles under the

sink. She noticed various jugs of pool chemicals. One caught her eye, a plastic bottle labeled Pot Perm. Hmm. She looked in the medicine cabinet. Yes, among other skin products, a bottle of glycerin. *Better living through chemistry, ha!*

She arranged, on the front of the desk, the bottle of potassium permanganate, the bottle of glycerin, and an ashtray. While the computer continued its upload, she searched the desk in more detail. Under the desk, Sokolov had taped a small revolver. She checked. Only one bullet. She placed it beside her on the desk. Now nothing to do but wait.

LELIA FORTUNE

After saying goodbye to his parents, Adam drove to the parking lot of a local mall. The lot was packed with cars, which served his purpose well. Nobody would notice him.

He parked and quickly searched the exterior of his car. Under the left rear bumper, he found what he'd suspected: a small gray disk with a magnetic attachment. He popped it off his bumper and placed it under someone else's. Obviously, that wouldn't fool the FBI for long, but it would at least give him some breathing room.

Back in his car, he took a deep breath. *God, I hate making phone calls.* There was no other way, though. He dialed a number. There was a certain person, he felt, who was gradually beginning to accept his unusual girlfriend. He could be a valuable asset. A gruff voice answered the call. "Anders."

"D-D-Detective Anders? This is …"

"I figured you would call. Are you familiar with Grant Park?"

"I am."

"Meet me there in twenty minutes. I'll be seated near the play area."

ADAM PULLED into a spot near the play area and saw immediately that this was an excellent location for his purpose. From this spot, he would have an unobstructed view of his car. Many children ran around from the slides to the swings to the monkey bars. Parents and other caregivers observed them. Nobody paid attention to the ordinary man in the rumpled suit seated on one bench and not even looking at the children. Adam caught his eye, walked over, and sat next to him.

"Thank you for meeting me," Adam said.

"You understand the FBI has the lead in this case. The kidnapping of a child is their purview."

"I know," Adam sighed. "There is a p-possibility that you will be no more willing to help Cara than Tanaka is. But you've been investigating Cara for a long time. By now you should know what she can do, but equally important is that you should understand her heart."

"Adam, Agent Tanaka is neither uncaring nor stupid. I've never met an FBI agent who didn't have a deep understanding of people, of human nature. You would have no way of knowing this already, but that business jet that crashed was fitted with a cockpit voice recorder and a flight data recorder. Tanaka knows what happened on the plane."

Adam looked at him curiously. Anders continued. "This is obviously between us, but he let me listen before he destroyed all copies of the audio."

"Why would he d-destroy the audio?"

"He feels strongly that the government should not learn about Cara. Nor should the media, or foreign interests."

"Oh. Wow." He could be so articulate.

"Are you aware that I've seen the kidnap video as well?"

"No," Adam said, surprised. "Did Sokolov send the video to everybody? He clearly wanted to create a commotion on our end, and he seems to have been successful."

Anders smiled. "Tanaka is still alive. I cannot envision Cara killing him. She's such a sweet girl. I have a hard time imagining her killing anyone. But certainly not law enforcement."

"What do you recommend I do next?"

"Officially? Go home."

Adam rose off the bench, ready to head back to his car. Anders reached up and pulled on his arm. He sat back down.

"I was saying, I cannot help you officially, but there may be someone who can." He reached deep into his pocket and withdrew a gold medallion two inches in diameter. "Years ago, I did a friend a favor. She gave me this. If you and Cara can find her, she'll help you."

Anders handed him the medallion. Adam turned it over in his hand, examining it. It was surprisingly heavy for its size. The engraving was worn, but he could make out on one side a fist surrounded by the words *Numquam Obliviscaris*, while the other side of the medallion showed a rough representation of a female face and the words *Verbum Meum Est Votum Meum.*

"Is this real g-gold?"

Anders nodded.

"It must be worth a fortune."

"Adam, this is much more valuable than a fortune. This is worth a Fortune." He pronounced the word oddly, emphasizing the last syllable and rhyming it with "cartoon" or "in tune."

"What does that mean?"

"Lelia Fortune. If anyone can help you, it would be her."

"How do I find this lady?"

"She's easy to find when you need her. You're headed up to Chicago, anyway. Look her up. Give her this medallion. She will help you."

Adam looked at the medallion again. "I t-took a couple of years of Latin. My guess is that this side, with the fist, says 'Never Forget,' and the side with the face says 'My Word Is My Vow'? Or 'Promise'?"

"Very good. Loosely it means 'My Word Is My Bond.' Lelia Fortune values honesty above all else. She respects people who do not break their word … for any reason. I recommend you never lie to her. She will know."

"I understand, detective. That is how I was raised."

"Good. Then you'll get along with her. When you see her, please give her my regards."

"I'll do that. Thank you."

"Good luck, Adam." Anders stood and shook his hand. His grip was firm.

Medallion safely in his pocket, Adam returned to his old Toyota. Before he drove away, he pulled out his iPhone, fired up the VPN app, then left a Signal message for Cara to update her as the two agreed before she disappeared. He was surprised and pleased that she answered almost immediately. They met at a truck stop. A quick embrace, then they headed toward Chicago.

"I didn't think you would come," Cara said. "I was about to steal a car."

"I t-told you I would stay with you forever."

"Yes, but that was before the FBI decided I was persona non grata. I didn't expect my boyfriend to stand with me against the federal government."

"It's okay," he told Cara. "Over time, you'll see you can trust me and depend on me."

As they drove, he updated Cara on his conversation with

Detective Anders. "I guess in retrospect, it would have been okay for you to be with me when I spoke with him," he said.

"We had no way to know. Agent Tanaka didn't seem very keen on me, so we worried that Detective Anders felt similarly. I confess I'm surprised that Tanaka destroyed the audio data. That was incredibly helpful and kind of him."

"Could he really have been worried you would k-kill him?"

"Who knows? Maybe."

An electronic message board along northbound I-65 was flashing an Amber Alert for Linnea. Adam's breath caught in his chest. Cara gasped. Damn Sokolov and his men for putting their little sister in this frightening position.

THEY PULLED off the highway just south of Chicago to refill the gas tank. While they were there, Adam searched for this Lelia Fortune. It was neither a long nor difficult search. A person with that name apparently lived in Glencoe, Illinois, about half an hour north of Chicago. He had no luck finding a phone number.

In less than an hour, they found themselves on a quiet residential street in Glencoe. Most houses on this street were visible from the car. The address they had, on the other hand, was on a simple light pole at the start of a long driveway. They could not see the house from the street. Suddenly, Adam was less sure of himself. He remembered the Amber Alert, steeled himself, and turned up the driveway.

A hundred yards later, they reached a large two-story modern house of white brick and stucco, surrounded by old-growth trees. The house featured picture windows on all sides, though oddly they couldn't discern the interior of the house through the glass. Adam parked to one side of the circular drive in front of the house. As they walked up to the front door, he tried to find his location on Google Maps. For some reason, he was unable to get a cell signal. Cara couldn't get a cell signal either. *This is not the time for technology to fail us. Damn.*

There was a heavy bronze knocker affixed to the front door. Adam did not notice a doorbell. He knocked twice and waited. Minutes later, the door ponderously opened, as though it were heavier than it appeared. A short, white-haired elderly woman, slightly stooped, stood in the doorway.

"May I help you?" she asked.

"I … I may have the wrong house."

"That is possible," she agreed. "For whom are you looking?"

"We were g-given the name of a Lelia Fortune." He pronounced the name the way Detective Anders did.

"I am Lelia."

"Yes, ma'am, but I may have made a mistake. This c-can't be where we were supposed to go."

"Perhaps you are correct," the lady said. "Or perhaps you ended up just where you need to be. Please come inside. I'll fix you both some tea. We can talk."

"We appreciate the offer, ma'am, b-but we're in a rush. It is literally a matter of life and death. The clock is ticking. I'm sorry, but we really can't stay now." He was getting anxious. He did not have time for a sweet old lady who was lonely.

She smiled at them. "Please, both of you, come in and talk with me. I insist." She took Adam's arm and gently led him inside. There was something about her, something in her eyes or her spirit, that was difficult to refuse. She led them to her sitting room and motioned to a loveseat by a low glass table. Two comfortable-looking chairs were on the other side of the table. "Sit. I'll get us something to drink."

The lady quickly returned with a silver tray, a small

teapot, and three little china cups. She set the tea service down on the table, poured them all a cup, and sat down in a chair opposite them. Then, she looked at them expectantly. Adam didn't know what to say.

"Here's to new friends." She lifted her cup and toasted them.

They returned the toast. "To new friends."

"Now then, what can I do for you?"

"Again, ma'am, you're very k-kind, but we have the wrong house. You can't be the Lelia Fortune we were told to see."

"Ah," she nodded. "Because I'm an old lady."

"No, ma'am, I didn't mean …"

She held up her hand to silence him, her affect suddenly businesslike. "Tell me, young man, do you have something to give me?"

"I was t-told to give … wait, how did you know?"

"Never forget. My word is …" she looked directly at his eyes.

"M-My bond," he said. He reached into his pocket and pulled out the golden medallion. Mechanically, he handed it to her. She took it, and it disappeared into her clothes.

"What is your name, young man?"

"Adam. Adam Samuelson."

"I see. And you, miss?"

"Cara Ferris, ma'am."

"And who gave you the medallion?"

"Detective Anders. He sends his regards."

"David," she murmured almost to herself. "Such a nice young man."

"You know him, ma'am?"

"He did me a favor many years ago. I owe him. It appears he's calling in his favor now. Tell me your story, Cara and Adam. Start from the beginning."

They told her about the home invasion and meeting

Detective Anders, about the school bus and the airplane and the hospital and Linnea's kidnapping, leaving out just a few details concerning Cara. Adam wondered at one point if there was something in the tea. Or maybe it was something about this person that made her so easy to trust. In any case, they told her pretty much everything.

"Okay, that brings us up to date. I believe I understand what's going on. I can help you."

"You can save Linnea?"

She laughed. "I'm afraid I'm much too old for field work. But every job needs the proper tools. I have what you need. Follow me, please."

Lelia Fortune walked over to a bookshelf and manipulated several of the books. The bookshelf slid inward and to the side, revealing an elevator. There was a small screen by the elevator door. The lady stared into the screen for several seconds, then the elevator doors opened.

She entered the elevator, motioning for them to follow. Adam wouldn't have expected anything deeper in the ground than a normal basement, but the elevator continued down. Finally, it came to a smooth stop. "We're here," she said.

They stepped off the elevator into what he could best describe as a large high-tech warehouse. They looked around in awe. The space was well lit and air-conditioned. Classical music played in the background. Metal shelves were filled with assorted handguns, shotguns, rifles, and grenades, all neatly arranged. Boxes of ammunition were stacked beneath the appropriate weapons. Other shelves held knives, scopes, and what looked like night vision gear. There were shelves of various electronic gear, shelves of tactical clothing and body armor, and even shelves of larger ordnance.

"Holy c-crap, ma'am! Excuse my language. What do you do?"

"I'm in sales. Technology sales."

"You're an arms d-dealer."

"That's what I said," Lelia Fortune answered primly. "Now then, follow me to my office. We'll make up a shopping list."

DRESS FOR SUCCESS

"Stand still for a moment so I can get your exact size."

Like an experienced tailor, Lelia Fortune unrolled a soft measuring tape, its edges slightly worn from frequent use. She began her assessment at his neck, jotting notes on a small pad in a shorthand Adam did not recognize.

"Ma'am, I don't understand how this is helpful. We have to help my sister."

"Son, David … Detective Anders asked me to help you. Part of helping you is keeping you alive. You will be of more use to your sister if you're alive. Now hold your arms out."

He stood and waited while Lelia completed her task. When she was done with him, she turned to Cara. "Now you, miss. Stand like he did."

Then things got strange. Adam saw she was measuring Cara, but then extending the tape a little. She did this several times, and then she stood back, looking at Cara and rubbing her chin. "Very interesting. I've not seen that before."

"Seen what, ma'am?"

"Cara, your suit will need to be elastic. I can do that."

Cara and Adam exchanged glances. Lelia Fortune must have somehow sensed that Cara grew when she changed.

"Wh-Why did you say her suit will need to be elastic?"

Lelia chuckled. "I've been doing this for a long time. And I've become very good at it. Now trust me."

Done with Cara's measurements, she asked Cara and Adam to wait briefly as her machines prepared their new clothes. Then she left them alone in the room.

"We still have no internet access," Cara whispered. "I'm worried that Linnea may be trying to reach us."

"I share your concern," he said. "I'll t-talk to this Lelia Fortune when she returns."

The wait was brief. Lelia returned, looking very pleased with herself.

"Here you go. Put these on, please. There are changing rooms right over there."

The new clothes fit perfectly and were incredibly comfortable, as though they were made for the two teens. Which, of course, they were. And they were black, very black: his and hers versions of black pants, black turtleneck, black belt, and black shoes.

"Come here and look in the mirror," Lelia said. "What do you think?"

"They're … uh … b-black," Adam muttered.

She heard him. "Yes, they're black. The perfect color for when you're off marauding somewhere. Let me tell you about these suits. This is the newest technology, developed right here in my lab. These suits absorb ambient energy and repurpose it. Unfortunately, the suits are not one hundred percent efficient because no matter how wealthy I am, I cannot violate the laws of thermodynamics. So note these suits will not make you invulnerable. They will absorb much of the energy from handgun rounds, though the impact will still hurt. Sniper bullets and military ordnance may kill you. Oh, and they're fire resistant, water resistant, puncture resistant and grapple resistant. You will also be very difficult to see because the suit blends with your environment."

"Fire-resistant, I understand. What d-do you mean by grapple resistant?"

"Run your hand over your clothes. You're slippery. Hard to grab."

"Ah, very cool. Anything special with the shoes?"

"You'll find running and jumping a lot easier than before. The shoes get energy from the suit. And the shoes are quiet. But this is not the Marvel Universe. You are not superpowered. You can neither jump off nor leap over tall buildings. Don't do anything stupid."

"And our heads?"

"Hidden in the neck area of the shirt. Head covering pulls up if needed. Similarly, hand protection is in your wrists. And let's see, there's more."

She handed them each a pair of sunglasses. "Try these on. The first sunglasses that are made for the dark. Wait, don't put them on yet. Let me get the lights."

Suddenly the room was completely dark. Adam could see nothing.

"Now put on your sunglasses."

Wearing the glasses, he could see Cara, he could see himself, and he could see Lelia Fortune standing by the light switches. He could also make out the furniture in the room. "Warm bodies cast a greenish glow, don't they? Now watch your eyes. I'm turning the lights back on."

"Yes, ma'am. These are awesome. But …"

"But you want weapons like you saw when you first came off the elevator."

"Well, yes. And internet. Do you have internet down here?"

"I'm sorry. How silly of me. Yes, follow me. Communications room right here."

"Can we use our phones?"

"Yes, they'll work in this room. Free Wi-Fi," she added with a laugh.

CARA GASPED. "Adam, there's a message from Linnea. I'm sure it's really from her. Ha, she's in his office. She sent this just a few minutes ago. But so far as I know, there's no way to send her a message directly."

Cara tapped at her iPhone. "The IP address is from Highland Park. I can't get more accurate than that."

"I probably can," Lelia said. She sat down at a computer workstation and typed rapidly. A map of northern Illinois, northern Indiana, and part of southern Michigan appeared on the screen. Superimposed on the geography, they saw a complex web of red lines. "Civilians aren't supposed to have access to this, you know. So don't go telling anyone." She zeroed in on the Highland Park area. "Here we are. Not too far away. Almost neighbors." She typed some more. "Look at this. Someone's sending a lot of data from a residence." More tapping. "To the FBI. Bingo. That little girl is something. I'd like to meet her."

"I'm sure she'd enjoy meeting you too, ma'am. B-But right now she's surrounded by armed, dangerous criminals who want to kill her."

"Yes, it's time to put your new suits to use. Son, I have a couple more things for you." She handed him what looked and felt like a small toy pistol. "Here, it fits in your belt like so. Nobody will notice it."

"I mean no offense, but it looks like a toy."

"It's no toy, at least not in the sense you mean. This new stun gun incapacitates targets with a disabling energy pulse.

Your suit powers it. Another of our newest products. And this will help you find cameras and electronic bugs and disable them." With that, she handed him a device about the size and shape of a small TV remote. "Just push this button here to disable nearby electronics. It works pretty well unless they're shielded. Think of it like a focused EMP."

"An electromagnetic pulse? In this tiny thing?"

"Like the other tools, it's powered by your suit. You can't use it too often, or it will overheat."

"Okay, but that little p-pistol, ma'am ..."

"Yes?"

"Why not a real gun?"

"I said earlier that part of helping you is keeping you alive. Another part is helping keep you out of jail. There's a place for lethal force, but if that's the only tool you have, that's what you'll use. Killing will change your life, and not in a good way. I have a sense that you know something of this, Cara."

"Yes, ma'am," Cara whispered. "That's why I asked Adam not to come with me."

"B-But then why do you sell actual weapons?" he persisted.

"Look, any successful businessperson will tell you the secret to success, if you call it a secret, is to find a need and fill it. Help enough people get what they want, and you will get what you want."

"Wait a minute. An arms d-dealer is quoting Zig Ziglar?"

Lelia stared him down. "You might take off your judge's robes, young man. I don't sell to just anybody. I help keep balance in the world. You need to know that life isn't always pretty. It isn't always, or even often, fair or right. It isn't politically correct. There are people who take care of problems—serious problems—that most of the world never knows about. For many years, I've supplied these special men and women with tools to do their job. The world is better because I've done so. I can look you in the eye and tell you I've saved thousands of lives through my work.

"My work has been lucrative. I own all this." She gestured around her massive warehouse. "And I've given millions of dollars to initiatives for hunger, for hospitals, and yes, even the Chicago Symphony. The public knows me only as that eccentric, rich old lady who gives gobs of money to various charities and arts organizations."

"I'm sorry. I didn't mean to c-come into your home, enjoy your hospitality and gifts, and then lecture you on morals. I have no standing, no right to do that. I … I guess I'm shaken up about my sister. And you've done nothing but be a b-blessing to me. Please forgive me."

She patted his hand. "The French have a saying when it rains: *Je ne suis pas en sucre.* I'm not made of sugar; I won't melt."

"Thank you, ma'am."

"You're young and optimistic, and I hope you always keep some of that idealism. Help make this a better world for the next generation."

As they spoke, Lelia was leading them back to the elevator. A few minutes later, they were at her front door bidding her goodbye.

"Thank you again very much for your help, ma'am," said Cara sincerely.

"I enjoyed your visit. Please come back with your little sister when this is over. Here, this is my card with my private number. Use it."

"We sure will. Listen, you might give the FBI a heads-up. You know, the c-cavalry is always good. Can you do that anonymously?"

"I can. Though Special Agent Tanaka is more your friend than you might appreciate."

"You know T-Tanaka too, ma'am?"

"It's my business to know. Good luck out there."

As the teens got back in Adam's car, they saw Lelia Fortune closing her door.

"Well, that was interesting," Adam remarked.

"I remember a conversation when you first approached me in the library, where you said people are interesting."

"You d-don't forget anything, do you?"

"Not about what's important to me." Cara looked more solemn than usual. He squeezed her hand.

"How far is that address?"

"Take a right here, then get on the highway headed north. We should be there in twenty minutes, traffic allowing."

A WALK IN THE WOODS

*A*s they drove, Cara tapped on her iPhone.

"Adam, I've been looking at satellite views of the destination address. It looks like quite a compound."

"I've never seen a house like the one we just left. That was insane."

Cara lifted an eyebrow. He sensed one of her trademark wry statements coming. "Yeah, that last house took the term 'finished basement' to a whole new level."

"That's the t-truth, literally," he said. "Can you see the best way for us to approach?"

"I'm thinking we park a mile or so away, and hike in. It's probably best to come in through the woods, from the side closer to Lake Michigan. I don't know how far out their eyes go, and we want our arrival to be a surprise."

"Sounds good."

They continued driving in companionable silence other than Cara's navigation. Adam thought it was interesting that although he was uneasy with the whole situation, he wasn't terrified as he would have expected. Here he was, facing off against his parents, the FBI, and a gang of vicious criminals. This was so unlike him; he hated conflict. But with Cara by his side, he felt he could take on the world.

"First thing we'll need to do is verify that Linnea is here. Any thoughts about that?"

Cara shook her head. "I don't know what to expect. We can't go in guns blazing … or I guess gun blazing."

"I …" he protested.

"It's fine. Ms. Fortune knew I didn't need a gun. But what I was saying is that we'd better be quite sure this is the right place before we do anything aggressive."

"Agreed. But how will we know where to look?"

"In the end, we'll have to play it by ear. Let's stay together as long as we can."

"I'm p-planning on forever."

This affirmation earned him a smile.

THEY PARKED Adam's old Toyota on a quiet side road, far from any houses. He locked the car, and they headed into the woods. Early April in Illinois meant trees were still mostly bare. They'd spent more time than they'd thought in Lelia Fortune's house. The sun was going down. It would be dark by the time they reached Sokolov's mansion.

"Phone on silent?"

"Check."

They jogged in the woods for about ten minutes, then he raised his arm to signal stop. Cara ran into his arm. "Oops, sorry."

"Do you notice anything, Cara?"

"I don't hear your footsteps, and I can hardly see you. Lelia wasn't kidding about these suits."

He looked at Cara, then at his own arms and legs. They

weren't invisible per se, but they were very hard to notice. Their suits somehow blended with the environment.

"I've never even heard of this technology, Cara."

"I haven't read about it either."

Cara and Adam flitted soundlessly through the forest, like modern-day specters. The shoes and the suit made Adam feel light. Even after running more than a mile, he still had not broken a sweat. The suit kept him at a comfortable temperature.

They continued following the coast of Lake Michigan, remaining inland quite a bit. Every so often, they stopped to verify their position by GPS. By this time, they were getting close to what they believed was Sokolov's compound.

Adam felt a buzz from his pocket, and it was not the pocket where he kept his cellphone. He reached in and pulled out the electronic bug detector. Part of the detector's face was a screen inside of which he could see an arrow that appeared able to rotate in three dimensions. He moved his hand to align the arrow with the detector, and he found himself pointing at a tree two or three body lengths ahead of him. Nothing about the tree struck him as differing from any other. He reached down, grabbed a handful of fine dirt, and tossed it in the air ahead of them. As the dust settled to earth, they could discern the laser light going between trees at about waist height and knee height. On closer examination, once they knew where to look, they could see the tiny lenses and mirrors embedded in the trees. Adam pressed the button on the detector and the laser ahead of them vanished. To be sure, he tried the dust trick again. The laser was off. They crossed inside the laser perimeter, and then he pushed the button again. The laser remained off. *So much for the element of surprise.*

Now they proceeded more carefully. Adam held the

detector in front of Cara and him as they walked, but it was silent. A few yards further, the forest broke. Ahead of them, they saw acres of manicured lawn, perfect as a golf course. Surrounding the lawn were two rows of tall fence, both topped with razor wire. Several thick wires passed horizontally along the fences, separated from the metal fence by ceramic insulators.

"The man does like his p-privacy," Adam whispered.

"Wow," Cara responded. "Any ideas?"

"Over makes more sense than under or through. I have an idea. Let me try something." They were still in the forest. Adam picked a suitable tree, crouched, and jumped eight feet onto a branch.

"I suspected as much," he said after lightly dropping back to the ground, landing on his feet. "With these shoes and these suits, we blow away any Olympic athletes who ever lived. We can clear both fences with a running start. My d-detector doesn't show any cameras nearby. Once we're on the other side, let's head for the bushes over there."

"Got it. See you on the other side," Cara smiled briefly, then looked serious again. She took several steps back, then ran at the outer fence. She soared high over the fences, landed gracefully in a forward roll, then lay on her stomach. Her suit made her difficult to notice in the grass. Adam duplicated her actions, though he didn't think his landing was nearly as graceful as hers. Then, without a sound, they glided into the stand of bushes. The bug detector remained silent for now.

They may have been silent to their ears, but apparently they were audible, or at least smellable, to better senses than theirs. A couple of large, mean-looking Dobermans ran toward them. *Shit!* The dogs approached, mouths open, circling as though unsure what to make of the two teens.

Then Cara glared at them and started in their direction as though to attack them. The two dogs promptly whimpered and fled.

"You have a way with animals, Cara," he whispered.

"I guess young children and animals can see the real me, even when my boyfriend can't or won't," Cara said.

"Love is b-blind. And I'm perfectly content with my blindness."

Ahead of them, on a low rise, Sokolov's mansion dwarfed the above-ground portion of Lelia Fortune's impressive home. "Damn. Whoever said that crime doesn't pay obviously never knew Sokolov. Now, how the heck do we get inside there?"

A guard armed with a sidearm and carrying an AK-47 crossed in front of their path, near the mansion.

Cara leaned closer to Adam. "Between the laser perimeter, the razor-wire electric fences, the Dobermans and the armed guard, I'm no longer worried that we have the wrong address. We should do whatever is necessary to get inside and find Linnea. Do your best with cameras. We should try to stay unrecorded, if possible."

"Agreed."

"I'd expect cameras are covering all ground-floor doors and windows."

"That rather limits our options," he said.

"Not really. I'll bet that even if their electronics sense our movement, these suits will make us difficult to notice on video. Motion-sensitive cameras record lots of dogs, squirrels, birds, and whatnot. We may well not attract any attention at all until we're inside and running into people.

"Given all the other security measures, I'd expect bulletproof windows. So breaking in through a window, as they did in your house, will be futile. I say we enter through a door."

"Sounds g-good. I love you for your brain."

"Yeah, right," he heard her mutter under her breath.

"Ready?"

She nodded. Without another word, they flowed up the hill toward the closest side door.

ANOTHER BAD DAY

Cara and Adam ran up to the door without challenge from any guards. His detector buzzed, so he pushed the button to disable the camera. He tried to open the door, but it was locked.

"Let me try," Cara whispered. From her pocket, she withdrew an odd-looking set of picks. She examined the lock, inserted and manipulated one pick without success, then added another similar-looking pick. She moved them gently inside the lock as though they were extensions of her fingertips. Satisfied, she turned the doorknob. They darted inside.

"Seven years living on the street. I learned a couple of things."

"Apparently."

The garage was pitch-black. They both donned their special sunglasses. A subtle alert from Adam's detector allowed him to disable another camera.

"Damn," he whispered. "An eight-car garage? And most of the bays are full."

"Adam, look. A Mercedes Guard. I didn't think they were real."

"I'm not a car guy. Why is it cool?"

"It's bulletproof. Bombproof. Fireproof. This is what you want to be driving when people are trying to kill you."

"Imagine someone being angry at Sokolov."

"I know, right? I'm shocked."

"We can admire his taste in cars later. D-Do you see how to get inside?"

Cara pointed across the vast garage. "There's a door over there on the other side. Let's go."

Just as they headed toward the far door, it opened, and a man stepped down into the garage and turned on the light. Cara grabbed Adam's arm and pulled him down. They hardly dared to breathe, though the man showed no signs of having seen them. Cautiously, they observed the man from their hiding place on the far side of the Mercedes Guard. He was smoking a cigarette, but his full attention was on the yellow Lamborghini in front of him. To his credit, and even though Adam didn't know much about cars, he had to admit the Lambo looked fast. The guard with the cigarette looked as though, in his mind, he was driving the luxurious yellow Lamborghini wide open on empty country roads and he savored it, stroking the plush leather interior the way one would touch a lover.

There was no way around it. They would have to pass the guard in order to get through the door. He would notice them and would then, at a minimum, sound an alarm.

"Sorry, buddy," Adam murmured. "Let's see what this pistol does."

He drew his stun gun, aimed carefully, and pulled the trigger. There was a gentle hiss from the pistol. The guard's body blossomed with a lacework of energy for a few seconds, and then he dropped like a rock. The massive garage was quiet once again.

Cara touched Adam's shoulder. He turned to look at her.

"Adam, I don't want to morph into that creature until we discover where they're keeping Linnea, so I don't get distracted and go on a killing rampage. Can you take care of anyone we come across until it's time for me to change?"

He tried to fake a confident smile, though he'd never been much of a fighter. In school, he always relied on either his height or his sense of humor to keep him out of trouble. Neither of those would help him here. "I've g-got it, Cara. Don't worry."

He decided he would use the little gun whenever possible, though he promised himself when this was over, he would get formal training in hand-to-hand combat.

"Let's go," he told Cara. He opened the door, and they found themselves staring several armed men in the face.

<<<<>>>>

LINNEA CROUCHED in the corner of Sokolov's office. She was uncomfortable sitting at his desk for a long period. Besides, she wanted to monitor the large window behind his desk. It didn't open, but it was at ground level and was therefore likely able to be broached by his henchmen. She also needed to stay near the door, since that was the most likely place for forced entry. The deterrent she'd thrown together wouldn't keep people away for long but would at least make entry more difficult and costly.

I'm gonna need help to get out of this mess. The longer I can delay, the more chance there is that someone will come for me. Cara? Are you there?

In the hallway, someone tried to open Sokolov's office door. When it didn't immediately open, they pounded on it.

A man yelled in a foreign language. To Linnea's ears, it sounded like cursing. Time for phase one.

Linnea opened the two jugs, one of bleach and one of drain cleaner, inside the plastic dry cleaning bag and emptied them into the bucket. *I hope this bag is airtight.* Immediately a thick cloud of yellow-green gas filled the bag and seeped under the door into the hallway. Linnea gently milked the bag to help the poisonous chlorine gas disperse outside the office door. Apparently, there were several people in the hallway, from the coughing and retching. She couldn't be sure, but it sounded like at least a few of them had hit the floor.

Just when she was feeling hopeful that she'd dissuaded the criminals from entering, she heard Sokolov's voice calling for a fan. *Not good.*

A couple of minutes later, the office door shook from a massive blow, and then another. *The door won't survive many of those.* Linnea opened the bottle of Pot Perm and emptied the dark crystals into the ashtray. She opened the bottle of glycerin and placed it beside the ashtray. *I must time this carefully. Potassium permanganate and glycerin react violently for several seconds before they burst into flame. I need to think of it like the timer after the pin is pulled on a hand grenade ... but with more fire than explosion.*

The vigorous attempts to open the door from the outside continued, without success. After a time, Linnea realized that Sokolov had reinforced his own office door to protect himself. This added structural strength was now working against him. Thus reassured, she took a few minutes to look around his computer. Perhaps she could discover more information that the FBI would find useful.

As Linnea worked, she vaguely noted that the blows against the outside of the door had ceased. Suddenly, to her horror, she heard the distinctive sound of a shotgun being pumped. She dove behind the desk just as the doorknob exploded in a cloud of shrapnel. The door burst open.

Mikhail Sokolov did not pause. He charged immediately into his office, overturning the bucket of bleach. His foot caught in the slick plastic dry cleaning bag so that he lost his balance and fell backward. The shotgun went off again, showering plaster from the ceiling. He lay stunned for just a moment, but it was long enough for Linnea to pour the bubbling, smoking mixture of Pot Perm and glycerin on his clothes and face. Sokolov yelled and tried to wipe the material off, but it stuck and burst into flame. In pain, he staggered to his feet, forgetting about the shotgun. His only thought was to grab the girl who had caused him so much trouble.

Linnea held the revolver with both hands as her parents had taught her, aimed at Sokolov's chest. He lunged at her. Just before she pulled the trigger, a burst of gunfire hit the large picture window from the outside. The window starred but did not break, but the sudden sound distracted Linnea just enough that her single round missed the target.

Oh, God!

The man roared in rage and agony. He leaped the distance between him and Linnea, grabbed her and threw her across the room. She landed hard, out of breath. Sokolov ran to her, his clothes still aflame, grabbed her by the front of her pajamas and pulled his other arm back to deliver a killing blow.

Linnea screamed in terror. As he punched, she twisted so that the blow barely missed her. She tried to pull free, but he was too strong. *The revolver.* In desperation, Linnea swung the empty revolver across Sokolov's face, trying for his eyes. He released her momentarily to clear his vision. She tried to run, but he leaped on her, smashing her to the ground. Linnea screamed again.

CAVALRY

*P*erplexed, the guards looked at Cara and Adam for a moment before they reached for their weapons. Adam's gun was already in hand. His goal was to disable them all before they could start shooting or sound an alarm.

He dropped three of the guards, but a fourth was able to reach him and knock the gun from his hands. The man pulled a knife, crouching and circling. He was quick and clearly experienced in the art of knife fighting. Without his suit, the man would have drawn first blood on Adam's right arm, then would have disemboweled Adam with a move he didn't see coming. As it was, the blade slid harmlessly along the suit, doing no damage. Adam kicked the man away, giving Cara time to pick up Adam's gun and shoot his attacker. She handed the gun back to Adam.

The teens looked around. They were in a room that had been set up as a monitoring station. All the outside and garage cameras played in real time on individual screens. Beside the screens was a small bank of control panels. Cara bent to examine them.

"Adam, we can turn off everything from here. The laser perimeter, the electric fences, the cameras, everything."

"Do it, and you get extra p-points if you can make it extremely difficult to start things back up again."

"Give me thirty seconds." Cara typed quickly at a keyboard. Adam was paying more attention to the downed guards, though none of them were moving yet. Soon she stood. "Done. They hadn't even changed default admin passwords. Too bad for them."

They passed through the control room and headed into the mansion itself. There were more rooms and more hallways than anyone needed. Searching every room would take a while.

"Adam, we're going to have to increase our first derivative if we expect to find Linnea soon."

"I know we need to move faster. And you know I have a thing for nerd g-girls who speak in calculus."

"I'm counting on it," Cara murmured under her breath.

As they ran down the hallway, a heartrending scream of terror and pain pierced the air. Linnea!

"Go," he said.

Cara darted forward, transforming as she moved. Within the space of a few seconds, his girlfriend morphed into a creature he had never even imagined. Now she was closer to his height and weight. In the form-fitting suit, her muscles were perfectly defined, like those of a bodybuilder. He'd never seen a goddess, yet he was sure they must look like this. He felt rather than saw an aura about her—raw, overwhelming power. She turned to look at him, almost sadly, he thought. Her face was perfect, beautiful, unscarred. He thought he saw something of Cara in her eyes. She still had Cara's long, thick, luxurious hair.

Moving silently and much faster than was possible for a

human, she disappeared from view around a corner a second later. Sounds of violence soon followed.

ADAM HAD problems of his own. Two men caught up with him. From a distance of about twenty-five feet, they began firing in his direction. Bullets struck him in his chest and abdomen, knocking him to the floor. Almost immediately he realized that although the bullets hurt like hell, they were not causing mortal damage. He stayed on the ground since he was there anyway, and further bullets would just knock him down again.

He pulled his little stun gun and fired back, taking a moment for each shot. Again, each strike anywhere on the targets' bodies covered them with a lacework of energy … then they collapsed. He stood up and quickly examined them. Both men still had palpable pulses and were breathing but were unconscious. He wasn't sure how long they'd stay that way, so he headed down the hall after Cara.

Following Cara when she was in God-mode did not require any tracking expertise. When faced with a choice of doors, choose the one torn from its hinges. He entered and looked around an opulent room. A massive chandelier hung from the ceiling, lighting a suit of armor against one wall. The armor grasped a spear as a live soldier might have done centuries ago. A dead soldier, one of Sokolov's henchmen judging from his uniform, hung impaled on the spear. Another man had been thrown against an expensive-looking red velvet settee; his arm, which had been completely severed, was lying on top of him. His skull was asymmetric and bloody. His eyes and mouth were still open, but he was dead.

As Adam crossed through the room, he thought about what Lelia Fortune had said to him earlier in the day. If his only tool were ultimate violence, then there would be very, very limited conditions under which he could use his tool. This is why she gave him the little stun pistol that he'd initially mocked as a toy. He could use the gun when necessary and not kill people. He felt deep empathy and respect for Cara, who refused to fight in school because she didn't want anyone to die, not even bullies.

Another hallway, more dead bodies lying haphazardly in Cara's path. A large electric fan lay on its side near where smoke emanated from a doorway. From inside he could hear the crackle of flames and quiet sobs. He pulled up the neck of his suit to protect his nose and mouth, and then he dashed inside. A man that he presumed was Sokolov lay unmoving on the floor by an enormous desk. On the desk, a computer workstation apparently was still uploading data. Sokolov's clothes were burning furiously, but he was beyond caring about pain. Random patches of flame burned around him, even without obvious sources of fuel. *What the hell had happened here?*

Cara and Linnea were kneeling together near Sokolov's body, embracing and crying. Linnea was still wearing her pajamas, and she was barefoot.

"We need to g-get out of here," Adam exclaimed. "Can you both walk?"

Cara nodded but did not answer. Linnea murmured, "I think so."

"I'll help you." He lifted his sister to her feet. She seemed surprisingly light and small. Her personality was so big, it was easy to forget she was just a little girl. She walked with an obvious limp, so he lifted her into his arms. Linnea wrapped her arms around his neck and laid her head against his chest.

"You and Cara saved my life again," she said.

They hurried toward the exit, retracing their steps. At one

point, a couple of men accosted them. Adam shot them with his gun, one-handed since he was carrying his sister.

Linnea, curled in his arms, quietly observed the carnage as they passed back through the house. Cara walked beside Adam, not saying a word. Her face was impassive.

As they exited the building, Adam could hear in the distance the thrum of helicopters.

"We n-need to get into the woods. We can't afford to be seen here." Cara and Adam increased their pace to a run. Seconds before the FBI helicopters appeared overhead, they vanished over the fences into the dark forest. Adam pulled out his little detector, but it remained quiet. The laser perimeter was no longer operational.

They made it back to the car without being challenged. Cara wanted to sit in the back with Linnea. Adam drove, heading back to Indiana.

At a rest stop, Cara and Adam changed back to their normal clothes. Their special suits and other devices folded nicely into their bags, which Adam stowed inside his day bag. They didn't want to hear questions that would be difficult to answer, such as how they got this equipment.

BACK HOME AGAIN

When they stopped on the way home to change clothes, Adam called and spoke briefly to his parents. No surprise that Katie and Stephen were outside the house waiting for their return, although it was now well after midnight.

Katie grabbed Linnea and held her as though she'd never let her go. Katie cried. Linnea cried. Cara stayed apart from them, a somber expression on her face. Adam felt huge, raw emotion in his chest and his soul, but he couldn't cry. Stephen shook his hand, then pulled him close for a hug. "I'm proud of you, son."

"Th-Thanks, Dad. That means a lot."

Adam could sense that Cara was upset about something, but for the life of him he couldn't figure out what the issue was. Linnea was home at last; they were all home safely. Katie and Stephen were happy. But Cara stood apart, shoulders slumped, head hanging. Her face was slack, and her eyes were red. She was silent.

Adam led her outside behind their house, down by the

creek where they had that revelatory conversation the previous fall and where they shared their first kiss.

"Just be quick, Adam. Get it over with."

"We're usually on the same frequency. But you've lost me here, Cara. Why are you so sad? How can I help?"

"Say goodbye and go. I understand. I'll be okay."

"Why would I say g-goodbye to you? Please help me understand what you're thinking."

"You saw … that horrible thing that's in me. You saw what I did. You can't pretend anymore I'm not a monster."

"Ah, I get it," he said. "Cara, look at me. I understand that killing is very serious and very p-permanent. But can you see that even with my high-tech marauding suit and my little stun gun, there is no way I could have reached Linnea in time? Had you not been there, and had you not changed, my little sister would be dead. We would be at her funeral now, rather than giving thanks for her safe return to us."

"But you saw me turn into a horrible creature. I killed … I don't even know how many people."

"Those men were standing b-between us and a young girl who was within moments of death. None of us are glad they lost their lives, but they gave you no choice. Thank God you were there for Linnea."

"But …"

"Besides," he smiled, "your inner monster is kind of hot."

"I was sure it would disgust you. I hate it. How can you stand that it's part of me?"

"Cara, you're not perfect. None of us are. We all have parts of us we keep hidden, parts that shame us. I've seen your secret, and I'm t-telling you I still love you. Look at my face. You'll see the truth.

"You're strong, Cara. You're a survivor. You're k-kind and intelligent and good. The writer and poet Khalil Gibran said that beauty is not in the face; beauty is a light in the heart. And you're beautiful to me. And I love you."

Cara looked at him, stared deep into his eyes. Then her face clouded. "I don't deserve …"

"Stop, Cara. Please. I love you. Come here." He took her in his arms, and she melted against his chest. He caressed her hair. Cara raised her face to him. He kissed her lips.

She sighed. "I love you, Adam. I thought I'd lost you."

"Won't happen. I'm not interested in life without you."

They walked back up to the house holding hands. Cara's eyes were already brighter, and she had a faint smile.

Expecting questions that would be hard to answer, Cara and Adam agreed between themselves that they would not talk about the medallion or Lelia Fortune unless they were forced. They had no opportunity to include Linnea in this conversation, though they didn't expect her to ask them pointed questions in front of law enforcement. Special Agent Vincent Tanaka and Detective David Anders met the Samuelsons at their home for a debriefing of sorts.

"What happened after the men took you, Linnea?" Agent Tanaka asked.

"I awoke in the back of a van. There were no windows. I had no way to know how long I'd been asleep, where I was being taken, and by whom. But my best guess was Mikhail Sokolov because we've irritated him so much. I remembered hearing that he was based near Chicago.

"They took me to a place I later learned was his mansion. They brought me to a windowless room where they tied me to a chair. Sokolov demanded that I make that video. I refused initially, but he slapped me, and I agreed." Katie gasped at this and squeezed Linnea's arm.

"I'm okay, Mom. Really. But I figured there was no point

in forcing him to injure me. I wanted to conserve my strength."

"After the video?"

"Sokolov and his men laughed at me and said they planned to kill me no matter what Cara did, and then they left me tied in the room. I escaped from the chair …" Linnea recounted what happened to her in the room.

Agent Tanaka shook his head slowly. "Damn."

Linnea continued. "I'd noticed a large air vent in the ceiling. I moved the table, put a chair on it and escaped through that vent. I set a bottle of sulfuric acid so it would fall if anyone opened the grate to chase after me. Unfortunately, as I crawled through the vent, it suddenly gave way and angled downward. I lost my flashlight, so I had to cross that part entirely by feel, in the dark. Eventually, by chance, I found myself above Sokolov's office. I lay in the ceiling above him, praying he would leave. Just then someone tried to enter the room where they'd left me. There was a loud explosion. From the yelling, it sounded like someone got hurt. Then someone turned on the light, causing another explosion and more screaming.

"Sokolov left his office to see what the commotion was all about. I dropped through the grate into his office, locked his door, isolated his computer from his network, and started sending all kinds of interesting information to the FBI. You got that, didn't you, Agent Tanaka?"

"Oh yes. The gentleman was quite compulsive about his record keeping. Some of the most … uh … creative financials I've ever seen. Records of who killed whom, when and how much he'd paid them. Details of all his various legal and illegal businesses. Yes, that information would have locked him away for life if he were still alive. You brought down a billion-dollar criminal enterprise, Linnea. Then what happened?"

"Again, I looked around to see what I could use. I found some chlorine bleach and acidic drain cleaner, so I made chlorine gas, which I fed under the door to dissuade people from trying to break in. That worked for a while, but then he got a shotgun and blew off the door handle."

"So he came in and got you?" Katie asked.

"Not quite that easily. You may not have known this, Agent Tanaka, but Sokolov had a passion for gardening. Many gardeners use potassium permanganate to kill pests on their plants. Sokolov also had an indoor pool. People use potassium permanganate to regenerate the sand filter in pools. Anyway, he had that and a bottle of glycerin, and you know what happens when you mix the two."

Stephen shook his head. "It's been a long time since college chemistry. What happens?"

"Potassium permanganate is a very strong oxidizing agent, and the reaction is extremely exothermic."

"In English."

"It bursts into flame. Very difficult to extinguish. When he entered the room, he slipped in the bleach and the large plastic bag that I'd used to direct the chlorine gas. I ... may have poured a bunch of Pot Perm and glycerin on him. His clothes caught on fire."

"But that couldn't kill him fast enough to save you."

"No. But it gave him something to do before he could use the shotgun. I'd found a revolver taped under his desk. It had one round. I could have ended it then, but some of his men shot at the window from the outside. It scared me, and I missed. Then he grabbed me and threw me across the room. He ran to me and was about to kill me. I screamed as loud as I could."

"And then?"

"That's all I remember, Agent Tanaka. Next I knew, my

brother and sister were there holding me. Sokolov was lying on the floor, dead."

"How did Adam and Cara show up in the middle of the armed criminals in time to save you?"

"Should I t-take that one?" Adam asked.

"Go ahead, Adam."

"You'd told us that Sokolov was based in the Chicago area, and like Linnea, I p-presumed he was behind the kidnapping. So we drove up that way. When Linnea reached out to us on Sokolov's computer, we weren't too far away. Then we arrived, saw lots of dead people and found Linnea."

"Hmm. Indeed."

"Sir?"

Agent Tanaka leaned forward. "I've been working at bringing Sokolov down for years, building a case that would hold up in court. He was a slippery bastard. He's bought off or threatened judges and prosecutors. Now he kidnapped your sister, who's just a child, and tried to kill her. I cannot express to you how little curiosity I have as to exactly how he died.

"You should know that I've listened to the cockpit audio from Sokolov's jet, so I can make an educated guess why it crashed. Possibly something similar occurred last evening in his mansion."

Cara stood, eyes wide with alarm.

"Please sit down and relax, Cara. If you'll allow me to throw your words back at you, we are not at odds, you and I. Surely you can believe that Mr. Sokolov had many enemies. My report will say that a criminal competitor arrived before you and decimated Sokolov's security. That is by far the most reasonable explanation for the condition of his mansion and grounds when our FBI agents arrived."

"What happens now?" Cara asked.

"With the information Linnea sent us, and what we found

in his home, we'll be able to close his organization and send his lieutenants … the ones who are still alive … to prison for a long time."

Detective Anders leaned forward. "Linnea, if I may?"

"Of course, detective."

"When I questioned you following the home invasion several months ago, you related to me the events of the attack until just before the attackers were killed, then at that point in the story, you told me you remembered nothing further."

"Yes."

"And just now, you gave us intimate detail of what was truly a remarkable escape, again stopping just before the point where the attacker was killed."

Linnea shrugged. "I'm sorry, sir. I'm just a little girl."

Anders snorted. "No, miss. You may be only thirteen years old, but you're definitely *not* 'just a little girl.'"

Stephen's eyes narrowed. He crossed his arms over his chest. "Just tell us what you're trying to say, detective. Cut the crap."

"Linnea, without a doubt, you are one of the most intelligent and resourceful kids I've ever met … or even heard of. I wonder, do you suppose your memory will ever work properly when Cara may be involved?"

Linnea looked the detective in the eye. "No, sir. It will not."

"I see." He nodded, paused. "That's remarkable. There's a saying, you know, that the ability to speak several languages is an asset, but the ability to keep your mouth shut in any language is priceless. You've figured that out early in life. This skill will serve you well."

"Should I thank you, Detective Anders?" Linnea asked politely.

"No need. But I'm thinking that you are going to grow

into a truly formidable adult, Linnea. You remind me of an old friend of mine. Hopefully, you can meet her sometime, if your parents allow it."

"She reminds you of me? She sounds delightful." Linnea grinned.

"Cara?" Katie said.

"Yes, ma'am?"

"I want to apologize to you for how I behaved after I saw the video of Linnea."

Cara walked up to Katie and gently took her hands. "You know, for the past seven months, you've been the mother I wish I'd had my entire life. You've made me feel like family. I'm told that sometimes family members argue." She paused. "I can't imagine how I'd feel if some sick bastard kidnapped my daughter and threatened to kill her. I would never judge you for what you did or said. I love you, you know …"

Katie's eyes grew moist. "Come here, Cara …" They hugged.

"We're good?" Katie asked.

"Always," Cara answered.

WORTH THE RISK

"Tell me one more t-time why the good Detective Anders wants to talk with us again?"

"Adam, be nice," Stephen admonished. "He said this conversation would be 'unofficial' and unrecorded, and he asked that our attorney not be present."

"How can this be a good idea?"

"I don't know how to explain it, son. He sounded different when he called me. More vulnerable. I guess I'm operating from a gut feeling more than logic."

"Besides," Katie broke in, "as famous as you kids are right now, you could probably run for office and win. I can't see that we have much to worry about."

THE FRONT DOORBELL RANG. Linnea jumped up to open the door, then paused and looked back at her family. "The last time I opened the door without thinking, it didn't go well."

"Go ahead, dear," Katie told her.

More sedately now, Linnea walked to the door and opened it. "Hello Detective Anders," she said.

"Well, hello, Linnea. It's a pleasure to see you again. May I come in?"

"Yes, please." Linnea gave him a shy smile.

Stephen rose to greet him. "Come inside. Let me take your coat." The two men shook hands.

"Thank you, doctor."

"Let's all sit at the table and talk. Would you like something to drink, detective?"

"Water would be great, thanks."

"I'll get it," Linnea said.

Anders looked around the oak dining room table at the Samuelsons and Cara. He tented his fingers and glanced briefly down at the table, taking a deep breath as he decided how to begin.

"Sir Arthur Conan Doyle's fictional detective, Sherlock Holmes, said that once you eliminate the impossible, whatever remains, no matter how improbable, must be the truth. When I first spoke with you, Cara, I dismissed out of hand your initial explanation for the death of the two men who broke into your home. In retrospect, I was wrong."

Cara regarded him, her face stone.

"Cara, please tell me again, as best as you remember, what happened that day when you were ten. It's difficult to talk about, and it's painful to hear … but it's important."

"My mom's boyfriend was drunk. I was alone with him. He grabbed me and touched me … my chest. Wanted to have sex. I struggled, slapped him. He got violent. Punched me, pulled a knife and cut me. Then he … took me. Is that what you wanted, detective?"

He shook his head. "I'm so sorry. What do you remember after that?"

"I must have lain on the floor for a while. I woke up, and … he was asleep on the couch. I felt dirty. I ran to the bathroom and wiped off the blood and vomit as best I could. My cheek wouldn't stop bleeding, so I had to hold a hand towel on it. I found some clean clothes to wear and ran away. Didn't bring anything with me but my doll, Emma. She was all I owned that was important to me.

"I ran, I don't know how far. I was weak. I was cold. Didn't know where to go. I was afraid to get help. I thought they'd send me back, and he'd kill me. Some men saw me and chased me. Finally, I was too weak to run anymore. I hid behind a dumpster in an alley. It was too much. I remember I prayed, I begged God or whoever for help, to protect me … to give me strength so that people couldn't hurt me. Finally, I fell asleep.

"I woke up to find a couple of men trying to undress me. I got angry …"

Cara's face reddened. She wiped sweat from her brow as she stared down at the table in front of her.

"I … need a minute. Excuse me." She pushed back from the table, stood, and headed for the kitchen.

I FEEL something moving in my chest. Spasms. I scream in pain. My arms and legs twisting and changing. This is not my body. Muscles. Power. Anger. No … rage. I need to kill.

I hear harsh, inhuman sounds and realize they are coming from me.

The men back down the alley in horror. I swat at the dumpster, and it tumbles away like a little toy. The two men break and run, but I easily head them off before they leave the alley. I grab the first one by his neck and his belt and throw him high against the wall. He slides to the ground with a dull thud and lies still, like a broken doll. His friend drops to his knees.

"Please, miss. Please, I'm sorry. Didn't mean no harm."

I take his head in my hands, and I squeeze. I feel his skull crush under the force of my grasp. Blood and gray matter stain the ground.

I run.

CARA RETURNED to the dining room, sipping a glass of water.

"I'm sorry. Sometimes the memories are overwhelming."

"I apologize as well," Anders replied. "I know it is tough for you to rehash this."

"Detective, I don't understand what happened to me after I fell asleep. I don't know what I am. I don't know if God answered my prayer … or someone else. But since that time, the rules have been different. And I started my new life, broke and homeless, with no adult I could trust to help me." She paused. "That's my story."

"Do you remember what time of year that was?"

"I believe it was fall. It was cold at night."

Anders was silent for a long time, struggling to control his emotions. Finally, he opened his briefcase, pulled out a thin folder and pushed it across the table to Stephen.

"Dr. Samuelson, this is a police report." Anders summarized it from memory. "October 23, 2009, two local men were found dead in an alley in Brooklyn, New York. One man's skull was crushed, the other had multiple trauma as though he'd fallen from a height, very much as Cara described. Elsewhere in the same alley, behind an overturned dumpster, police found a bloody doll with child-size fingerprints in the dried blood.

"Cara … fingerprints on the doll match yours. DNA from the blood on the doll is a match for yours. Cara, you were in that alley seven years ago."

The Samuelsons were stunned.

"How long have you known?" Stephen asked the detective.

"For several weeks."

"Why didn't you say anything before now?"

"I was trying to make sense of it. But now the school bus and airplane incident pushed me to move. May I share a story with you?"

They all nodded.

"I was fourteen years old. My sister, Isabella, was about your age, Cara. You would have liked her. She was smart and funny, and she was protective of me. I loved her.

"One day, I came home from baseball practice and found Isabella on her bed. Someone had stabbed her to death. The police never found the killer. After that, my world fell apart. My folks ended up getting divorced. I went far away to college and never returned home."

Anders looked around the table at the Samuelsons, meeting each person's eyes. "I blamed God. I doubted my Catholic faith. Haven't been to church since then. I devoted my life to solving unexplained murders. That's why I couldn't leave you alone, Cara.

"The fingerprint match took a long time … weeks to search through old archives, not knowing exactly what I was trying to find. When I found the match with the child in New York, I confirmed it with DNA. The DNA confirmation was a lot faster, of course, since it was just the two samples."

"Who else knows?" Stephen asked.

The detective shook his head. "Agent Tanaka has an idea, though I don't think he knows about the alley in New York. He told you he heard the cockpit audio from the airplane. He let me listen to it, and then he said he would destroy it and all copies. He agrees with me that this isn't something our government should know. Cara, that man in Boston, in the park … I have reason to think he had been stabbing young girls for many years, including my sister. You stopped him."

"I don't understand. How could you know …?"

Anders smiled grimly. "Let's just say you'd have to ask Isabella about that. I've come to believe that you're here for a divine purpose, Cara. I wasn't able to help my sister, but I decided I can at least help you. Dr. Samuelson, the folder I gave you is the only record of Cara's past. I don't want it back. I never filed a copy with headquarters. It could cost me my job if they ever find out, but you're worth the risk, Cara."

"Thank you, sir," Cara said. "And thank you again for taking a bullet for me."

"I didn't know it wasn't necessary. That hurt like hell, you know."

Cara smiled. "It's the thought that counts, detective."

"One last thing before I leave," Anders said.

"Yes?"

"Special Agent Tanaka feels certain this isn't over for you. He deleted the cockpit voice recorder from Sokolov's jet, as I said, but he's worried there may be an offline copy somewhere or you may have attracted attention from our government … or, heaven forbid, another government.

"You may need me again. I will do whatever I can to help."

ACKNOWLEDGMENTS

Thanks go to my wife, Teresa, and my kids, Benjamin, Andrea, Hannah, Olivia and Jacob for their encouragement and understanding. Thanks to Jennifer Blum and Karen Adolph for believing in my ability to write. Thanks to John Beam for his knowledge of school buses and related student safety procedures, to Justin Beam for his aviation expertise and to Captain Fred Ilnicki of the Indianapolis Metropolitan Police Department for police matters. Thanks to Kathie Myers for insight into FBI procedures and to Daniyal Habib for guiding me through the arcane world of the American legal system. Thanks to Rocco Blum for his help with Latin translations. Any errors are my own.

Special thanks to LeeAnna Groves, Julia Robertson, Dee Bloom, and Teresa Beam for making the book stronger with your insightful suggestions.

ABOUT THE AUTHOR

Eric Adolph is an emerging author of young adult magical realism. He and his wife, both retired physicians, have been married for over three decades and live in Indiana. They have five adult kids and, at this writing, two exceptionally cute and brilliant grandkids.